The Haunted
Lost Rose

The Haunted Lost Rose

Charlotte's Voices of Mystery Series

C.L. Bauer

The Haunted Lost Rose, Copyright © 2023 by C.L. Bauer.

This book is a work of fiction. Names, characters, businesses, organizations, places, events and incidents either are the product of the author's imagination or are used fictitiously. Any resemblance to actual persons, living or dead, events, or locales is entirely coincidental.

For information contact:

www.clbauer.com

ISBN: 978-1-957015-02-6

First Edition: February 2023

10 9 8 7 6 5 4 3 2

Charlotte's Voices of Mystery Series

The Haunted Lost Rose

Dedication

To all those strong women who come from strong families, and to those voices that lead us to our destiny.

Chapter One

Atlanta, Georgia, Thanksgiving morning

As Max Shaw crept out of the bed, he searched for his trousers in the darkness. He'd stayed longer than he planned. Truth be told, he never stayed the entire night or ever had a woman sleep over at his place. Waking up next to a woman created a commitment that he didn't want in the life he had created for himself. Besides, he needed to make his flight to New York City. This mandatory trip was the only remnant of the family he once had. When he was seated on the plane, he'd be just one step closer to finishing this holiday season's obligation. He hated this time of year.

Max heard a sigh. "Honey, come back to bed."

While tugging on his pants, he quickly threw on his shirt and turned to smile at the naked woman stretched out on the bed. The few hours they'd spent together had been beyond good, but there was no way he'd change his plans for her. "You know I can't." He didn't need any complications, especially from that luscious body. He was drawn to the tall, willowy type with legs that could wrap forcefully around his hips. She was the full package with ample breasts and long hair down to the middle of her back. She was perfect and always looked as though she had her own makeup team and wind machine following behind her. But she was needy. He knew the type. First, she'd want him to stay, then she'd want him to whisper words of love, and eventually she'd want a ring. That wasn't a life for him right now. Entanglements only caught you up in a web of promises to be kept and responsibilities that needed to be met.

The thin blonde hit the empty side of the bed. "You never stay, Max. You wait until I'm asleep, and you leave like you have a train to catch."

Max buttoned his white shirt and grabbed his jacket and tie from a nearby chair. "It's a plane I have to catch. You know I'm very busy."

"Just once I'd like to wake up in your arms."

Max flashed a quick smile and blew a kiss. *There's several women who want that, honey.* "Maybe someday. I really have to go." He leaned down and kissed his girlfriend of three months. At his age, she wasn't really a girlfriend. She was the woman he saw or was draped on his arm at a mandatory cocktail party. This one was a former pageant winner, and she'd graduated from a well known business school. Her arms wrapped around his neck and began to pull him down to linger. "No. I have to go. This is the one time of the year my mother insists I'm sitting at that blasted dinner table."

"Then take me with you, darling. I'd love to meet your mother."

Max stood up quickly and looked over her body as though he'd never seen it before. He examined all of her attributes, committed them to memory, and shook his head dismissively. "Honey, you wouldn't want to meet her or know her. I'm saving you from a terrible fate. I'll call you this weekend."

"When you get back, maybe we can go somewhere warm, just the two of us. Wouldn't that be great, baby?"

He found his keys and phone on the dresser and turned to face her one more time. "Um, about that." He found the doorknob and opened the door for his escape. "I won't be back. I'm going from New York to my next assignment in Missouri. I have just a few weeks to move. We had some great times, and you're a great woman. I'm sure you'll find someone to go on that trip with you. Take care of yourself."

As he shut the door behind him he heard the thud. He didn't know what object had just landed on the wood, but he winced at the sound of the impact. He'd dodged a bullet with that one, literally. But he did hear the words uttered before.

"Maxwell Shaw, you are a sonofa–"

Max's limo waited downstairs. His usual driver held the car door open. "Airport, Max?"

"Yes. Do you have my luggage?"

"Yes, sir. I also have your boarding pass, laptop, everything."

Max entered the vehicle and slumped back. He could sleep on the plane. "Thanks for doing this. I appreciate it on Thanksgiving morning."

The driver laughed. "With what you're paying me, this is no problem at all. My wife loves you, but I bet you've heard that from a few other women."

Max only offered a smile as his response. In a matter of minutes they were on their way to Hartsfield and to a direct flight that would have him arriving in New York City in time to be caught in the parade traffic. But all he had to do was eat a lavish Thanksgiving meal and listen to his mother and sister prattle on about this social event or that debutante. He could also meet his mother's newest boyfriend. She'd met him in Greece. He was an artist. Last year's man of the moment was an actor from Barcelona.

By late evening, Max would wander down into midtown to find his favorite tavern. He'd talk sports with the locals, and he'd call his dad. He missed him, in fact he was one of the very few people in his life he did miss.

That wasn't true though. His new assignment was taking him to a city that held fond memories for him, and people he did miss when he thought about them. His life had taken such turns lately that thinking about anyone but himself was a challenge. But the times had been good there, and the friends had been even better. Max said he would never return to the city of his childhood, but he'd asked for this assignment and was offered it because of his connections and past work on sensitive cases. Once and for all, he needed the truth of so many things.

Chapter Two

Kansas City, Missouri, the day after Thanksgiving

The real estate agency wanted an independent assessment of the property. Two inspectors arrived on a cold November day expecting less than a couple of hours of work.

"So how was your Thanksgiving?"

"Turkey coma, and I tolerated my mother-in-law," Jerry Palmer said as he shut his car door. "Have I told you that my wife thinks we should add onto the house so her mom can live with us?"

His associate, John Davies shook his head. "I thought your wife's mom was a former Olympian?"

"Yes, but I was fed this bull about mom aging, and suddenly my wife wants to be prepared for the inevitable. Hell, she'll probably outlive us." He took a few quick photos of the parking lot and sidewalk. "Didn't this place used to be a country club of some kind?"

John followed slowly behind. "Yeah, a few years back. They shut it down, and since then it's been vacant. As soon as we get the photos and make a few notes, we need to get back to the office and get this report together for Tom."

John looked up at the chimneys before they headed inside, but Jerry stopped him. "Did you see those curtains wave up there on the third floor? Look at that second window. See."

John shook his head. "Rats have probably set up a condo in that attic, and the wind is blowing through the opening they've made. It's just a draft. Come on."

Jerry followed behind John as he placed the key in the lock and opened the door. "I don't feel good about this. I've heard this place is haunted."

"Jerry, that turkey coma did a number on you. Get a grip. It's broad daylight. Besides, I didn't take you for someone who believed in ghosts."

"It's not that I believe in them, but I don't want to meet them either. Exactly why does the realtor need this done?"

John took a photo of the front door and began making his notes. There was a little warping on the solid wood door. What a work of art it was. "The wealthy family selling it wants to know what kind of shape it is in; kind of a last look around, I guess. They haven't lived here for years. Tom mentioned there might be an interested buyer."

Jerry placed his clipboard and phone on the small desk in the hallway. He blew on his hands. "Damn it's cold in here." He looked above the hand carved wainscoting to the art deco style chandelier. "The craftsmanship in the woodwork can't be done these days, and this fixture is made from hand cut crystal. Wow, the things this old girl has seen."

A cold wind blew through the house. "Did you feel that? That's not normal." Jerry really had a bad feeling about this now.

John headed deeper into the building. "Jerry, you're starting to freak me out, and I don't believe in that stuff. Let's just get our job done."

"What the heck?" Jerry saw a fresh red rose laying on the marble mantle.

John walked quickly back into the entry room. "Now what?" He stopped and followed Jerry's view. "What the hell?"

"Exactly. What is that doing here? I thought you said no one lives here and hasn't for years."

John shook his head. "I'll tell Tom about this, but that shouldn't be here. Maybe a couple meets up here to fool around. I'd pick a hotel, but you never know about people, do you? Let's get this done and get the hell out of here."

Less than thirty minutes later the two men nearly ran from the house. They heard tapping on the third floor. Two doors shut quickly behind them on the second floor, but that had been from the draft, hadn't it? They smelled a perfume that seemed to follow them from room to room. On the second floor, there was the aroma of a pungent cigar. As they locked up, they thought they heard a shriek.

Once in the truck, Jerry started up the vehicle quickly and sped out of the driveway. "What are you going to tell Tom?"

"Nothing. Absolutely nothing. But I'm not going back into that house ever again."

Jerry was smug in the knowledge that he had been correct. "We won't even talk about that rose, right?" That place was haunted, and if it wasn't, someone was in that house. He didn't really care either way. He wouldn't be going back in there ever again either.

"We did our job. We didn't even see a rose."

Chapter Three

Kansas City, Missouri, January 4th

"Charlotte! Wake up."

"Charlie, get up!"

My eyes opened when I heard their voices, but I shut them again. Was it really Monday? I just want a few more minutes of sleep. No, I can't because it's Monday. I opened my eyes slowly. "I'm awake," I said out loud. "You don't have to keep yelling at me. You two are better alarms than my phone. And we've discussed how inappropriate this is. Isn't there something else you two should be doing? Maybe you could join an angelic choir?"

I should be grateful for the extra help in the morning, well on some mornings. This wasn't one of them. The sun wasn't shining. I looked out my bedroom window and saw the snow swirling. It was January in Kansas City, Missouri. Yuk! Why did my family not settle in Florida or maybe even Hawaii? Why hadn't I moved?

"Charlotte!"

"Charlie!"

"I'm up. See? I hope you two are happy." My brother and mother were the punctuality police even now from beyond the grave.

When had I heard my first ghost or spirit? I wasn't quite sure, but I wasn't in grade school yet when a dead person contacted me. I was innocent of any fear, and it seemed like a very normal occurrence. I realized that something was very wrong when I told my mother, and she hugged me tightly in my arms and said not to tell anyone what I had just heard. As an adult, I kept myself busy enough to shut out most communications from the other side of life, the dead side. But my mother and brother were daily voices in my head.

I swung my legs over the side of the bed and felt the cold floor. I detested winter. Why did you like the cool floor on your feet in the summer, but the same temperature of a wood floor in January would absolutely begin your day off on the wrong foot? I smirked. That was a good joke, and there was no one to share it with in my home.

I headed into the bathroom. I needed to meet up with a client at the old Taylor Club by nine. The remainder of the day I'd be busy cleaning up the work that wallpapered my desk. I showered, dressed, and ate a toasted english muffin with a tablespoon of peanut butter. Right about now, I was missing yesterday's breakfast at Dad's. The man knew how to cook, and I could use his scrambled eggs and ham instead of a limp muffin with a childhood favorite spread. I wasn't missing all the time spent with my family over the holidays. I loved them, but it was time to go back to work. My two sisters-in-law, my three brothers, my older only sister Jane, her husband, two nieces and four nephews were my everything, but too much of a good thing made me a very snarky little sister and aunt. I cooked and shopped more than I ever did during the year, went to church four times, saw my youngest niece's Christmas concert, and had a bout of flu.

Grabbing the bag with my laptop and small purse in it, I headed into the garage with a new attitude for the year to come. As I pulled out of the driveway, the snow was no longer swirling, it was falling and beginning to stick on the streets. I called into the office as I headed to the Taylor Club.

"O'Donohue Real Estate."

"Good morning, Meg. I wanted to check in."

"Charlie, how are you this morning?"

"I'm cold, and I really don't think I'll warm up until July. Is your husband in?"

Meg laughed. "Your brother is in, but he hasn't had his coffee yet. Do you still want to talk to him? Do you have a death wish this early in the week?"

My brother Tom needed a caffeine drip line throughout the day just so he didn't turn into a mutant grizzly. I'd already warned him he'd end up with kidney stones if he kept up the routine. If he hadn't had any coffee yet this morning, I would have to be careful with every little word I said. "Sure, I'll be the sacrificial lamb, but why hasn't he had his caffeine yet? Did you two get into the office late on a Monday?"

There was a pause in the conversation as Meg cleared her throat. "Charlie, it's our anniversary, and well, we lost track of the time this morning."

What on earth? What were they doing? Oh! My face suddenly warmed. I should say *yuk* as any self respecting little sister would do. Instead of responding in a disgusting manner at the very thought that her brother ever had sex, I chose to be the adult I was, at least claimed to be. I even chuckled at that thought.

"Happy anniversary," I added quickly. "Put him on the line. I'll talk to you later."

Meg giggled. "Yes, you will. If this snow piles up like they say it will, I'll keep you updated. Here's your brother."

"Are you headed over to the old club?" Tom was abrupt in his question. There was never a salutation or wondering about how his sibling was. I could be stuck in a ditch, and he'd tell me the address for our next showing.

"Yes. I'm about five minutes away." I always answered in turn. If he wanted to be businesslike then I was too, even if it was his wedding anniversary. Why did they get married in January? I remember. He had those six weeks in-between deployments.

"Remember, he needs to know that the zoning is reverting to residential unless he applies to the city. He will have a heck of a time with the residents if he plans on anything but updating it into a single family house."

I rolled my eyes. "Yes, I remember. I talked to Councilman Johnson last week, and he met with Mr. and Mrs. Martin. The three of them went over everything, and the Martins assured him they were going to turn the club into their home, all ten bedrooms of it."

"Good. We don't want to get jammed up with this sale. Check in with me after you meet with Mr. Martin."

I felt like saluting, but he wouldn't see it. Geez, sometimes he treated me like the little sister I was or the soldier I wasn't. "Yes, sir. Talk to you later. Bye."

The large flakes of snow fell harder as I drove past the art museum and entered onto the long driveway. No one would be shoveling this baby. There was a light tire track or two guiding me. Apparently, Mr. Martin was waiting for me. I was five minutes early.

The windows and roof of his car were completely full of the white stuff. I hurried up the concrete trail. There were no previous footprints to shield my steps. What the heck? When had he arrived? My client's car was parked near the sidewalk, but it looked as though it had been there forever.

I expected to meet him at the front door, but he wasn't there. I turned the knob. The door was locked. I used my key and entered the structure.

"Mr. Martin? It's Charlotte O'Donohue. Where are you?"

Silence was my only answer. I yelled again. Nothing. Oh come on. This was weird.

I entered the room on the right and felt a cold wind through a partially open window. Heading to close it, I noticed a red rose laying on the marble mantle of the massive fireplace. "That's strange." I shut the window tightly and placed my bag over on a corner desk.

"Mr. Martin?" I shouted as I walked through the mammoth dining room with its built-in cabinets. I checked the kitchen and the butler's pantry. I walked back into what had been serving as a small ballroom.

"He's in here." I heard the words. I shook my head. It was the wind.

"I said he's in here."

I stood still. My body was completely frozen from fingers to toes. My head throbbed. The damn headache always came on when something awful was happening or when I heard someone from beyond. "What did you say? Where?" I shouted out.

"He's where I used to read to my pup. Take care, dear girl."

I breathed out and a stream of frosted air left my body. Slowly, I walked further into the dark. I knew it well. It was my favorite place in the mansion. It featured a floor of black and white tiny tiles imported

from Europe in the early 1900's. The room had one
wall of windows that overlooked the terraced gardens.
I visited this house when it was a tennis club. Mom had
taken Janie and me to a mother-daughter tea. It was a
special day, but it had been the day before a very awful
day. I shook those thoughts away as I peered around the
corner. On the floor of those tiny tiles, I saw the soles of
two shoes. The body was between the sitting room and
what I thought used to be a sunroom.

"Oh no." As I rushed in, I saw Mr. Martin's body
stretched out on the cold floor. He was face down and
too big to turn him over. I crouched down to touch
him, but he was cold to the touch. I only knew how to
do what I saw on television. Grabbing his arm, I felt
nothing. I touched his neck. There was no beating or
pulsing of any kind.

"I said he was here. He's departed."

I looked around, but saw no one. Of course. I was
listening to someone who was part of this house.

"I can see that." I pulled my phone out of my pocket
and hit 9-1-1. "Do you know what happened to him?"
I yelled out the question but received only silence once
more.

"Hello, I'm at the old Taylor Club, and I've found a dead man, my client. I'm a realtor. Yes, the old Taylor Club. I'll be waiting."

I looked around the body. Nothing was out of place. Nothing seemed to be disrupted in the room. No window was broken, no table overturned. I stood up and moved away from his body. The tremors began to take over, shaking me to my core. I leaned up against the brick wall of the room beneath a framed painting.

Needing a distraction, I turned to look up at the piece of art. It featured a lovely woman seated in a Queen Anne chair as she held a small dog and a book in her lap. The woman was sitting in this very room. Her dress was white with a small red and coral bloom print. At her neck, the dress tied with a red bow to the left. Her eyes were a piercing color of green. Her hair was sunshine blond. The painting was unfinished at the bottom, her lower figure was only outlined.

"Is this you?" I asked out loud.

"Once." I heard the voice fainter than before, or perhaps it was another voice. If walls could talk! Perhaps they could in this old house.

"Thank you for being here with me. I haven't been with a dead body before, well not since..." I stopped muttering. I was shaking from the cold, my fear, and my memories.

I heard a soft laugh. *"Dead. Only another time, another place."*

I walked back to the hallway to wait for the police. "Maybe for you, but for me this is not a normal day in Kansas City." I glanced back at the red rose on the mantle. "And who left that?"

"Be careful." Those two words shook me to my core. I heard the sirens. I rushed to open the door.

"Charlie?" My brother, the police sergeant, stood in front of me. His face was distorted in a mixture of shock and fear. "They said some real estate person was here, but I didn't realize it was you. Tom is going to have a heart attack. Where's the body?"

"Nice to see you too, Sean. He's in the sitting room. I'll show you." I led him to Mr. Martin's body. I stood back watching the oncoming swarm of officers and emergency workers do their jobs. But my client was still dead.

Sean headed toward me with his own version of "this is so awful that you had to see this" face. He opened his arms and wrapped me up in them. "Let's hope the detective doesn't get this case."

That hadn't even occurred to me as a possibility until Sean mentioned it. "He won't. He can't." As if on cue in a very bad mystery movie, our oldest brother, William Padric O'Donohue, Jr. stood next to us, looming over me with his bear-like frame.

"Charlie, what the hell?"

"Good Morning to you too, Paddy," I greeted him as I turned out of Sean's arms. On a good day, this brother was particularly intimidating with a perpetual scowl and large build that could intimidate a grizzly bear. On a bad day he could replicate the second coming of the devil.

My formidable brother, the oldest of us all, the most serious, the most intelligent if only in his own mind, the biggest, the fastest, stood stoic, and scowled. "Charlotte, where did you find the body? What time did you arrive? When did the victim arrive?"

The questions, his inquisition, seemed to be endless, but I just kept answering. I even mentioned the fresh red rose which was now half-frozen in the cold house. Paddy insisted I show him. Finally, he slid his arm over my shoulders as we stood in front of the mantle. The detective morphed into my strong brother.

"Are you okay, babe? You can tell me if you and that guy were, well, close." My brother leaned his head on top of mine. I pulled away quickly. My face showed my indignation. Paddy cowered just a bit.

"How dare you! He was our client. How can you even think that? And I'm not okay, especially now that my brother has accused me of having an affair with a married man." I walked a few steps away from him. Brothers! "I need to call Tom and tell him what happened here. Excuse me, Detective O'Donohue, but I need to inform my employer that I'll be a little late." I stopped shaking somewhere in between exasperation and frustration with my DNA sharers.

I stepped closer to the window for a little privacy to call Tom. "Tommy, I'll be late. There's been a problem at the house."

"Great, Charlotte. I have the Sloanes coming to discuss the house search, and with all of this snow predicted, we will shut it down. What happened? This was supposed to be an easy thing today."

I bit my bottom lip, a habit I had from the time I learned to bite my lip. I swiped away a drop of moisture on the edge of my nose with my glove. "Tommy, I found Mr. Martin. He's dead. He was dead in the house when I got here."

There was a brief silence before his voice roared. "Jesus, Mary, and Joseph! What the hell? Are you okay, honey? Are you there alone? Have you called Sean or Paddy?"

I nodded, but Tom couldn't see that. "They are already here," I whimpered. "The entire bloody police department is here. Oh Lord."

"What? What's wrong?"

I rubbed the frosted window to see clearly. "The news stations are coming down the backstreet. This will be all over Kansas City by tonight, and our names will be connected."

Tom swore again. "Tell Sean and Paddy to keep your name out of it. Tell the stations we were just representing the owners in the sale or better yet, just avoid them. Then, get out of there as soon as you can."

"Okay. I will as soon as they release me." My voice quivered, but I just couldn't make it stop. My body shook uncontrollably again either from the cold or the shock. I hung up and walked slowly behind Paddy, touching him on the shoulder.

As he turned around, his face softened. He was seeing a scared little sister, not the woman who just found a dead body in an empty house. "Charlie, what do you need?"

"Tom says Sean and you can keep my name out of this? The television stations have their vans arriving. This could kill our business."

Paddy cocked his head at my use of an interesting verb. "Ms. O'Donohue, we can question you later. I just need you to write down your contact address and phone number." Always the professional, he handed me a pen and paper. "You can sit over there." He pointed at the window seat.

I sat down and slowly wrote out information that my brother already knew, but he always did everything by the book. Sometimes he could be such an arse! Why did all the men in my family have to be so serious? Our dad wasn't like that. Mom hadn't been like that. What happened to all of them?

It was terribly uncomfortable on this seat. Something was sticking up through my heavy winter coat. With no cushion, it might be a splinter of wood. I stood up quickly after hastily writing down all of my information and looked down. I ran my gloved hand across the area. It wasn't a piece warped by years of neglect; it was a key wedged into wood. I looked around at the crowd of investigators.

"Um, anyone?" My voice wasn't very loud. I should've known no one would hear me. It wasn't the first time people didn't listen to me. Did I want them to? Really? I looked down at the key. "What do I do with you? You might have nothing to do with all of this. Then again, you might."

Slowly, I reached down with my gloved hand and began to manipulate the item, pulling it to the left and then to the right. I plucked it out of the window seat after a few seconds.

"Please don't tell."

I looked around, but no one was watching me. "Why?" I whispered.

"Help me."

When I was small, most voices assured or informed me, but this was the first time a spirit asked for my help. I knew I should hand the key over to one of my brothers standing just feet away from me, but I stuck it into my pocket. Even I surprised myself with that move. I was from a family who revered the law and everything legal. I was an attorney even if I wasn't currently practicing law. But what if this key had nothing to do with all of this around me? But what if it did? This spirit needed my help. Help for what?

As I turned around, I bumped into Sean. "Charlie, why don't you go home? This must have been a shock for you. Just go rest."

"Thanks, Sean. I have to drop by the office first. But I think I'll go see Dad. I really don't want to be alone right now." I shoved my gloved hand into my pocket to keep my hold on the key. What the hell was I doing?

Sean looked out the window behind me. "You know, that's probably a very good idea. With all of this snow piling up, it might be better if Dad had you, and you had Dad."

"Lucky for me, I have a packed bag in the back of my car." I punched him in the shoulder. "My brothers make me do that."

Sean smiled. "They sound like brilliant men."

"Right. Keep telling yourself that. They were boy scouts. They make me prepare for anything." Although none of them had ever prepared me to discover a dead body in a house I was selling!

Sean gave me a brief hug, and Paddy waved to me as he watched me exit the house. I noticed that the rose was still on the mantle. I quickly pulled out my phone and shot a photo. No one would even notice if I took the flower, but my brothers would kill me if I moved evidence. As it was, I was already leaving with an item that might be related to the murder. Maybe it was an additional house key? Or maybe someone had dropped it years ago in that old window seat, and it didn't mean anything to anyone? But the voice didn't want me to tell. My thoughts raced as I battled with the secret. I shut my eyes and made my final decision. I was leaving the house with it. I pulled my coat closer to me as I walked down the sidewalk. I slowed my steps after my first slip. The snow was slick to walk on. I carefully passed more and more police, news reporters, camera crews, and others before I arrived at my car.

As I began to slide uncontrollably toward my door, a black gloved hand held me up.

"Whoops," I yelled. "Thank you so much." The gentleman was holding me up in his arms, and I felt as though I was at his mercy for some reason.

"You're welcome." His voice was low. I heard some sort of an accent, but I just wasn't sure what it was. I looked up slowly to gaze into the prettiest brown eyes. They were the color of my favorite candy bar. They were large, offering a girl enough room to get lost in them on a rainy day. Heck, on any kind of day. His dark hair was wavy, windblown, and had hints of a white hair here and there. Mmm, I never was that fond of salt and pepper hair, but just these little touches looked good, well looked great on him.

He was still holding me up, when I stiffened and reached out my hand to my car door.

"Here, let me get you to the door." He slowly pushed me closer and made sure I had safely made it inside the vehicle. "Have a good day, Ms--"

"O'Donohue, Charlotte."

He smiled. His smile could very well melt every snowflake on my coat. In fact, I was warm all over. "Ah, O'Donohue, as in every O'Donohue in this blessed city?"

I nodded. I just didn't have the ability to speak right now as he smiled again.

"And I suppose you all know everything about everyone just like a large Irish family should?"

I cleared my throat. Come on, get a hold of yourself. "We wouldn't be Irish if we didn't. We all know secrets, but we just tell only one person."

He nodded knowingly. "And that person tells another, and before you know it, everyone in the world knows everything?"

I nodded again and smiled like some goofy teenager. "It seems as though you've caught on."

"I've only been here a short time, but I catch on very quickly." He looked toward the house and pointed. "I need to go in there."

"Then I need to warn you that there are a couple of those O'Donohue men in there."

"I bet I can guess which ones. One of them called me. It was nice to save you."

Save me? Right, from the fall. He began to shut my door, but I braced my arm against it. "I didn't get your name."

He shook his head shyly, and smiled again. He seemingly thought that could distract me. "No, you didn't. Sorry, occupational hazard. Be careful out there." He closed my door very unceremoniously.

I watched him pull his coat's lapels up around his neck. He shoved his hands inside his pockets and began to walk toward the house. He turned around once to look back at me. I smiled like an idiot just in case he could see that far. Then he disappeared into the structure. I also saw a curtain move in one of the windows on the third floor. Then I saw another curtain flowing freely on the second floor, but I also saw a shape, a dark form. The curtain was pulled back and then fluttered back into place. It was nothing, probably just a draft, wasn't it? I was only lying to myself. I knew what I saw. The spirit haunting that house was very concerned with the man who was entering the old Taylor Club, but I was more intrigued by the stranger.

I bit my lip. "Who was that?"

Chapter Four

By the time I'd survived the interrogation of Tom the Hun at the office, keeping both the realtor key and my discovered one, and actually walked through the door at our family's home, I was exhausted.

"Dad," I yelled as I entered. "Where are you?"

"In the kitchen fixing you a hot lunch. I hope you are sleeping over tonight."

Something smelled good. Our father always had culinary skills, but now retired, he had become a master chef. He said cooking always did calm him, but now he didn't need a stress reliever. He did it just for fun.

I hung up my coat and dropped my work bag and overnighter in one of the chairs in the living room. I kicked off my boots and thanked my mother for carpeting over the cold wood floors. I retrieved my cell phone from my new designer purse. At Christmas, we all pulled names to focus on just one gift for one person. This year we all had chipped in for an additional gift for Dad. It wasn't glamorous, but he was in love with his new dishwasher. I was in love with my bright green leather bucket bag from Sean. Jane had told him which one I wanted, and he proudly announced Christmas Eve night that he just purchased it at an area outlet mall just three hours before. I didn't care. I loved a good purse, that and a peaceful, beautiful bathroom with a deep tub could buy my heart and my body.

As I arrived in the kitchen, my father was tasting a sauce from a small pan. He was wearing jeans and a Notre Dame sweatshirt. My childhood memories of him always included a shirt, tie, and a jacket he immediately flung onto the hook in the hallway after he entered through the front door.

Now, I enjoyed spending time with him, and he had the time to spend. He'd been so busy working when I was little. Most nights, he'd come home late. I remembered him lifting me from Mom's arms and into his. He carried me up to bed. Some nights, he sat on the edge just watching me sleep, well pretending to sleep until I actually did. I had different memories than the rest of the kids in our family. I was the baby.

He turned around as if he knew I was watching him. He probably did. He seemed to know everything.

"There's my Charlie. You are going to love this."

He held out the spoon for my own tasting. I blew on the sauce and then brought the utensil into my mouth. "That is amazing. What is it?"

"A bolognese I've been working on. A friend of mine from years ago used to make this sauce. I never did get the recipe so I've been experimenting. I think I've got it. The pasta is almost finished. Grab a couple of plates, will you?"

I headed to the cabinet and gathered up the plates and utensils. "Where's the dog?"

"Mickey is visiting with Mrs. Blane."

My father began to serve the food as I placed the silverware on the table. "Since when does he do that?"

"Since Mrs. Blane has been feeling a little blue." He handed me a full plate as we sat down. "Her son died of cancer a few weeks ago. That's when Mickey and I began to visit. Her son used to drop in on her during his lunch break. I noticed early on she didn't care if I was there, but Mickey was her ticket to a little happiness. I drop him over there, and I pick him up around three. We need to pray."

I bowed my head. Dad said a prayer of thanks

slowly. He always added a twist at the end just to make sure we were all listening. "And please watch over Charlotte. She's always getting herself into the darndest pickles. Amen."

"And I could say the same about you, Judge O'Donohue," I spat out. I looked down at the full plate and couldn't be mad for very long. "I have been so cold today. This really hits the spot."

"I'm not a judge anymore, but you still get yourself in trouble."

I quickly stuck my tongue out at my father and mimicked his statement. "I don't get myself into trouble, trouble finds me. Apparently."

"Apparently," he murmured as he passed me the salad. "It already has a light dressing on it."

"If this is lunch, what did you have planned for dinner?"

"I made chicken soup yesterday so you get leftovers." My father passed a piece of garlic bread in my direction.

"Dad, are you always cooking?" I was thankful he did, but he needed to get out of the kitchen once in a while.

"No. I still play poker on Thursday night with the retired police chief and his bunch. Of course, this weather may change my schedule. Friday lunches are with the women at church. I could play cards every day of the week if I wanted, but that gets old and so does the conversation. Next week I'm going with Lucille Danby to the opera. I try to keep myself busy. When spring comes along, you'll find me out in that garden. I've decided I want to try my hand at growing watermelons."

"It seems like you may have a better social life than me," I grumbled.

"And whose fault is that? All you do is work."

I pushed back from my food. I was already getting full from the rich sauce and the heavy pasta. "And there's no one in this city to date. Dad, you know we're related to half of the Irish families in Kansas City. I don't want to fall in love with my cousin. Besides, I haven't met one man that's worth my time. It's better to work." There was one man, but I would never see him again. I would call Sean later to ask him if he knew the stranger.

"And to avoid getting your heart hurt?" My father's soft blue eyes stole through my aching heart.

"What really hurts is the stomping of my heart, Dad." He didn't respond. He nodded his head. He knew all too well how much that hurt.

"But, Charlotte, isn't it better to have a little bit of love, rather than none at all?"

His soft voice was a salve on my heart. I knew he never used that tone a day in court, ever.

"You know I've tried, and look where that got me. I just don't seem to get the right one. I think Mom got the last really good man." I smiled, grabbing his hand on the table. Mom had left us way too early when she passed away from cancer two years ago. We all thought it might devastate our father, but he soldiered on. Perhaps in the middle of the night, when none of us saw, he collapsed into hysterics or tearful regret, but he never showed us that side. He worked another year before he retired. He was now adjusting to being a widower and a retired judge. His daily schedule was filled with a calendar of card games, lunches, and in the spring, gardening.

"Dad, do you think Lucille Danby is after you? You are a catch."

He threw his head back in laughter. "A catch? I have

a bum knee. I cheat at cards. I am a creature of habit and schedule, and I never deviate. Besides, I have too many kids."

"What does that have to do with dating Mrs. Danby?"

"She hates family. She told me herself. Her husband and she just had each other. They never wanted anyone else. She just misses going to the opera, honey. That's all, and that's all it will ever be.

"But you need to know we would all be okay with you dating someone, heck maybe even marrying again."

"But I wouldn't be," he quickly answered. "I had your mother. I'm good with just being a grandpa and the best dad I can. No more talk about that now."

When my father ended a conversation or a discussion, it ended. I knew when to stop, besides the man was cooking for me. I didn't want my private food chain to end because I asked too many questions.

"I did meet this man today at the Taylor Club."

Dad began to clear the dishes as we finished our meal. "He's probably a cop if he was there."

I joined Dad at the sink. Out the window, we both saw the snow piling up. You couldn't differentiate the street from the yard. "I'm not sure. He was getting there as I was leaving. He didn't dress like a cop, and he hasn't lived here very long. He dresses well, and he has a little bit of an accent, definitely not from around here."

"Sounds like he made an impression on you." Dad scraped the dishes and began to load the new washer.

"He saved me from falling, that's all." Well, and the fact that he was the best looking man I'd seen in ages.

"Have one of your brothers track him down. They used to ask me to do that when they were dating."

"But you never helped them, did you?"

Dad laughed again. "Maybe once or twice. Paddy found Linda that way after her family had moved away. He needed to find her, and I knew a man who knew a man. He had the new address and phone number in two days. Now, what are we doing with the rest of the day?"

"I have some work to do, but all of it is on the laptop. Why don't you go get Mickey and visit for a bit while I work?"

"Sounds like a plan," Dad answered quickly. "That will give you time to call one of your brothers to check on that guy."

I swatted him with a kitchen towel. He laughed

as he left the room, dressed in his coat and boots and departed the house. I wouldn't call the boys. Besides, if I did, I would wait until tonight, after they were away from so many open ears.

Later, after Mickey returned home and the soup was eaten, Dad stoked the fireplace. I bundled up in one of her mother's afghans and stared into the blazing fire. Dad handed me a large cup, and I took a quick sip.

"Exactly how much whiskey did you put in this coffee?"

Sitting in his special large leather chair, my dad toasted me. "Just a touch. Remember when Monsignor Ferity used to say 'I drank just a touch'?"

"But he was drunk by then." I toasted my father. "To Monsignor Ferity."

"To himself," he answered. "Have you called Sean or Paddy yet about that guy?"

"Dad, you need to get a life. I'm not interested in dating or getting married."

Dad's brows narrowed. "I had and have a great life. We are attempting to get you a full life."

"Dad."

My father placed his coffee mug on the coffee table.

"Charlotte, I'm serious. You can say you don't want to date or get married, that's fine. But you need to get out. You've taken care of me for two years."

I began to debate his statement, but his hand flew up in the air to halt my stammering.

"I know what you did. Maybe your siblings don't, but I know. You stopped by to ask a question. You dropped in to see if I needed some milk because you were going to the store. You made your way here every night for three months after your mother left us because you were on your way home. I'm not daft, Charlotte. I love you for what you did. But now, it's time for you to live again. I realized a long time ago that you were hurting as much as I was. We had a one-two punch with Conor first and then your mother."

I began to cry as I heard his words. He was the wisest man I knew, possibly the only wise man I would ever know. "Dad, I needed to do what I did. I promised Mom I would take care of you."

"Not forever, Charlie. You've done your duty, and it has been appreciated." He stared at me, searching for something in my face. Mickey heard my cries and sat below my chair. "Charlotte, find out who this man is. Maybe he's the one?".

I wiped away the tears in my eyes. "He kept me from falling."

Dad smiled. "Exactly. Charlotte, live a little."

What on earth? I took another drink of coffee and placed my cup on the side table. I picked up my cell phone and hit Sean's number. "Are you happy?" I asked my father.

He clapped his hands in appreciation. "I will be when you give me a grandchild."

I shook my head and looked away from him. "I'm just interested in discovering who he is. I don't need to have his child." I hit my brother's number. "Sean, I have a question."

"How are you feeling? Paddy and I were worried about you."

"I'm fine, thanks. Sean, I need to know something."

I heard Sean sigh. "I can't tell you anything about the case."

"Sean, there was this man who saved me from falling on the ice. Do you know who that was?"

Sean laughed. "I could use a little more detail. What did he look like?"

I knew exactly what he looked like, but describing him to my brother was going to be a challenge. "He was wearing a black wool coat and black gloves. It was a longer coat. He was about six feet, maybe a little taller. Dark hair and brown eyes. His hair was wavy with a few gray streaks, just a few." I stopped short of telling Sean how good the man smelled, and that his close shave was perfect. Heck, he was perfect.

"And he came into the house?"

"Yes, and he wasn't one of the newscasters or any of their crew. He said he'd been called by one of you."

"You'll have to let me think. He came in after you left. I think he talked to Paddy." I could almost see what he was seeing. Sean had this unique knack to pull up information with his photographic memory. It took him a little time, but I knew he was figuring it out.

"Got it. He's a prosecuting attorney. Wait, I've got it. He's a federal attorney."

"He's a United States Attorney?" I asked as my father's head shot up from the fire he was stoking.

"Yes, that's it. He's fairly new. I hadn't seen him before, but Paddy knew him. I think Paddy contacted him for some reason. I was busy working to pay too much attention, but he did look familiar. He wasn't there long. You'll have to call Paddy."

"Fine." My answer was short and abrupt. I wasn't going to call Paddy to ask about some guy.

"Did he do something to you?" Sean asked with concern.

"No, I just wanted to thank him again for keeping me upright on the ice. That's all." I could see my father shaking his head in despair. "Goodnight. Take care."

As I placed the phone down, I began my defense. "Don't even start. He's a United States Attorney which means he's a busy man. He probably has a family." And what the heck was he doing at a local murder site?

My father said nothing. He stood up and yelled for the dog. "Mickey needs to go out. I'll be back."

His absence gave me the opportunity to hit my head softly with my right hand. "Stupid, stupid. I don't need anyone anyway." Keep telling yourself that, Charlotte. I focused on the fire to block any thoughts from my mind.

Dad returned with a slightly wet dog and two glasses of straight whiskey. He handed me the glass and kissed me on the cheek. "His name is Shaw, and he'll be here for dinner on Saturday night. Make sure you look pretty and are on your best behavior."

I opened my mouth, but nothing came out. I downed

the whiskey, coughing from the burning in my throat.
"Dad!"

"Daughter?"

I leaned my head back on the chair. My family knew
everyone and everything. They were going to be the
death of me yet.

I was feeling no pain as I walked up the steps to my
old bedroom. I never tried to keep up with my father
while drinking whiskey or any similar libation. There
was that one time, only that one time. I learned my
lesson after keeping up with him until the fourth beer.
I couldn't stand to look at a bottle of Harp until just a
few years ago. He always said he drank with the best; I
wasn't even mediocre.

Mickey followed me into the room. The slightly
overweight collie jumped up on the bed and curled up
on one side.

"I never had to share my bed with anyone before,"
I announced to the quiet room. "Mickey, down." I
directed with my hand. The dog closed his eyes. "Crap."

My head was spinning a bit when I sat on the edge
of the bed. The bedroom window was frosted over.
Maybe the dog would be beneficial? I climbed under the

covers with my sweats on. I wasn't going to change. I wasn't even removing my socks.

As Mickey's backside wiggled closer, I stretched out and closed my eyes. Hopefully, I wouldn't make it into the office in the morning. Nope, I knew I wouldn't make it into the office.

My thoughts churned in my head of Mr. Martin's dead body, the rose, the key. I still had that key, and I needed to compare it to the house key. The police and even Tom hadn't asked for the one they knew about. And who left that rose? Why did she need help? That woman's portrait was unfinished, but it was hanging in that room. She told me to be careful.

"Mom, what's going on here?" Mickey's head popped up to look at me when I spoke out loud. "It's okay, boy. I'm just trying to talk to my mom. Don't you remember her?"

Oh, that's right. Mickey was never Mom's dog. Five years ago, Dad walked through the kitchen door with a bouquet of roses in one hand and a puppy in the other. Mom pitched a fit. She threw every argument at him including that now that all the kids were gone from the house they didn't need another thing to take care of and feed.

Dad's argument won. The dog had no family. He was being fought over by a very wealthy couple, and eventually they both just dropped the pup in the federal courthouse for some reason. Dad noticed the little guy waiting patiently by the front desk, and as he described it, it was love at first sight.

"Remember, dear. I fell in love with you that way," he argued. "I think I need him, and he needs me. There doesn't need to be a reason to bring more love into your life."

Mom had hit a few pans and walked out of the kitchen. But she never said no, and soon Mickey won her over. When she was dying, she realized why the dog was there. He would give Dad a reason to wake up each and every day after she was gone.

I patted the dog's head and soon drifted off to sleep. My visions were numerous. I never called them dreams. I could see things. I could hear people, and tonight it was no different than many other nights.

"Mom, are you here?"

"Charlie, what are you doing at your father's?"

"Snow."

"Charlie, you found a dead body."

I shuddered. I felt the dog grow closer to me. "Yes, and I talked to a woman."

"A beautiful woman. The rose."

"Yes, I found a rose."

"No, Charlie, she's Rose."

I understood. "I met a man."

"You know him, Charlie, and so does Sean."

"Mom…" My mother was gone from my thoughts. I gasped as my eyes opened. Tears were streaming down my face. It was an awful feeling to be speaking with her and suddenly she would be gone.

Mickey woke too and placed a paw of comfort over my body. "I think I know him. I knew him." I stopped talking and returned to slumber, this time without any visits from the beyond.

I felt Mickey leave the bed as I looked over at my phone. It was almost seven in the morning, and I smelled sausage. Even though I had a slight headache, the sausage actually made my stomach grumble. I headed downstairs to see what the old man was up to.

As I entered the kitchen, I was greeted by a fully set table.

"Have you been cooking since daylight?"

"Good morning to you too, daughter dear. I planned this perfectly." He looked out the window, and I followed his gaze. "You aren't going anywhere today. Tom called and said for you to work from here. The news is saying we have about twelve inches. The city wants everyone to stay off of the streets so they can get this mess cleaned up. It sure is pretty though. Have a seat."

I did as I was told and was awarded with a plate of pancakes and sausage. A cup of hot coffee and a glass of orange juice followed.

"I could get used to being treated like this," I announced as I began to drizzle warm syrup onto my plate. I loved syrup on sausage.

Dad sat down at the table. "You should be treated like this. Find a man who will fix you breakfast, and you've found the right guy."

I dropped my fork. "Father, dear, you just implied that a guy should fix me breakfast after I sleep over?"

My father took a large bite and continued to chew, avoiding the question completely. Then he winked. He knew exactly what he had done.

I waved my fork in his direction. "You're going to

get yourself into trouble saying things like that, you big leprechaun."

"Saying things like that is how I got all you kids."

He won the discussion one more time as he always did.

Chapter Five

After the leisurely eaten breakfast, and frankly, quite a bit more than I ever ate any morning during the week, I headed upstairs to dress. Mickey followed me into my old bedroom before I shut the door. He jumped on the bed and settled in while I pulled out a heavy sweater and a pair of jeans. I dug deep down into my bag and found two pairs of clean underwear and socks. Good. I wouldn't have to do laundry today.

Mickey began to whimper. "What's up big guy?"

He hid his head under one of the pillows.

"Charlotte."

My mother's voice was soft and low. "Yes, Mom."

"Key."

I reached over and patted the dog's back. "It's okay, boy, it's just Mom."

"Key."

"Oh, the key." I stepped over to my old desk, and to the key I uncovered, looking it over carefully. There were no markings, but it seemed to be older than the key I had for the door for the Taylor Club. I went to my purse and pulled out the other key. This key was newer, still holding a little of gloss on its sides, but the teeth were identical to the older key. Funny, the police hadn't asked for my key. But I hadn't offered it either. My brothers would kill me when they discovered their mistake. As usual, it would be my mistake. I should have read their minds and known to hand it over. But the spirit needed help.

Who had embedded the key into the window seat? And did it actually fit the mansion's door? As soon as this awful weather passed I would make sure to check it out if I could get past any police tape.

I pulled on my clothes and brushed my hair. My jeans were a little tight today, but that was expected after the holidays. One day I wouldn't worry about the ten pounds I packed on every year that took me until May to remove from my hips and belly. I looked at my face in the small mirror in the bedroom. My freckles were showing. I didn't need to cover them with any foundation today, and I wasn't washing my hair either. No one was seeing me from the comfort of Dad's living room. Let it curl!

Mickey watched me closely as if I was a stranger, but to him, I was. I was already on my own when he had come to live here with mom and dad. I looked around the room at my past. This space hadn't changed much since the day I moved out. I opened the closet door and saw a few pieces of clothing left behind, just in case. There was a poster still taped to the side of the door.

"Bye, bye, bye," I sang out loud. I pulled it off the door, but despite being careful with the tape removal, one corner began to rip. "Well, crap." Fine, I was over that group anyway.

I was still thinking about my knight in a dark coat who had saved me from a bruised butt. His features were almost movie star quality. With that deep dark hair and eyes, he was hard to forget. I hadn't thought about a man this much since, well since never. Even when I was engaged to the man I would not name, he never conjured up this kind of intrigue or warmth all over my body. I hadn't had a date in months and that was when I went out with one of Sean's police officer friends. It had been a one and done with a handshake at the end of the night and probably both of us deleting each other's numbers off of our cell phones before I even reached my couch.

I jumped on the bed and hugged Mickey. For once, he was receptive, placing his paws around my neck. "You'd be a better boyfriend than some good looking, mysterious stranger, right boy?" Why was I still thinking about him? I should be thinking about that key.

"I'm going out to shovel some of the sidewalk." My father yelled from the bottom of the stairs.

I jumped off the bed, and Mickey followed. "No, you are not. Let me borrow your shoveling jacket and boots. I'll do it."

I ran down the very familiar stairs and grabbed him just as he was leaving the house.

"Dad, don't you dare. I mean it." I held out my hand as I demanded his jacket. He shrugged and began to remove it. "And I will need those boots too."

He made some sort of a noise of disgust and shuffled into the living room to sit down. Slowly, glaring at me occasionally, he pulled them off.

"They'll be too big for you. It will never work."

I grabbed them quickly and pulled them on. "I have very thick socks on. It'll be fine. In fact, this will work out better than if you went out there."

He slumped back into his favorite chair and watched me prepare for the outside elements. "I don't know how this works out better. What does that even mean, dear girl?"

I finished zipping up the heavy coat and pulled his cap out of the pocket.

"It means Jane won't kill me for allowing you to shovel. I'm saving myself and you too." I smiled sweetly at my ingenuity.

He laughed loudly and pointed. "That's clever, but what's so funny is how you look right now."

I answered with a toothy smile. "I'm choosing to ignore that. I'll be back."

"You look like that cartoon character Elmer," Dad shouted.

I saw myself in the hall mirror before I headed out into the winter wonderland. Of course, my father was correct. I did look like the cartoon character as he went hunting for "wabbits". Who cares? It wasn't like I was going to meet the love of my life out there.

As I made a path down the few steps and onto the sidewalk, the snow was heavier than I expected. Why did it always look so pretty as you were drinking by the fire? The reality was setting in very quickly that I needed to encourage my cheap father to hire someone to do this for him. Maybe I needed to take him to buy a snow blower?

Knowing that the city sidewalk had to be cleared within a certain amount of hours, I trudged my way there first. I'd work my way back to the house. Yes, being a judge's daughter meant you knew a lot of little quirky ordinances, some were real and some Dad just made up to scare us to death. The boys were all especially afraid of some law that included placing the toilet seat down, and what materials you could take into a bathroom with you. Ironically, that was the first "law" they looked up when they were old enough to know better.

I began to put my hips and back into it. In a matter of minutes I realized I wasn't visiting the gym nearly enough. I'd cleared a few feet of snow and came closer to the street. The plows had already been through leaving a three feet high white stack of hardened snow in their wake. I wasn't going to touch that monster. On the street, some of the solid precipitation had transformed into black slush from the anti icing application applied. With the sun hitting the surface of the streets, at least a few of them might be passable by tonight. Of course, they would refreeze with the dropping temperatures, and we'd be back to square one tomorrow morning. Oh, the life of living the winter months in Kansas City!

And exactly why was I still here? I was the one who would move to Florida and be some big attorney down there. I knew exactly why I hadn't followed that dream. Death had entered our lives and changed everything. I leaned on the shovel and looked back at the house, at my home.

As I thought about why my life was still here, and frankly took a breather from the shoveling, I heard a car racing down the street. I turned my head to see what fool was driving that fast on a residential, ice and snow covered street, and that's when a wave of ice and black snow pelted my face.

"Oh my Lord! You did not just do that," I screamed out loud as I wiped my face with Dad's coat sleeve. "Un freaking believable."

The car slowed down and stopped in the middle of the street. It began to reverse until it was even with where I stood. I moved my shovel to use it as a weapon. The window rolled down slowly to reveal a man in sunglasses.

"I'm so sorry."

I pointed the shovel at him. "Well, you should be. What the hell were you doing driving that fast?"

"I'm late. I'm sorry. I shouldn't be. Can I clean the coat for you?"

I shook my head. "No. Just slow it down, buddy."

The man looked up at the house and then at me. "Judge O'Donohue still lives here, doesn't he?"

I didn't say anything as I continued to wipe the gunk from my eyes. When we were kids, Dad and Mom instilled in us the fear of God, frankly the fear of just about everyone we didn't know. While I was in high school, Dad was the judge on the trial of members of a syndicate. He didn't speak of the three-months long case, and we were warned not to speak to anyone, especially strangers.

I surveyed the car. It was a midnight blue Jaguar. Who drove a Jag in the snow? I guess I could tell him the truth and then memorize the plate number? Sure, why not?

As if he knew I was struggling to respond, he removed his sunglasses. "I've known him a long time. I just wanted to make sure I knew where the house was. I'll be joining him for dinner on Saturday."

Holy Mother of God! It was him. It was the knight of saving my butt! Crap. I look like a cartoon character.

"Yes, he still lives here." I had no other words. Obviously, he didn't recognize me from yesterday's murder site. Good. When I met him at dinner, I would lie and tell him we had hired some neighbor kid to shovel the snow.

"Good. Again, I'm sorry about the snow. Take care." He placed his sunglasses on his face, his window went up, and he was gone in a few seconds. I leaned my head down on the shovel.

I sure do hope he buys the story about the neighbor kid.

Chapter Six

A few nights later, Tom and I entered the funeral home for Mr. Martin's memorial service. Given that the Martins had recently moved to our city, I was surprised when I saw the crowd. Apparently, they'd made friends quickly, and there was another visitation down the opposite hallway. I usually avoided funeral homes. Of course, every human tried to stave off the inevitability of death, but for me I never knew who would try to talk to me. Lord, please don't allow Mr. Martin to invade my thoughts. We signed the guest book. I heard a voice, but it wasn't our murdered client.

"Hi. Hello. What's going on?"

The sweetest middle aged man was waving at every visitor. As soon as I saw his transparent form I knew. His smile faded as he was ignored, but I made the mistake of smiling back at him.

"Can you hear me? Oh, you can!"

I managed a slight nod.

"My family is down there. Could we talk?"

I touched Tom's arm. "I need to use the restroom. I'll be right back."

"I'll wait for you."

"Thanks." I followed the signs. My little man was speaking as fast as he could. His name was P. Russell Farmington. He'd been driving his car. He hadn't been feeling very well and was driving to urgent care when something happened.

I entered the restroom and luckily there was an outer room with a sofa and a couple of chairs. First, I did my own search of each stall to make sure no one was around to overhear. I sat down in one of the chairs and began to whisper. "Mr. Farmington, what do you need me to do for you? That's how this usually works."

"*I've never been in a women's restroom. This isn't right.*"

"Don't worry about it. What do you want?" I needed to meet up with Tom and get out of this place before more requests came from beyond.

"*I don't want to go in there alone. Could you take me to my family?*"

I stood up immediately. I'd had this happen before. When one of our aunts passed away unexpectedly, I was surprised by an elderly grandmother who was just as surprised that I could hear her. She wanted to go to her family. I had to tell Mom about the encounter. God bless our mother! She lied and told Dad that she knew the woman. She held my hand as we escorted my spirit to her own visitation. I needed to do the same for Mr. Farmington.

As I exited the restroom, I avoided Tom's path of sight and walked in the opposite direction down to the other gathering. My talking spirit rambled on nervously as I stared into the large salon. "You have a lot of friends and family," I whispered.

"I was very blessed. Thank you. I know where to go now."

I saw a transparent form suspended above. It hovered over the family in front of the casket. Before I turned, I thought I saw him wave. The funny thing was I noticed a little girl wave back at him. She pointed at the spirit and tugged at the coat of the woman who sat next to her. I wasn't surprised when the woman held the girl's hand and calmed her down. I understood.

I rejoined Tom and explained that I thought I'd known the man's son from law school. Practice makes perfect in anything, and I was becoming a perfect little liar. As we walked in, Tom informed me that Mrs.

Martin was considering a pullout from the sale. It was completely understandable. That historical mansion and former country club was easily managed with her husband's salary as an investment broker, but now she had no idea what the financials looked like, and she wouldn't know until the accountant and the family's attorney went over all the details.

"She looks like she hasn't slept in weeks," Tom whispered as we stood in the receiving line.

I nodded. She did look weary, but her three children standing beside her looked completely lost. The Martins were a nice couple, and it had been easy working with them. The two boys and one girl looked as though they had lost their very best friend in the world.

As we came closer, I could hear Cynthia Martin explaining that the real estate agent found her husband. Me. She admitted to the man she was speaking to that it had been a shock. She hadn't even known he was meeting the agent. Me! She was wondering if the police had looked into the agent. Me! What? She knew her husband couldn't possibly be having an affair with the agent. What? But you never did know what really was in one's heart. I did, I wanted to scream. I wasn't having an affair with your husband.

Obviously, my brother heard the discussion too. He placed his hands on my shoulders. "Just be gracious. You know the truth. She's just grasping at anything to explain the loss. We know that feeling."

I bit my lip and stood straighter. I nodded. I would be me, well I'd be a silent form of me. It was suddenly our turn to express our condolences. Only minutes earlier it would've been so much easier.

"Mrs. Martin," I said as I held out my hand.

She turned her head to look at her oldest son. "This is the woman." She focused back on my face and glared. "I can't believe you showed up here, after what you've done."

Before I could get in one word, Tom pushed me to the side and took my place. "We just wanted to say how sorry we are. You take your time, and I'll talk to you after things settle down."

"You mean after they've arrested your sister? Oh, we'll be talking alright! You'll be talking to my attorney, and Ms. O'Donohue," she paused and pointed her finger at me, "will be talking to you through prison glass while she's serving her time for murder."

"That's enough," Tom calmly said. He said nothing more as he pushed me away. He held me under his arm as he shielded me from the darting glances and flurry of gossiping murmurs. I held my head down and just saw our shoes moving on the funeral home's carpet.

"Tommy, let's get you two out of here safely." I heard a low voice, and then another body on my right side. It wasn't until the lobby near the front door that Tom released his hold. The other man and he greeted each other with a warm embrace.

"Dad told me you were in town, but I just didn't believe it. You said you'd never come back here."

"I guess you really shouldn't say never, right?" the stranger commented. All I saw was his back when I finally lifted my head.

As I was brushing away my tears with a tissue, my brother made the introductions.

"Max, you remember Charlie, don't you?"

It was like a magician's reveal at the end of his show as he turned to face me. His smile didn't fade as he searched my face. It was him. It was the stranger, my knight, and the man who had swamped me with dirty snow and ice.

"It can't be. This is Charlie O?"

"Yep, all grown up, and we have a real estate

company together," Tom said proudly. In actuality, it was his company, and I just worked there, but he was a good brother, and an equally great employer.

I could see that everything was coming together in his little brain. He hit his forehead in realization.

"Your sister and I have been running into each other this week. I saved her from the ice the morning of the murder, and then I splashed snow on her while she was shoveling your dad's sidewalk. Sorry again about that." He touched my arm.

He touched my arm, and I realized something too. Oh my gosh, he touched my arm. I was no giddy teenager, but I knew there was something going on. Mom had told me about love at first sight, but I never believed her. Yet, this man of mystery evoked something within me. I just wasn't certain of what that feeling was.

"I'm sorry, but other than those two incidents, do we know each other?"

Tom and he shared a laugh at my expense. I hated when men did that. It always made me feel inferior as though they knew something I didn't, and I was stupid because of that.

"Charlie, don't you remember Max?"

I surveyed my stranger. It wasn't a difficult task, in fact, it was quite delightful. His brown locks weren't quite as unruly tonight as they had been flying in a winter wind. His caramel brown eyes had softened. His nose was beautiful, oh heck he was beautiful, and he was tanned. Who was tan in January in Kansas City? He was impeccably dressed with creased pants, shiny shoes, and a tight tie.

"Max? I'm sorry, I don't think I do." But I did, a little. I had a few memories boiling up, but they weren't the best ones.

"Max and I played football together all four years in high school. He came over to our house all the time, Charlie. He stayed with us one summer."

Nope, nothing. I remembered one of Tom's friends who used to call me…

"Charlie O, I can't believe you forgot me."

Realization became that crappy reality our little memories attempt to protect us from. "Now, I remember. You called me that because I was built like a blockhead cartoon character."

In fact, he had also added the description *Melon Head* a few times. I suddenly determined why I had placed all those memories in the "do not disturb" part of my brain. I hated Max.

He looked up at my face and then ran his eyes down my body slowly. Suddenly, I felt more vulnerable than I had when Mrs. Martin verbally attacked me. "You are certainly not built like a melon head now. Sorry about all of that. Kids will be kids."

I suddenly knew we would never date, never marry, never have children, never, ever have sex. I felt very slimy, almost victimized for a second time tonight.

"No, kids don't have to act like that. I never did. I was nice to everyone. I was nice to you, and you were mean. You were mean because you were cool, and you could get away with it," I lashed out as any normal kid would do. I was angry, perhaps more from the tongue lashing I'd received from the widow, but my assault had been on a most deserving target.

"Ouch," he said as he pretended to be hurt. "I suppose I deserved that." He turned to Tom to continue a conversation. "Can I have someone walk you two out to your car?"

My brother who was usually serious, became even more, if that was possible. "We should be fine. I drove. All those things Mrs. Martin said, you know they aren't true, right?" Tom looked over at me with a comforting smile.

Quickly, Max's eyes darkened. His charm vanished. "We are looking at it from every angle, and I really can't talk about it."

"Wait a minute," Tom said as he held his hand up. "You can't tell me you all suspect Charlotte? She's done nothing wrong. She only found the body."

Max shrugged. "We have to follow the leads."

"There are no leads," I shouted. "I haven't done anything. Why don't you look at who left that rose on the mantle?"

"What rose?" Max looked away from Tom and directly at me.

"I told everyone about it. There was a freezing rose on the mantle in the club, the house, whatever."

"I'll look into it, thank you." He looked at me as though I had burst his blue balloon he'd bought at the carnival with his own money. "I'll make sure that it is in the report. I'll also have a detective check in with you to follow up with another statement."

"I did one with Detective Blalock over the phone the afternoon after the murder," I answered.

He smiled through clenched teeth as though he was losing his patience. "Then you'll be doing another one."

Tom, the ever-protective brother, grabbed my arm and pushed me toward the door.

"See you around, Max. I need to get us home and out of here before things get any more tense than they already are."

"Tom, don't be upset, but your sister should probably have a legal representative with her when she gives this statement, and it will be in person this time."

I thought Tom was going to tackle him on the spot. "Don't worry about that, she will, plus she has her own law degree."

Max took a couple steps back, placing his hands in his pocket. He was uneasy with the confrontation. "I'm just doing my job, Tommy."

"And exactly what job is that?"

"I'm a federal prosecuting attorney."

I could physically feel Tom tremble as he heard those chilling words. He said nothing. He opened the door and fed me out into the night air. We said nothing as we walked quickly to the car.

Once inside the vehicle, he turned the car on and sat staring into the night.

"Charlotte, you and I both know they don't bring in a United States attorney for just some little old run-of-the-mill murder. I just thought Max was there helping the police in some capacity. I'm going to suggest that until this thing is settled, you move in with Dad."

"You're overreacting, Tom. I'll be fine," I answered, but inside I was shaking. My very confident brother was frightening me. He was worried, and if he was worried, I should be too.

"He's a bloody United States Attorney. He never gave up in football. He never gave up in any competition. He even broke my nose one time, and that was when we were playing flag football."

Tom was scaring me down to my core. I remembered something very important.

"He may be all that, but he's also coming to dinner on Saturday night. Our father is trying to set me up with him."

Tom's shocked face landed on the car's wheel. "Saints preserve us."

Yes, indeed.

Chapter Seven

I survived the lengthy interrogation, supposedly a statement about the murder, but it was certainly a questioning of the "gotcha" format. They even made me go downtown to walk through the building almost like a "perp walk", meet with a Detective Marino, and flee out of the building feeling frazzled and befuddled, and every other word that describes sheer hell.

Along the way, my legal representation was greeted by many who missed him in court. We ran into many of his old friends. Dad was definitely in his element. Then we ran into Paddy. My own brother pretended to not even notice me. Dad and he talked briefly in the hallway, and I slumped against a wall as I perfected my talent of invisibility. Over the years, I'd become very good at blending in and going unnoticed. During the lunch after Conor's death, no one saw me sitting in the corner for over an hour. I liked being the wallflower; attention only made me aware of my flaws and insecurities.

My voice was weak and wavering after thirty minutes of time-sensitive questions. Finally, my father tapped his hand on the table in front of us.

"Detective, let's make this easy for you. Tom and Charlotte O'Donohue were the man's realtors. Charlotte clearly had a meeting set up with Mr. Martin that morning. There is proof she called her brother on her way there. It was beginning to snow. Mr. Martin's car was parked in the lot before her arrival. The door was locked. She went in and discovered the man's body. What more do you want?"

The detective coolly searched through the file folder in front of him. "What about the rose he gave you?"

"No, the rose was on the mantle when I arrived. He didn't give me a rose."

"Did he ever give you flowers?"

My father's hand slammed down on the wood. "There wasn't anything going on between them except for the sale of a house. Drop it."

The detective placed a piece of paper in front of Dad. "Why do I have a receipt for flowers delivered to Ms. Charlotte O'Donohue from the victim?"

I was incensed. "He was thanking us for finding the house for his family."

My father looked over the receipt and handed it back to the interrogator. "Come on. He was thanking her."

"But he singled her out. He didn't send the flowers to the office, or to Tom O'Donohue. He sent them to her, to her house. That seems pretty intimate."

"It was the holidays. He knew the office was closed," I admitted. "Besides, I was home sick with a stomach bug. He knew because Tom had to take the previous tour with him because I wasn't feeling well."

"Then why were you there with him that morning?" He was definitely laser-focused on pinning this on me.

"I told you. We were meeting one more time, and I was making sure that he understood the surrounding residents were fine with the structure being a single family home, but if he had any ideas about turning it into a club again, a gallery, or bed and breakfast it wasn't zoned for that. You can check with Councilman Johnson," I insisted.

The detective turned over a couple more of the papers in front of him. Finally, he pushed back from the desk. My father patted my hand and whispered that everything would be okay. But then it wasn't.

"Ms. O'Donohue, when was your last relationship?"

"What?" My face was possibly as red as the mysterious rose.

My father stood up quickly and packed his old briefcase. "We are done now. Come on, Charlotte."

"We think it's relevant in this case."

"And I don't," Dad announced. "Detective, we have sat here." He stopped and looked at his watch while I gathered my purse and coat. I didn't dally when my father said we were leaving. "We have sat here for over a half of an hour. Unless you have some serious questions, going forward, you will need more than hearsay to question my daughter. Is that understood?"

Detective Marino stood up slowly and eyed my father as if he were a lion going in for a kill. "Oh, I understand. I understand that you think you still have some pull around here. You are deeply respected, Judge. Please don't place yourself in a situation because your daughter got herself into a jam. Maybe she should hire another attorney?"

The judge smiled. "You're right, there is another attorney, a friend of mine, who might do a better job for her." The detective nodded at the admission, but then

Dad continued. "But he's busy right now serving on the United States Supreme Court. She'll have to just settle for me. Have a nice day, Detective."

Dad hustled me past the man and out the door. I hadn't realized I was holding my breath until we departed the offices and headed into the hallway. I ran to a chair, sat, and I bent my head down.

I felt Dad's pants leg on the exposed skin between my skirt and the boots I was wearing. "Charlotte, are you going to pass out?"

"No," I whispered. Passing out was an option, but death might be simpler. "Dad, what is happening?" I lifted my tear-stained face to his soft eyes. "I haven't practiced law, but I can tell when things don't feel right."

"I think they're just trying to clean this up quickly. Maybe they're lazy? I don't know this detective. Has Paddy or Sean said anything to you about all of this?"

"No. I don't think Sean is involved at all, and you saw Paddy. I'm not sure he's still my brother." I blew my nose and began to cry harder.

But Dad chuckled. "I can tell you what your mother would say about that. She'd say your brother's head

was so large she never thought he'd make it through
the birth canal. She'd add that the big head didn't insure
intelligence, especially in your brother's case. He was
always a handful."

I leaned my head on his shoulder, and he gathered
me in his arms. "It will be okay, kiddo. Trust me. But
if you did kill him you need to tell me now so I can
prepare a case for you."

I shoved away. "Dad, how can you even think I
might murder someone?"

My dad stood up, extending his hand gallantly down
to me. I stood up slowly, still begging for an answer.
"Jane and you grew up with your brothers. Desperate
people can do desperate things. I learned that a long
time ago."

"But murder?"

As we began to walk out, he continued to hold my
hand. "Your mother, who was a saint, threatened to
murder me on a regular basis, especially anytime she
discovered she was pregnant."

Our mother did have a temper, in fact she was the
one we feared the most. We didn't want to disappoint
either one of them, but Dad was more distant working

long hours and traveling. Mom was there with us. She knew every little thing we did; she saw every little thing we did.

"But she never did kill you."

As he held the door open for me, he let go of my hand and patted my back. "No, but she made plans. I found a few of them. One involved a car bomb, another was some plot with the lawn mower. There were six times she plotted my demise."

He'd said it so seriously, but I was laughing through my tears. His years as a judge made him almost impossible to read. He could keep a straight face better than anyone I'd ever seen. "Dad, thanks for making me laugh."

"I'm happy I did, but I was just proving that anyone can commit murder if they are pushed."

I shook my finger at him. "You shouldn't kid about Mom. She can't defend herself." But I knew better. Maybe I could ask her later?

As stoic as a cold-hearted judge could be, he answered. "I wasn't kidding. I'll show you some of her plans when we get home. There are even detailed drawings, but some are done in crayon."

Either he had called my bluff, or he was not kidding. "Seriously? Mom? Didn't that worry you, that there might be something wrong with her?"

Finally, he smiled. "Hell no. I didn't blame her. It was her way of remaining sane in a house of crazy. I probably would've done the same thing. Besides, she couldn't live without me, and she knew I couldn't live without her."

We walked toward the car in silence. He was living without her, but today I saw the loss in his eyes more than any one day except that awful day when she closed her eyes the final time and never woke up again. A little of him had died with her, but he did live on for all of us kids. For me, I was happy he was still next to me. I needed him now more than ever.

Chapter Eight

"What were you thinking?" I pulled the standing rib roast out of the oven and checked the temperature. I was questioning my father once more about the dinner party tonight. He never rescinded the invitation to Max, the federal attorney and bane of my existence .

Dad was busy whipping his mashed potatoes. "I'm thinking I invited him over. As I recall, you wanted to meet him."

I rolled my eyes as I slid the meat back to cook for twenty minutes more. "Do not put this on me! That was before he accused me of being a murderer."

"So, let's convince him you aren't one."

Dad was too calm about this entire crazy episode of my life. I was a nervous mess ever since the funeral home fiasco. This morning, we heard from a friend at the newspaper that Mrs. Martin was sharing her theories about my involvement in her husband's death to anyone who would listen. She had already been interviewed by the newspaper and two television news channels.

I grabbed my glass of wine from the kitchen counter and took one drink and then another. "You know, my entire life could be over because of this. I might lose my realtor license, my law license. Not that I use it."

Dad turned from the potatoes and wagged a finger in my face. "You should. You would be a great lawyer. You'd be amazing with families."

"And that's another thing. Don't hang your hat on me having a family anytime soon."

"Stop whining."

My mouth gaped open. "Seriously, Dad? Don't you think I have a right to complain?"

Dad turned his attention to his new wine cooler, turning a bottle over to read a label.

"You do, daughter dear, but you shouldn't. It's not very attractive, and I want you to look great tonight."

"Damn it, Dad. I may be fighting for my life, and you've invited the vampire into our home to suck my blood." I filled my glass with more wine.

"Wear a cross and carry some garlic." He continued the preparations of the meal as I stood defiantly with arms crossed and face reddening.

He was saved from my wrath by Meg's voice. "Where are you two?"

"We're in the kitchen," Dad answered.

In a few minutes, Meg and Tom joined us. She extended her arms out and held me, patting my back to comfort me. "You poor dear. How have you been? This is an outrage. Don't you worry, Charlotte. We are all behind you."

Still in her embrace, almost suffocated by her attention, I looked at my brother and whispered the word "help". Tom shrugged and headed to the refrigerator for a beer. My brothers were always there for me, but sometimes they let me hang in the wind for a while, flaying about like a helpless puppet.

Finally, I pulled out of the suffocating love fest and thanked my sister-in-law. Funny, no one ever mentioned how ridiculous it was that anyone thought I could kill someone in cold blood.

Tom took a long drink from his bottled beer. "Dad, why exactly are we still doing this tonight?"

"I wondered about that too. From what Tom said, Max hasn't been that friendly," Meg added as she grabbed her own wine glass and borrowed my bottle on the counter to pour her own drink.

"Charlotte wanted to meet him." He offered no other explanation.

"But Charlotte has met him, and she doesn't want to have anything to do with him," I replied. "I've changed my mind. Isn't a girl allowed to do that?"

Dad completely ignored me and continued working on dinner. The doorbell rang. We all froze in place. Dad turned around to see three paralyzed figures.

"Oh for God's sake. He's not Satan!" He threw a towel on the counter and walked out of the kitchen.

"I'm not sure about that," I murmured.

Tom cocked his head in thought. "I'm with you, sis. He might be the devil."

Meg drained her glass. "And your father is inviting him in right now."

"I'm doomed," I admitted. We all knew our father was a brilliant man, but we were wondering if he was slipping a bit.

We heard laughter in the hallway. Dad's laugh was unusually loud. I could hear the deep tones of my stranger, who wasn't very strange to me now. "Come on in here, Max. We're not formal. Everyone is in the kitchen," Dad said as he entered ahead of our guest.

"As I remember, we always ended up in the kitchen, especially when your wife was making those pecan cookies. I loved those," Max said calmly. He had no idea what he was walking into. If you couldn't handle the heat in the kitchen, maybe you shouldn't be in it, even if you had been invited?

Max smiled widely as he saw us all gathered on one side of the kitchen. "Meg, my gosh. It is so good to see you again. How many years has it been?"

Always gracious, Meg hugged him. We all understood that she was a hugger. Of course, there were those times, Mom had called her a hanger, but that story was for another day.

"A long time, especially since you missed our wedding."

Her statement took the oxygen out of the air. Max nodded and pulled away.

"I'm so sorry, but I was deployed. I hope you did get my gift." That smile was back on his face. I wanted to punch it off of him.

"Yes, we did. Thank you, but that was years ago. We all **used** to be so close."

I shuddered. Meg had emphasized that their relationship was indeed in the past.

Max seemed to take it in stride. He shrugged and

leaned back on the kitchen counter. "I sure hope that we can resurrect our friendships now that I'm living here."

Dad winked at me, and I turned away. It was ironic that the devil was speaking of resurrection.

"In fact, I need to pick your brains. I want to buy a place, and I'd love to use your real estate agency."

Usually, we would be excited to obtain a new client, but all three of us just looked at him and blinked. Dad broke the awkward silence by asking Max what he wanted to drink. The two of them talked as Meg, Tom, and I, one by one backed out of the kitchen. Meg and I made sure everything was ready in the dining room as Tom turned the television on searching for a football game.

Dad announced dinner was ready and soon we were all seated together. God help us. Our father took his place at the head of the dining room table. Tom and Meg sat in their usual places, leaving the devil and I to sit next to one another. Earlier this week, I would have been smiling and giggling at every word dripping from his lips. I only hoped I didn't accidentally touch his shoulder.

After a quick prayer of thanks, we began what I

was labeling, the last supper. In my head, I continued to analyze him. He smelled good. His cologne or aftershave was light, not overpowering. Since he was left-handed, his right hand was placed to the side of the plate. His tanned hands were beautiful; his nails were well manicured. There were no tan lines except where his watch was located. He wore no rings. Again, usually that would've excited me, giving me some sort of hope for a future. I wouldn't date Satan, not this time. I'd been to hell and back after my last dance with the devil.

Dad carried most of the inane conversation. Thankfully, the football game on the television offered a modicum of noise but was overshadowed by Dad's story about the trial of a monkey. Tom, Meg, and I nodded nicely. We had heard that story so many times, but apparently it was a first for Max. He laughed so hard I almost found him attractive again. Almost.

Dad eyed us all. I figured we would get a good talking to once our dinner guest departed. He wasn't happy with us. I could see the disappointment in his eyes and could almost hear what he would say. "You all are better than this. You were rude. I raised you better than the behavior you exhibited tonight." He'd say it all. It wasn't like we hadn't heard it before, but usually we, the good children, didn't participate in this sort of behavior.

Thankfully, everyone finished their meals and Dad took Max into the living room to watch the game. He suggested to Meg and me that we could bring dessert to them.

"Why don't you have to get the dessert?" I whispered to Tom as Meg and I began to clean up the kitchen.

"Because I'm drinking." His head was shoved inside the refrigerator searching for his next beer.

"And you're a man," Meg admitted. "Your dad always becomes this macho guy in charge when there's guests, especially this one. Don't you see that **the judge** is cooking up something? He's playing with Max."

I stopped scraping the plate and faced Meg. "You're telling me, Judge O'Donohue is working Max?"

My sister-in-law nodded in her superior insight. "You two should've known. You both grew up with him. He has this tell. He laughs at everything, and it isn't just a chuckle. It is a full belly laugh. Your mom used to roll her eyes whenever she heard it. She knew he was up to something."

Tom and I searched each other's faces. "Is it possible that your wife knows our dad better than we do?" I asked.

Tom placed his arm around Meg. "I believe so. She is a smart one."

After he placed a kiss on her neck, she nudged him in the ribs. "You better say I'm smart. I got you through economics in college, remember?"

Tom evaded her glare. "I think I'll go join the men."

As he exited, a towel hit his back. I looked to Meg for an answer. "When did he become so obnoxious?"

"When he was fifteen." Meg remembered that summer very clearly. That was the first time she had put her eyes on Tom O'Donohue. She was the new girl in town. Her mother had convinced her to go to the local pool, even if she had to go alone. It would be an opportunity to meet some of the other teenagers in the neighborhood.

She walked to the pool three days straight. She stayed an hour swimming laps and drying off. Then she walked back home. On the fourth day, she went earlier in the day. She began swimming her laps and ended up running into a boy who was playing some form of dodge ball in the pool.

Meg had taken in a lot of water, gasping for air as she removed her swim goggles.

"You could've hurt me, you jerk," she yelled. The boy's back was right up against her front.

When he turned around, still grazing the front of her swimsuit, she was staring into the greenest eyes she'd ever seen. She remained speechless when he smiled.

"I'm so sorry. Are you okay? What can I do for you?"

Meg blinked several times, unable to say anything. Tom waited for her to respond. Finally, he turned to the other players.

"Max, I think I hurt her. You take over," he suggested as he threw the ball to the other boys. "Come on, let me get you something to drink." He lightly touched her back and moved her along in the pool. He even helped her up the stairs, taking her by the hand to follow him to the concession stand. "What can I get you? Water? A soda?"

"I like orange soda," she stammered.

"Hey Gail," he yelled for the young lady behind the counter. "Do you have orange soda?"

She did. He ordered two drinks, grabbing both of

them, and guiding her over to the picnic table in the shade. "I really am sorry." When he handed her the drink their hands touched and that was it for Meg.

"I shouldn't have been there."

Tom laughed. "Yes, you should've. We should've been more careful. If my mom and dad found out that I'd hit a girl, they would bury me in the backyard."

Meg finally smiled. She took a quick drink and lost herself in those green eyes.

"I don't think I know you. Are you new to the neighborhood?"

Meg nodded. "We just moved in last month, after school was out."

He extended his hand. "I'm Tom O'Donohue."

She grasped his hand. "I'm Meg O'Mara." Now she noticed his freckles. He was adorable.

"Super. Meg O and Tom O. That's perfect. Now, tell me all about yourself."

She never made it back into the water that day, and the remainder of the summer she had a partner to walk to and from the pool. He was still her partner and always would be.

Nearly twenty minutes later, we "little women"

joined "the men", entering with plates of the pecan pie that Dad had baked.

As the judge held court in his big chair, Tom was sprawled on the couch, leaving Max on the smaller sofa. Meg quickly took her place next to her husband, leaving me next to **him.** Usually, I didn't think of hurting anyone, but as my darted glance hit Meg's eyes, I could see how one could be pushed to do it.

Max seemed relaxed. He smiled as I handed him his pie and sat next to him. Even I was a little more forgiving now that I'd been fed and had the opportunity to cool off a bit.

"So who is winning?" I asked.

"Pittsburgh," all three men answered together.

"Do we care who wins?"

Tom answered while Dad and our guest began eating their pieces of pie. "Yes, we do. The Chiefs would do better against Pittsburgh than New England."

"New England's quarterback can pull any game out," Max added to the conversation.

"He's good, but I loathe him," Tom admitted.

Max nodded and continued to eat. I thought I saw him looking at me a couple of times, but if I turned he would know that I knew he was looking at me. What a mess!

I decided I would be nice. "What kind of home are you looking for?"

His head turned so quickly in my direction I thought he'd hurt himself. "I'm not sure yet. I know I don't want a townhouse. I had one in Atlanta, and I really didn't like it. It had a great rooftop patio, and a super view of the Atlanta skyline. I guess I know what I don't want."

I put on my agent persona, making it much easier to talk with the devil. "Do you have a preferred location?"

"I don't want to be too far from my downtown office, and I'd like to be near a park. I run every day."

Of course he did! He had to be one of those athletic, dedicated runners. He probably ran alone because no one wanted to run with him.

"How many bedrooms do you need?" Suddenly, my face seemed warmer. How many bedrooms do you need was a simple question, but once the words had left my mouth they seemed to take on more importance in an uncomfortable way than they should. Max began to smile. My face had to be red.

"I'd like a nice master, and maybe a couple more?

I'm not sure. I'd like a guest room for my dad when he visits."

Ah, the devil had a father. He had not crawled out from under a rock. Besides, he couldn't do that. He was far too clean and handsome, yes handsome. I was beginning to see the same man who had been my savior from the ice.

"How's your mom, Max?" Tom asked as he began to pick up plates around the room.

"You know her, she's always excellent. She's still living in New York City. She loves the snow."

"If I were her, I'd be at her house in West Palm Beach," Tom interjected as he left the room.

"I'd be at the house in the Virgin Islands, if I had time," Max murmured.

I looked back at him as he leaned back on the sofa. "How many homes does your family have?"

"I'm not sure. My dad has a place in Georgetown near the Potomac, and my mother has an apartment in New York, a Paris flat, um, I'd have to look at the list."

I looked over at Dad, and he just winked. I directed my attention back to our guest. "Does she collect houses?"

He chuckled and leaned up to intently watch a play on the television. "My dad and I think so. We live much simpler lives."

I nodded. "That's good to know when we are trying to find you a place. Simple then? Do you have a simple budget?"

"Nope," he answered without looking at me. "If I find something I like then I'll buy it. The budget doesn't matter."

I shook my head. He was a perfect client with no particular budget. Except I couldn't get a read on him. If my father played his games, I read people. Max was a blank page, offering me no education on his personality.

"We usually send new clients a checklist to fill out. That's our first step to determine what you need. We could narrow down your perfect location, and then we go out and see houses." Now, I was more comfortable, slipping into professional Charlotte.

"I'd like to do that as soon as possible. I've been staying in a rental, and that's getting real old real fast." He looked at me quickly and then returned his attention to the last minutes of the football game.

"Yes," Tom screamed as he jumped off of the couch.

"Touchdown, Pittsburgh, and with that, we don't have to face New England again."

"And we gain home field advantage," Dad added.

"Really?" Max asked. "You know I can get us tickets."

Tom and my father suddenly forgot about my plight completely. "That would be fantastic," Tom admitted. Dad agreed.

Max clapped his hands. "Done. I'll get those for the game, for the five of us?" He glanced at Meg and me.

"I don't like football, remember, Max?" Meg's face scrunched as though she smelled a pungent fragrance. "I hated it when I had to watch you both play all those years ago. Then, this one," she said as she pointed at her husband, "had to go and play in college."

"So that's a hard no for you Meg," Max acknowledged. His attention fell on me. "Well, Charlie, are you up to a game with the guys?"

I saw my father nodding in an affirmative manner. Really? "Sure, why not?"

"Wonderful, then the four of us. Tom, we can figure out all the details later next week."

Tom nodded and headed out to the kitchen. Meg

followed. I had no idea why, but Dad and I were left behind with the guest.

Dad cleared his throat, gaining Max's attention. "Max, do you think that would be appropriate for Charlotte to go with us? I mean, the detective made it seem that she's your number one suspect. By the way, why is a United States Attorney overseeing a local murder investigation?"

It seemed as though Max's demeanor completely changed. He stiffened his back as though he were at attention, or being reprimanded by a teacher. "I think it will be okay. The detective is looking at every angle. Once they present their case, then I may have to distance myself from, well, it just depends on the outcome of their investigation." Now, he looked at me and smiled slightly. He turned back to Dad. "I'm not at liberty to say why I'm overseeing the case."

"It's not just because of the house?" My father's question hit a nerve of some kind. I saw a vein roll on the side of our guest's neck.

Max laughed nervously. "Well, there is that."

What? What about the house? I didn't know if I could wait until he left to know the answer. My sight line with my father yielded me no answers. But I didn't have to wait too long before the devil himself provided what I needed.

"The Taylor Mansion, Club, whatever you want to call it, was my family's home. My mother is a Taylor. I lived in that house." His tone was flat, non-emotional. He said nothing, but he said everything in his dispassionate statement.

"Oh," I answered. I couldn't come up with anything else.

"So now you know my secret, Charlie O." He smiled that smile, and I felt my heartbeat quicken, just ever so slightly.

Dad stood up. "How about some coffee?"

Max looked down at his watch. "You know, I really should be leaving. I have witness statements for another case I need to review by Monday. This was great to reacquaint myself with all of you. Thank you so much sir." He stood up and shook Dad's hand.

It wasn't until Max had put on his coat and was heading out into the winter night that **the judge** stopped him at the door. I stood behind my dad for protection from the cold.

"You know, Max, I've learned over the years, that

if a man has one secret, he probably has more. Those pesky little things can ruin a man if he's open for blackmail. Luckily, for this family, we have no secrets. Have a good night. Come again."

Max looked at my father in the most peculiar way. He looked as though he had been caught, and I saw a small amount of fear. He nodded, waved, and ran to his car.

Dad shut the door, and I hugged my father as tightly as I could. "Have I told you how much I love you? I don't know what all that was about, but you scared him."

He patted my back. "No, Charlotte, I just fired the first shot. He'll be back." Dad closed his eyes and held me tighter. "I love you too. I'll do anything for you, even destroy a young man I used to love like a son. If I have to, I will.

Chapter Nine

I managed to talk my way out of moving back into the family home, for now. I woke up Monday morning in my own bed. I pulled clothes to wear to work from my own closet. I made coffee in my own kitchen. I took a sip of the much needed caffeinated beverage and took a deep breath.

Last week was insane, but this week will be calm and hopefully mundane. I would be at my desk by nine and line up a few meetings for the week, steering clear of the Taylor Club, but I did need to drive by and see if the police tape had been removed.

My cell beeped. Dad's photo popped up. "What's up, Dad?"

"Are you dressed?" he asked seriously.

For a second, I thought maybe he was attempting a bad joke, but he seemed worried.

"Yes, why? What's wrong? I can hear it in your voice."

"You are going to have company in a few minutes.

Don't worry, and for heaven's sake, please do not say anything, good or bad." His tone made my skin crawl.

"Dad, just tell me." My voice was barely audible.

"The police have a search warrant for your house. You know the drill. Just let them in and step back. Go where they tell you to go. Do everything they say. I'll be there as soon as I can, and I'll call Tom and update him. I'll be there." He hung up on me.

I stood in the middle of my kitchen shaking and holding my phone. When there was a sudden knock at the door, I jumped.

The pounding became harder as I made my way to the front hallway. I saw several large figures. As I unlocked the door, I could see the police uniforms and Detective Marino with a paper in his hand.

I could hear my heart beat out of my chest as I faced them. I needed to stay cool.

"Ms. Charlotte R. O'Donohue, we have a warrant to search your house, lot, car, and every item within those areas and associated premises. Please step back and allow us to enter." He handed me the document. The swarm entered, tracking in snow and muck from the yard. I looked out to see more police cars arriving. They headed to the backyard. The neighbors would definitely bring this up at the summer block party…if I could attend and not phone in from jail.

I was still standing in the hallway with my back plastered against the wall when Max walked through my doorway. He closed the door and leaned against the opposite wall.

He had the audacity to smile. "Charlie, just remember to breathe. It will be over soon. I promise."

He looked every bit the devil that he was. He was dressed in black from his shoes to that beautifully tailored overcoat. He folded his black-gloved hands in front of him. Black was a good color for him, and for funerals. Sadly, I thought I was attending my own wake. I tried to breathe, but I was breathless. It wasn't because of him and his charm anymore. I was building up an immunity to his good looks. I'd taken an examination of my feelings toward Max and had decided I was attending far too many bridal and baby showers. Hormonal flutters were tapped down when you were facing prison time.

I said nothing to him. He continued to examine me. Did he want me to break? I had nothing to hide.

Detective Marino stepped in front of our stare-off. "Ms. O'Donohue, I need the keys to your car, your purse, and your laptop. They're all included in the warrant." He held out his hand.

I looked down and around my body. "I don't have any of those items on me. May I get them for you?"

Max nodded at the detective, and then the detective agreed. Marino was Max's lapdog! Max was the puppet master of this event. I nodded just for fun and walked into the kitchen with my shadow. Handing my phone off to him, I then grabbed my purse and laptop and placed them on the kitchen counter. "Oh, and my car and house keys are in my purse. Have fun." Dad didn't say I had to make it easy on them.

I didn't wait to see his reaction as I stomped off. I returned to the hallway and saw Max sitting in my living room. "Why don't you join me while they do their job?" He extended his hand out to invite me to sit in my own house.

I thought I couldn't commit murder, but perhaps I could? I wanted to kill him right now. Our mother could scare you to death with just one look. Did I have that talent? Instead, I looked around to search for implements of destruction. There was a fireplace poker. That would do the trick, and it would leave a dent in that hard head of his. Instead of doing the deed, I plopped down on my own couch and began to look over the papers in my hands. When I looked up, we began our contest of who could stare at each other the longest.

"I'm sure they won't find anything," Max commented as he removed his gloves and placed them on **my** coffee table. He was certainly making himself right at home, in **my** home. What was the most infuriating was the notion that he looked more comfortable in my home than I did.

I said nothing. It was only a few minutes before my father rushed into the room. He hadn't even shaved or combed his hair yet this morning.

"Mr. Shaw, could I see the warrant and the affidavit?" He directed his question to Max. When I was a little girl, I never knew what my brothers' friends' names were. In fact, I'd made up nicknames for all of them. My name for Max had been *Poop Head.* I was a little girl, afterall. Most of my names weren't exactly Shakespearean.

Max pointed toward me, and I handed my dad the

papers. He sat down next to me on the couch and began to study the document. He looked up occasionally at the younger attorney across from him. Then my father pulled out his glasses. Crap, it was serious when he did that. "Judge Symones signed off on this?" Dad asked.

Max only nodded. My entire life was in jeopardy, and he just nodded. For what seemed like an eternity, Max and I continued to play our stare and avoid game while Dad read. Eventually, he placed his glasses and the papers onto the coffee table in front of us. He folded his arms over his still buttoned coat and sighed. Just sighed.

"You are looking for a murder weapon. My daughter doesn't even know how the man died."

Max's left brow rose. He stopped looking at me and focused on the judge. "Doesn't she?"

Dad turned his attention to me. "Charlotte, did you see a weapon near Mr. Martin last week?"

"No, and he was lying on his chest. His head was turned to the left. I knew he was dead. I know what death looks like." Dad winced. He knew too. We knew the coloring; we knew the smell; we knew the loss.

"Did you move the body to see how he died?"

"No. I checked his pulse, but that's all. In fact, I left the area and called the police immediately," I answered my father.

Max leaned his arm on the bolster of the chair and leaned his head up against his hand. He appeared to have a headache. Good. I hope it is a really good one! But of course, the headache was a retired federal judge. And that's when I remembered how I knew the name Shaw. When I was a little girl, Dad had a very dear friend who used to be an FBI agent. He eventually moved to Washington, D.C. and became the head of the agency. Max's dad was FBI Chief Edward Shaw. Dad talked to him over the Christmas holidays.

"Did you ever go back to the body?" Dad questioned again.

"No," I answered emphatically, but did I? The fog of uncertainty from so many questions began to mist my memory.

"Was the house locked when you entered?" Dad just kept the questions coming.

"Yes. I didn't understand though. Mr. Martin's car was parked there, and it looked like it had been for some time. I unlocked the door. How did he get in?" I began to search my memory for more details.

"Maybe you gave him a key so you could meet him there at any time?" Max asked. He never lifted his head.

"No, a client never has the key until it's their home," I snapped back. "If you knew anything about me, you would know that I'm always a professional."

Max's eyes narrowed. "Were you professional when you attacked your boyfriend over two years ago?" He was emotionless; a devil robot.

I began to answer, but Dad's hand stopped me. "What is going on here? Really? You know damn well what happened to her. The newspaper ran with that outrageous photo to get even with me. It was a bad time in our lives when my wife died. The boyfriend in question was a pretender. He tried to take advantage of my daughter. She threw a beer in his face at a Westport bar. I have this feeling you've had that happen to you once or twice. He grabbed her arm as she was leaving, and Charlotte decked him. You've probably had that happen to you too."

Yikes, Judge O'Donohue was in the house. I smiled smugly, but Max didn't move a muscle.

"She threw a punch. If she has anger management issues, she could become violent again," he murmured.

"My mother was dying, you ass, and he said terrible

things about my dead brother. The man who will not be named was awful to me. He used me in the worst way," I screamed out before Dad could stop me. Max sighed in response. "You sanctimonious ass."

"Charlotte Rose." Two words from my father's mouth shut mine, but Max wasn't backing down. He seemed formidable, challenging my father or me to slip up. I really wasn't sure to whom he was issuing the threat.

"Judge, can you trust your daughter? Are you certain you'd know if your daughter was having an affair with Mr. Martin, any man, or just sleeping with someone?" Max's heated gaze swept over my entire body. I felt a betrayal of my body as I warmed from the top of my head to the soles of my feet.

Dad nodded. "Yes, because Charlotte doesn't lie to me. Besides, Max, I believe affairs are in your wheelhouse." Dad smiled. "We all know it isn't the sleeping that gets you in trouble, right Max?"

Max's composure broke. He clasped his hands and then unclasped them. He wanted to do something. Instead, he cleared his throat and smiled at me. "I bet you wouldn't tell if you were with the right man, would you?"

Dad clenched the side of the chair. "I believe you have an agenda, Mr. Shaw, and I don't want my daughter caught up in whatever game you are playing."

I felt like bait for the catching of a prized catfish. What agenda? And could we go back to making Max feel uncomfortable about his love life?

Detective Marino arrived in the nick of time, entering the room, holding evidence bags with several knives contained within. "I think we have all we need." He showed Max the bag of knives and another one that held my cell phone.

"I need my phone for my business. And what about my laptop, and my purse?" I saw another detective holding the other items. "My driver's license is in there and so many other things."

Grabbing his gloves from the table, Max stood up and turned his attention to us.

"Today, you might want to take the day off. I ensure that you'll have everything back by the end of the day. I'll drop them off personally. Thank you for being so accommodating."

"Dad," I pleaded.

He patted my hand. "It's just one day, Charlotte. Relax. They'll do their tests, and copy the information on your phone and computer. Max will bring them back tonight. He promised."

My jaw dropped. Now, he was trusting **Max**?

Max began to leave the room. He stopped as though he had one more thought. He walked over to Dad and leaned down to shake his hand. "Thank you, Judge. I'm sorry about all of this, but I have to verify every piece of evidence. See you Sunday?"

Dad grinned. "Of course. I'm looking forward to it."

"We're on the club level so you won't get cold," Max whispered in my father's ear. "Oh, and there's food."

Dad nodded. Max nodded at me. Then he was gone, finally. I laid my head back in despair. "I think I'll go back to bed."

"You know, that may not be a bad idea." Dad looked out into the kitchen. "Um, yes, go back to bed. I'll talk to Tom. Later, much later, you can put your house back together."

Both of my hands balled into fists. I hit them down onto the cushion. "Are you kidding me? I just cleaned yesterday! Damn you, *Poop Head*!"

"Right now *Poop Head* has no jurisdiction over this case. The local police and DA should be handling it, not a federal prosecutor who obviously is after something bigger. I wonder what the Martins were up to?"

"They were involved in something that resulted in Mr. Martin's murder? I can't believe that. You'd make me feel better if you'd spill on your accusation of Max and a woman." If Dad could translate Max's comment that I would lie if I was with the right man, I'd be in heaven.

"Women, Charlotte, and it's not important."

I had learned in my lifetime when the conversation ended with my father. The discussion was abruptly and permanently tabled.

As soon as Dad left, I locked my door, took a brief glance of the chaos left from the devil's minions' visit, and went to my room. I took off every remnant of professional Charlotte and dressed in my favorite pajamas. I removed my discounted designer pillows, pulled back the covers, and slid in.

I drifted off to sleep quickly. It was time to sort things out. "Mom, are you there?"

She arrived, wearing one of her favorite outfits. I always liked her in the casual tan pants, and the palm tree design on her v-neck shirt. It reminded me of the last family vacation at Clearwater Beach. Dad had told her we could go anywhere, but she wanted to go back to a familiar beach.

"Charlotte Rose, you made your father mad today."

I nodded. "I'm sorry, but they're trying to railroad me."

Mom snickered. *"That's an old term."*

"I'm an old soul. You told me that a long time ago when I first told you." I stopped short of saying anymore.

"You can say it, Charlotte. You told me you could talk to the dead."

I nodded my head. "Mom, help me."

"Charlotte, help yourself. You can do this, and try to be nice to Maxwell. His life hasn't been that easy."

"He's being mean to me."

My mother's laughter filled my room. *"You used to say that when you were little too. Your family loves you. I love you. Listen to the woman. Listen to Rose. You'll find the answer."*

"But, Mom…" I sat straight up in the bed, gasping for air. I grabbed my head. Max had somehow transferred his mother of all headaches to me. "Thanks for sharing, *Poop Head.*"

True to his word, Max Shaw stood outside my

house at six in the evening, holding all of my worldly work possessions. I greeted him at the door, still in my pajamas and fuzzy slippers. I opened the door, then shuffled into the living room to plop my body in the chair he had sat in that very morning.

Max placed all of my things on the coffee table, and then without asking, he took a seat across from me on my couch. "We have everything we need, and thank you for your cooperation."

"Uh huh."

"I'm just searching for the truth."

"Uh huh."

I began to chew on one of my fingernails. It was a nasty habit that I long since had abandoned, but today seemed a good time to pick it up again, especially in front of the federal attorney.

"Charlotte, I'm really sorry, and this time answer me." His tone was a little louder and much more demanding.

I stopped slumping, sitting erect in my chair. We were staring at each other again. I knew what I was looking at, but I wondered what he was seeing. I looked absolutely awful with my medium-length hair pulled into two ponytails on either side of my ears. My makeup was nonexistent. My pajamas were baggy, hiding any form I did have. I didn't even have a bra on. Usually, I would never allow a man to see me this way, but who really cared? I didn't. Obviously, he didn't either.

"What exactly do you want me to say, Mr. Shaw?"

He ran his hand through his hair and clenched his hands together in front of him. He looked as though he was praying.

"I don't want you to take this all personally."

If I had been drinking something, I would've choked. "You must be kidding! How should I feel? I'm not happy about any of this. You think I killed a man. Your detective thinks I was fooling around with my client, a married man. You think I'm holding something back." I snapped my mouth shut. I hadn't told anyone about the key. I was holding something back.

"Did you ever think that by doing everything by the book, I'll prove you innocent?"

I shook my head. "So now you're doing me a favor? I am innocent, *Poop Head*!"

That broke the ice. He looked as shocked as I felt. We both broke out in laughter.

"Gee, I've missed that so much," Max kidded. "You

were so cute when you were little." It was then that he finally examined my look. He burst into laughter again, pointing at my pajamas. "What the heck are those?"

"Birth control?"

He wiped away a few tears. "Yep, that outfit would certainly slow down a romantic night with me. Slow down, but not prevent." He stopped laughing. He focused on my face. I was focused on his lips. How had I not noticed those luscious lips? Stop. He wasn't the man I originally thought he was. He was not a knight in shining armor. He was a devil in a black overcoat.

He stood up quickly. "I should leave, and let you get back to whatever you've been doing. Again, thank you for your cooperation, Ms. O'Donohue."

I stood up too. I wanted to make sure he made it to the door without searching my hallway for guns. "Not my pleasure, Mr. Shaw."

He grimaced and headed to the door. Before he turned to leave, he smiled. "You know, on second look, those pajamas might just--" He stopped and lowered his voice. "Take care, Charlotte."

I pushed the door closed and locked it quickly. My heart was beating faster again. He called me by my name. He didn't call me Charlie, Charlie O, or even his term for me, *Melon Head*. He hadn't looked at me as though I was a block head. I liked how my name sounded like a song when he whispered it. My name sounded like some exotic term when he said it. I liked how he formed the words. No. He was the devil. No, I liked him. I had always liked him.

Chapter Ten

I drove by the Taylor Club at least a dozen times before Sunday. On Wednesday, the police tape had been removed, but there was a security guard on the property. Thursday, the guard was sitting in his car eating his lunch. On Friday, I got cold feet when I saw a woman walking her dog on the nearby sidewalk. By Sunday, I decided to wait a couple more weeks before I tried the key in the lock. In the meantime, to save myself, I avoided speaking to my detective and police officer brothers. I suspected my own father knew I was holding something back, but I was hoping that he thought it was about the rose I had seen. I showed him the photos. He jotted down a few notes to ask the police what they had seen, or if they had bothered to take photos of the mantle.

By the time Dad and I reached Tom's house, I was exhausted just from sheer worry. What if the key was an integral part of the investigation? What if the murderer had hid it in the window seat on his way out? I was basically interfering in a murder investigation, but was I? I justified my decision not to turn over the key as it was my only ace-in-the-hole.

Besides, Rose needed my help. I was delusional. In reality, it was another piece of evidence, and it would be looked upon as if it were in the hands of the real murderer...me! I couldn't tell them a ghost had asked me to keep it secret.

Tom and Max were waiting for us in the driveway as we pulled up. Thankfully, the devil didn't look so much like a demon today. He had on a brown leather bomber jacket with a peak of a Chiefs' red shirt underneath. Tom looked like one big Kansas City fan. From top to bottom, he was attired in red and gold. Meg waved to us from inside the house.

The two old friends had already decided Tom would be driving. It seemed as though they, including my father, were putting everything aside from the last two weeks. I remained unusually quiet as they all joked, and Dad reminisced about their bad behavior in high school. My mind wandered, imagining what it might be like in prison. Could I practice law in the federal pen? I bet Mr. Shaw knew the answer to that.

We were nearing Arrowhead Stadium when the conversation turned toward Max's family.

"Max, when did your parents divorce?" Dad asked. I glared at him for the rude question, but he ignored me completely.

Max turned back to answer. "They haven't. After all of these years, they remain separated, but not divorced. Neither one of them will ever remarry, but from a legal basis they should iron everything out. Heck, I'd do it for them. It might be a mess when either one of them dies."

"You just have your sister, right?" Tom asked as we pulled into the tailgate fog from all of the grills in the parking lot.

"Yes, hey turn into that lane over there," Max directed as he placed the parking placard onto the rearview mirror.

Tom slowed down to be checked in, and we were directed to our parking space, very near to the stadium. "Gee, Max, do you think we're close enough?"

Even my father was in awe, and it took a lot to impress him. I sighed. If the seats were good, the two of them might throw me under the bus for future playoff tickets. As if he could read my mind, Max explained the location of the seats.

"Just wait until we get in there. We're in a suite on the club level, complete with food, liquor, and heat. It's a long way from that time you took us to the game in that snow storm, Judge," he said. I could see him take a glance at me very quickly, then turn around in the passenger seat.

"You made me happy when you mentioned heat," Dad added. The man was absolutely glowing with happiness. "That was a cold game, but you two had won those tickets. The Chiefs were terrible back then, but I didn't have the heart to tell you boys no."

My head bobbed back and forth as I mimicked my father. He didn't have the heart to tell them no? He never had a problem telling me no. I couldn't go to this dance. I couldn't go to that party. I couldn't get a ride from anyone but my sister and Paddy, not even Tom! This bromance was making me nauseous, and we hadn't even made it into the stadium.

I was completely invisible as we entered. The devil was offering them so much. It was then that I realized I was the sacrifice for the day. I might as well remain in the parking lot waiting in line for my position on the spit.

I figured I might as well enjoy myself after we entered the suite. Tom and Dad were already seated with their plates and beers as I looked over the buffet. I studied the pasta, but then I had to choose between the brat or the steakburger.

"You could have a little bit of everything." His low voice rumbled near my ear. As I looked up, I nearly hit Max's nose.

"Sorry. I don't think I can eat all of it."

Max grabbed a plate and handed it to me. "Why not? By the way, when did you grow up? I mean when did Charlie O leave and this lovely woman Charlotte arrive?"

I looked up to watch his mouth and those lips. I didn't know what to say. Was this his attempt at being nice, or was he playing me? After my last exploration into love, I definitely had lost the ability to trust.

"Probably in college," I answered slowly. "I was playing a lot of tennis then and working. I still have my melon head."

He acted as if I had wounded him. "No you don't, and I'm sorry about that. Boys will be--"

I stopped him with my hand touching his chest. "Don't even say that. We went through this the other night. You and Tom were evil to me. You don't know how many times you made me cry."

I became uneasy as his eyes followed down to my hand. I could feel his heart beating. I pulled back quickly. I knew I was blushing.

"Charlotte, I never want to make you cry again," he whispered.

Yikes! How could the timbre of his voice send a charge to every nerve in my body? If just the sound of his voice could do that to me, what if he touched me, really touched me? I shook that off very quickly, and selected the brat, bun, sauerkraut, and brown mustard. I kept piling on food. I hadn't eaten baked beans in two years. I kept my head down and sat next to my father, completely distancing myself from Max Shaw.

"This is going to be great," Max announced as he took the seat next to me. His leg touched my leg. I looked at him as though he were some alien. He took a large bite of his own brat. He winked at me as he swallowed.

Thankfully, it was time to stand for the National Anthem and the beginning of the game. The first half of the game was the longest two football quarters of my life. Max talked over me to Dad and Tom. In fairness, he did attempt to include me in the conversation. If I was truthful with myself, it might have been a long half, but I was having one of my best days in the last few months. During the break, everyone in the suite mulled around.

Max could be quite charming for a *Poop Head*. He made sure that Dad talked to the city's mayor, the state governor, two other federal officials of something, and even the team's owner. Tom and I grabbed beers for the four of us as the two political monsters made their way through the room.

Tom's head tipped up in their direction. "Look at him. Dad is having the time of his life. This is the happiest I've seen him in a long time."

I looked in their direction and saw the same thing. He was happy. "I know. I hate that Max is the one who is doing it."

"Don't say that. It will be okay, I promise."

I took a drink from my beer. "I appreciate your assurance, but that detective is still looking at me as a killer. Max has to be pulling those strings."

"I don't think so," Tom whispered. "I think he's on a different track. Something else is up. You may just be the distraction."

Me? A distraction to Max Shaw? I snorted. "You must be kidding. That man is way above my pay scale."

Tom's eyes narrowed. "What the hell are you talking about?"

I suddenly realized we were discussing two different things. "Um, nothing. Just the case."

My brother was eyeing me suspiciously. "You aren't falling for him, are you? He's the same guy who called you *Melon Head*, remember?"

I nodded. I needed to keep my mouth shut. There was no need to tell my own brother that just Max's touch could warm my body. When I looked at Max's shoulders I wondered what his bare chest looked like, and that led my thoughts to…Tom just wouldn't understand.

As the two of us sat down, Tom nudged me. "Besides, I need to talk to you about something."

"What?"

He sat closer to me and whispered. "I have looked all over the office. Meg has too. Please tell me that you have both keys for the Taylor Club."

"No, I don't." Surely, he didn't know I had that old key, did he? My brother didn't hear dead people. On a daily basis, we were all lucky he heard the living ones.

"So, you had the key that day to let Mr. Martin in, right?"

"Yes, and I put that key into the file. Mr. Martin was

somehow already in the house when I opened the door. Tom, should that key go to the police?"

"I'll ask Max, but I think it was just an oversight that the police didn't take that one from you. I had another key in the packet when we met with the Martins three weeks ago. It's gone. I just don't know if I should tell Max."

"Tell me what?" Max was leaning into our conversation and over me. Dad and he had joined us.

"How much this means to Dad today," Tom lied. My brother looked at his friend and lied.

Max saw his beer and toasted Tom. "No problem. It's just good to connect with you all again. I've missed this." His hand waved in a circle, encompassing the three of us.

The game began, and it looked as though my brother had swallowed a small animal. It seemed ironic to me that a family of mostly law-abiding adults could suddenly turn to lies when placed smack in the middle of a murder investigation.

Most of the conversation for the remainder of the game involved the Chiefs. How could they pull off game after game at the last minute? The city of Kansas

City was having a collective heart attack every time they played.

When the Chiefs took the lead, Max nudged me. "I hope you are having a good time, despite everything surrounding the Martin investigation."

I nodded, but I didn't look at him. I couldn't. My left arm was on fire as his sleeve touched my arm. It was hard to lie to someone who was being nice to you, especially someone like him.

Surprisingly, he leaned closer. His mouth almost touched my ear. "I know you're holding something back. When you're ready, just tell me. We can figure this all out together."

I didn't flinch. I didn't breathe. I didn't respond.

"Do you want to tell me why you've been driving past the crime scene?"

I still stared ahead. Were the security cameras turned on now at the house? We weren't informed. Or was he having me followed?

"No, I don't. Do you mean your old house?"

"Yes. I'm talking about the place where a man died. A place that you seem unable to stay away from."

Out of the corner of my eye, I could glimpse a little

bit of a smile, a very knowing smile. "We still need to get you a home," I stated coolly. Two could play his little game. I was my father's daughter.

He nodded. "Yes. I'll stop by the office tomorrow. Will that work?"

"That should work. We're usually in every Monday."

He turned his head to face me. "Except for **that** Monday." His smile faded. He studied my face. I refused to break.

"That was a special case."

We remained seated as Tom and Dad shot up out of their seats over another touchdown.

Max lowered his head toward me. "Indeed it was."

I absolutely hated him being this close to me. I hated what he did to my psyche, to my body. I was so warm I didn't even need the sweatshirt I was wearing, but stripping wasn't an option. It would just give him more fodder in his investigation.

By the end of the game, I was more than ready to walk in the cold to the parking lot. Thankfully, Tom sensed that something was wrong and hung back to walk with me while Dad and Max led the way.

"Are you okay? You seemed to be involved in some serious conversations with Max."

"Oh, you have no idea." My loud exclamation made Dad and Max turn around as we continued to talk. "Tom's being a moron."

They smiled and headed on. Tom hit my arm lightly. "Thanks for throwing me under the bus."

"Your friend needs an invitation to learn humility. It seems we both need to be worried about Mr. Shark up there." I pointed at Max. "He's dropping by the office tomorrow under the auspices of finding his dream home."

Tom hung his head. "My friend never espoused humility. I'll give him the key we have and tell him about the lost one."

I was thinking the same thing myself. Tomorrow, I needed to tell a federal prosecuting attorney about my discovered key. As long as I was in the land of the living, the ghost would have to understand.

Chapter Eleven

Meg was aware that Tom and I were on edge. It was not just the usual Monday blues. She said nothing as she placed hot coffee in front of both of us at the conference table.

"You two look like death warmed over. Maybe this caffeine will perk you up." Sitting at the head of the table, she opened her files. "We have a fairly slow week so I expect both of you to shake some trees for clients, and I need you to clean up all your paperwork. I've begun compiling everything for taxes with the accountant. I just want to make sure nothing is hiding in your offices. I don't want any secrets around here."

Our focus on our coffee cups was broken. Both of our heads shot up in shock.

Meg had gained our attention. "Ah, I knew there was something. Your Dad had a great time yesterday with Max, but you two looked like you'd been to a funeral. Do you want to talk about it?"

"**No!**" Tom and I answered.

Meg stood up, grabbed her file and phone, and began to walk out of the room. Our eyes followed her, surprised at her abrupt departure. She turned around before she entered the hallway. "If you won't talk to me, then you'll talk to your dad."

As if they had masterfully blocked out a scene for a film, our father walked in, perfectly on cue.

"I haven't had to give you two a dressing down in years. You were always the good kids. Now, what the hell is going on?"

Dressed in his Sunday pants, a shirt, tie, and a cardigan, he strode in and sat in Meg's seat. Both of his arms rested on the table, his cool blue eyes looking from Tom to me.

"Fine. I'll begin. I know something is going on. Max knows something is up. Secrets don't help anyone, especially your attorney. By the way, Charlotte, you owe me a dollar if I'm going to be your representative." He held out his hand.

"My purse is in my office."

"Get it to me before I go to bed tonight. And you--" He turned to Tom and opened his hand again. "I think you may need to give me a dollar too, unless you want to tell me about something?"

Tom reached into his pants pocket and pulled out two one dollar bills. "I'll pay for Charlotte too, if that's okay?"

Dad actually took the money and stuffed the bills in the pocket of his sweater. "I'll take it. Now, spill Thomas."

"The police never asked for Charlotte's key to the Taylor Club. I'll see if Max needs it today. But, I noticed that the extra key for the property is missing from the office. I've searched everywhere for it. I had it the week before Martin's death when the couple was here in my office."

"Is that all?" Dad asked quietly.

"For me, yes."

They gazed over at me. "Charlotte Rose, spill."

"I, I'm afraid about how this is going to look," I stammered.

"If Max finds out first whatever you're hiding, it will be worse. I can guarantee that. The boy is not an idiot, and he doesn't appreciate being played for one."

"I found a key, not Tom's key. After the police came, they wanted me out of the way. I sat down in this window seat, and it felt like I was sitting on something.

No one was paying attention to me. I got up, and I found a key stuck into the wood. I pulled it out. It seems to be very old, but it also matched the one I had. I've been trying to get back to the house to see if it fits in the lock."

My father dropped back into the chair, his eyes closing as if he was in prayer. I felt the tears begin trailing down my cheeks. Tom reached for the tissue box behind him on the shelf and placed it in front of me.

"You do not go back to that house," he instructed without opening his eyes. "Tom, you will hand over the one key. Marino or Paddy goofed up on that. You will tell Max today about the missing key. Give him the exact date of the last time you remember seeing it. You tell him who was in the room, and who wasn't in the room. You tell him how the Martins were acting, and you tell him where your sister and your wife were during that meeting. Do you understand?" He finally opened his eyes to look straight into his son's face. Tom nodded. "Good, now go pull anything you have on the Martins, and write down all that information so you don't get it wrong. There is no room for any mistakes. I want to talk to your sister alone. Close the door on your way out."

No, don't close the door, Tom, I pleaded with my eyes. As the door closed, I braced myself for what was to come. He wouldn't raise his voice. He never did. He just made you feel so bad.

"Of all of you six kids, you, the baby, have never done anything that really disappointed me. Until today. Paddy has always been the one I needed to watch. He seemed to have this need to prove himself. I'm still surprised he lived through puberty. Then Jane was the one who had to sneak out all the time. It wasn't that she didn't like us, she just wanted to be somewhere else. I thought for sure she'd end up pregnant. Tom and Sean were the party boys. Your mother and I lost a lot of sleep over the two of them. But all the boys have pulled out of idiocy. Tom is more reliable than the sun coming up in the morning. Conor, he seemed to be an angel, but he needed that danger. I couldn't save him. His death left your mother hopeless. She never fought hard against that cancer. She wanted to be with him. And then there was you."

I dabbed at my eyes as he reached out for my hand. His large paw enveloped it.

"My baby girl, you were the surprise. You were spunky, but you were so sweet." He pulled away from my hand. "And I never, ever thought you would be the one who would hide evidence in a murder investigation."

I sniffed and blew my nose. "Daddy, I thought I could handle it. I thought I could find out--"

"Find out what? You aren't some amateur sleuth, Charlotte. Do you think Max is an idiot? He knows something is going on. Oh, I don't think he believes you are the murderer, but he knows you have been less than forthcoming. You will do the same as Tom. You'll tell him everything. You'll hand over that damn key today."

"Yes, Dad." My words caught in my throat.

"I'm your attorney consulting you right now. Your dad is too disappointed in you." He pushed away from the table and walked behind me. "Now, get yourself together. Max will be here in a little bit. You need to be the usual professional, confident, honest woman I know you to be." He patted me on the back. "I love you, and I believe in you. Make sure Max believes you too."

He shut the door as he left, leaving me alone in the room. He always did that. He would come into your bedroom, talk about your transgressions, and leave you alone in your thoughts. It was usually awful in your head. Lonely.

"Mom, I need you," I said out loud. I heard nothing. Even Mom had left me. Conor too.

"Rose is the key." I heard it plainly.

"What?"

"Rose is the key."

The door opened quickly with my father filling the frame. "Charlotte? I heard voices. What's going on?"

I couldn't answer. But I think he knew. I had told him once about who I could hear. He nodded and left me alone again. In a few minutes, I heard Max's voice. Dad and he were discussing yesterday's game, and then Dad said he needed to leave.

I was surprised as the conference room door eventually opened and Tom entered with Max.

Max seemed happy, but when he saw my face, he became sullen.

"Max, have a seat," Tom directed.

The federal attorney sat down across from me as Tom took his place at the end of the table. He placed his briefcase in front of him. "I have a feeling this isn't about finding me a house."

"No," Tom admitted. "I'll compile a timeline for you. I'll also be giving you a copy of everything we had on the Martins, and details of the last meeting I had with them. I was alone in my office with them. Meg and Charlotte had already gone home since it was nearly seven. I keep packets on all of our clients. We have one key for the agent. Meg keeps those in a safe, especially when we're dealing with a high-end property. I keep another key in my file in my locked cabinet."

Max sat silently, listening. He shared his looks between Tom and me.

Tom continued. "So, during that meeting, everything was fine. The sale was going forward. Charlotte was checking with a city councilman on the zoning stipulations. I discussed with them that it was only zoned for a single family residency now. It couldn't be used for a bed and breakfast, a country club, an event space, or a gallery. They seemed to understand. They left, and Mr. Martin was setting up another tour with Charlotte. He called the next day and made the appointment. I'll have all the dates for you. But, that night I realized the key for the file wasn't in there. I couldn't remember if I realized that before the meeting or not, but definitely, when I put it away that night, it was not there. I figured Meg had it or I had placed it somewhere else. I made a note to look for it the next day."

"But you didn't find it," Max stated seriously.

Tom sighed. "Max, I forgot. It was Friday morning, and I had a call about a Mission Hills property. It was a big sale. I blew it off. Then, it was the New Year holiday. In fact, I forgot about it until just the other day when I opened the packet again. I'm sorry."

Max pulled out a pad of paper from his case and began to write notes. "Tom, I'll need all that information as soon as you can. I can have someone from my office pick it up when you have it ready. Anything else?"

Tom slid a key in Max's direction. "The police never took this one from Charlotte the morning of the murder. We all forgot."

Max sighed as he picked up the key. "That was sloppy." Max made another note and turned his head first toward Tom and then to me. "Now, is there anything else?" Tom nodded negatively, and my eyes began to well up.

"What do you need to tell me?" Max nodded to Tom. "Would it be okay to speak with your sister alone? I promise I'll be nice."

Tom searched my eyes. "It's fine," I answered. He left the room, but not before he gave me a soft kiss on my head.

It was just Max and me. That sounded very strange and very frightening. I dabbed at my nose.

I could feel him studying me again. His eyes were a little softer, but he looked every bit the prosecutor searching for the truth. "Charlotte, what do you need to tell me? Why do you keep going over there?"

"To see if I can remember something, anything that might help," I yelled out. "I didn't kill him. I can't live like this with people thinking I was fooling around with him, that maybe I killed him."

"Let me get this right," Max said as he leaned in. "You are trying to be some kind of an investigator? You are trying to prove your innocence?"

"Yes. Detective Marino is ready to send me up the river."

Max began to laugh at my expense. I threw a tissue at him. "Sorry, but you sound like some character in an old movie. He isn't trying to send you up the river. He's trying to get to the truth."

"But you even alluded to my guilt. You all brought up what happened with my last boyfriend. You think I have anger management problems, don't you?"

He smiled. "I think you're an O'Donohue. What did the jerk say that was so bad?"

I hadn't talked about it for so long. Once I had told the entire family, that first time, I told them it would also be the last.

"He said many things. He used me to gain connections through Dad, and we were planning to marry before we broke up. He left town, but was visiting when Mom was dying. Dad told me to go out with friends, and we ran into him. When he said that the world was a better place without my brother Conor in it, I lashed out and threw the beer on him."

Max drew in a breath. His smile faded. He picked up his pen, tapping it on the paper. "You showed great restraint pouring that beer on him. I probably would've knocked him out."

I laughed. "If you'd been around, I would've let you do it, but I left the pub after I did it, and he came after me. He grabbed my arm. He was hurting me, and he said some things about me that I won't repeat. That's when I slugged him."

Silence filled the room. Max tapped, and I sniffed. I needed to tell him about the key, but I couldn't. Dad might not talk to me for a few days, but he didn't need to know, for now. Nor did Max.

"Charlotte, the police tape has been removed. I can have someone meet you there."

"No, I just want to walk around the exterior to see if I can think of anything."

I noticed Max's frown. Did he suspect I still wasn't telling the truth? "Fine. Do what you need to do. There's security making the rounds. If anyone says anything, you tell them I gave you permission." He fumbled in his briefcase and removed a business card. "Here, take this. It has my office and my private phone numbers on it. Call me if you remember anything, and I mean anything. I need to know more about the Martins and how they interacted."

"Tom worked with them more than I did. Mrs. Martin seemed very aloof. She said the right things. She seemed to be acting."

Max began to write. "Do you think she had something to hide?"

"No, I just thought she was uncomfortable about the move here. She apparently didn't want to leave Atlanta, but her husband had insisted. He told me that she wasn't very accepting of the position he was taking here."

"Ah," Max murmured. "I'll check into his job and into her."

"Was he really having an affair with someone?" Finally, I had stopped the waterworks, but my nose was stuffed up from so much crying.

"I haven't found any evidence of it. She really made a show at the funeral home."

"It was unbelievable. I almost thought the lady did protest too much."

Max packed up his pad and pen and closed the briefcase. "You do have a point."

Before I began to consider confessing to him about the key, I decided we did have one more piece of business. Dad would just have to forgive me. Hopefully.

"Now, what about your house? Have you figured out which area of town you want to live in?" Sales would be down because of this fiasco. I might as well get the money I could, and apparently Max had enough of it.

"I'm still not sure. I know I don't want to live downtown."

I frowned. "But there's some great places down there now. I think you'd love a loft."

"No." He offered no other explanation.

"What about the Union Station area? You'd have great views."

"No."

I folded my arms. "Max, where do you want to live?"

"I'm more comfortable around the Plaza, but I don't want to live on the Plaza. Unless, there's parking. I had to park on the street in Atlanta, and I'm done with that."

I began to think of a couple of properties already. "I have some great places. I know you said the budget wasn't a problem, but do you have a range?"

He grinned. "My range is unlimited. I do like a good deal." He looked down as if he was embarrassed. "After all, I'm just a government worker."

I snarled back in my attempt at a strange grin. Now who was lying and not telling the full story?

At that moment I justified my duplicitous behavior. If Max Shaw could have his secrets then so could I. As Max left the room, I stayed behind to think. I needed a plan to soothe my father's rant when he realized I hadn't told Max about the old key. And then I thought of something…Atlanta. The Martins and Max had been living in the same city, and they both were moving to Kansas City, almost at the same time. Now, who was keeping secrets?

Chapter Twelve

I just couldn't go up to the door of the Taylor Club. Two days in a row I sat in my car in the parking lot. I just looked at the house, studying every window, hoping that I'd hear something, or someone. I needed to go up to the door and check the key, but I just couldn't gather up the nerve. By Friday, I stopped my daily drive-by.

Sunday, I was helping Dad in the kitchen while everyone else gathered in the living room. Paddy, his wife Linda and their two boys were fortunate enough to be attending the football game in person. That left Tom, Meg, Sean and me to watch the championship game with Dad.

I was putting the vegetables around the dip when Dad presented his bombshell.

"You didn't tell Max."

I looked up in shock. "What?"

"You heard me. You didn't tell him about the key."

How in the world could the man possibly know that? He hadn't said something to the attorney, had he?

I continued to work on the dip, avoiding him completely. Dad finished the chicken wings.

I always stuck my tongue out when I was focusing intently on a project. This was no exemption.

"Charlotte, the key." My father's voice had intensified.

I looked up quickly. "Rose is the key." My statement was a shock. My father wondered if I'd lost a screw; I was wondering if I was losing my mind.

I placed both hands on the kitchen table for support. "Dad, you know how I hear things?"

"Yes. Go on." He was always uncomfortable when I actually spoke about my talent, and right now I was using this fact to distract him from unloading on me.

"There's a woman at the Taylor Club, and she says the rose is the key. Interesting, huh?" I knew if I acted nonchalant it would throw him off. He believed that I could talk to and hear dead people, but he wasn't comfortable with it.

"Yes." He moved the wings onto the counter and placed the plates on the kitchen table. I began humming. If I kept this up, he would probably think I'd lost my mind. Sorry, Dad, but a ghost begged me to keep the key secret. I needed to check that door and get into that house. Maybe the woman would talk to me again.

Sean entered the kitchen. "Are we ready? I'm starving. How was the game last week? You went with the trust fund baby, right?"

Dad swatted him with the towel from his shoulder. "You don't need to call Max that."

I licked the dip off my finger. It was my guilty pleasure during a football game. "Is Max a trust fund baby?"

Dad rolled his eyes. Sean dipped a carrot into the dip. "Didn't you know, Charlie? His mom is an heiress. She's never worked a day in her life, and Max didn't need to either."

"But that's not how he was raised," Dad added. "His dad is one of the hardest working men I know, and always has been. If you'll recall, Max has worked since the day he turned sixteen."

Sean shrugged. "Oh yeah, but if I'd been him I wouldn't have worked. I would have moved to the islands and worked on my tan."

Dad added a spoon to the crock pot of meatballs. "You've never been fond of work, Sean. In fact, do you work?"

Sean acted as though an arrow had struck his heart. "Dad, how can you hurt me like that?"

"Easy. He knows you," I giggled.

Sean grabbed another carrot. "I am deeply hurt."

Dad ignored his comment. "Go tell everyone we're ready to eat." He turned back around to me as Sean left the room. He pointed a finger in my direction. "I'm saying this only once. You are playing with fire if you think you can get one over on Maxwell Shaw. The sooner you come clean about the key, the rose, your ghosts, the quicker you can get on with your life. And you do need to get on with your life."

He left me with the dip to wrangle the family on his own. I was speechless. He hadn't screamed. How did he know I hadn't told Max? Did he just know me that well? He was my dad, but when did he become so perceptive about his youngest daughter? I needed my mom right now, but I wasn't hearing her sweet voice. I did hear the herd of family members ready to grab a plate before the game began.

By halftime, Meg was curled up in Tom's lap. They sat in the chair Mom used to sit in when she would knit. As I remembered, she never did make anything, but she just knitted. Meg's eyes were closed. How could she sleep during the game?

Sean sat on the ottoman in front of Dad. They were drinking some of the best Irish whiskey.

"What are we doing about our St Pat's Day float this year? We need to get on it," Sean suggested.

"Paddy and Linda have already begun. We'll go to work after the Super Bowl. I think Paddy has the form completed." Dad took a drink and nodded toward me.

I had the entire sofa to myself cradled in one of mom's afghans. "Paddy even has an idea this year."

Sean moaned. "Wonderful. As long as I don't have to be a leprechaun again, I'm in."

I laughed. Before we knew it St. Patrick's Day and the annual parade would be upon us. If I wasn't in jail. "But you're such a cute little green man."

He grabbed a pillow and threw it in my direction. It bounced off the sofa and flattened a standing photo frame.

Meg woke up, and we all looked toward our patriarch. He rose from his chair, said nothing and walked over to the frame. It was a photo of mom with all of the grandchildren. We all watched as Dad kissed the photo and lovingly set it on the table. He didn't look in our direction but left the room.

"Sean, he is angry," Tom commented. "Sometimes I wonder how you can possibly be a police officer."

"Sometimes Sean wonders about it too," Meg murmured as she outlined Tom's chin with her finger.

"I don't need this abuse." Sean downed the remainder of his whiskey. "I have friends who do that."

The doorbell rang, and Dad yelled that he would get it. "Come on in. The half is just about to start. Put your jacket here. You were working late."

The five of us all had questions, and then we heard the other voice. Sean and Meg smiled; Tom and I grimaced. I sat up straight.

"I have a lot to catch up on," Max answered as he entered the living room. "Hello everybody."

Sean was the only one who stood to greet him. What was the deal? Were we going to have weekly visits from a United States Attorney just because I hadn't told him about a darn key?

"Max, how the heck are you? Sorry, I didn't get to talk to you much at the crime scene. Frankly, I didn't recognize you. It's been a long time." The two men shook hands and hugged briefly. Max looked around the room at the rest of the family.

"Hello all. It's so cold out there." He blew on his hands and rubbed them together. He walked right over and sat down next to me.

"Hello, Charlie."

"Hi." He was taunting me. I knew it. He hadn't changed after all of these years. He was just an older version of his *Poop Head* self. He could've sat next to someone else, or taken over the smaller sofa, but there wasn't a good view of the television from that area.

"Max, is whiskey good for you? Or beer? Coffee?" My dad was the host with the most.

"Whiskey is good."

Dad motioned for him to come into the kitchen. "Get yourself some food before you settle into watching the game. We sure had a great time last week--"

"What the hell is Dad doing?" Tom asked. "It's like he's adopted Max."

"I thought he really was my brother for four years," Sean joked.

"Shush. I think he's here to spy on me," I whispered.

Sean was perplexed. "Why should he want to do

that, Charlie? Do you have something to hide? Please remember that I am a cop."

I looked over to Tom. He was shaking his head, warning me not to say anything.

The game began, and Dad and Max sat down during the kickoff. Max dug into his food, stopping occasionally to say something about the Chiefs' offense, and to take a drink of his liquor. At one point, Dad and he toasted each other from across the room.

What alternative world was I living in? Whose father was he? Mom and I would talk about this sometime later tonight. Max was suddenly becoming my new brother. That didn't sound very good in my head. I never had the thoughts about my biological brothers that I did when I looked at the devil. I never wanted to see any of my brothers naked, nor in a shower...

"Judge, you make the best chicken wings," Max announced as he wiped his mouth with a napkin.

"They weren't too spicy for you? I can change the recipe a little if they are."

All of us, including Meg, stopped watching the game. Our attention fell on Dad.

He noticed. "What? Did I do something?" He

sounded innocent, but he knew exactly what he was doing.

I heard Max laugh lightly. "Your dad is very nice to me, and it is very much appreciated, especially the good food."

"So, Max," Meg began. "When do you want to buy your home? Immediately, I hope?"

Max had just taken a drink. He paused before he spoke. "As soon as possible. I really want to be settled by spring, summer at the latest."

"Wonderful. You know the three of us will be doing our best for you." Meg was certainly being nice. Apparently, she noticed how our client pool had suddenly dried up too.

Max looked directly at me. "You said you had a couple of places in mind?"

"Yes, not too far from here. One is just a couple blocks away."

Max nodded, but didn't say a word. He stood and retreated back to the kitchen. He would soon be my father's favorite if he cleaned up his own dishes! Sean certainly didn't do that.

We were intently watching the last quarter of the

game when Max entered the room again. The score was tight. He was hardly noticed. Hardly, except I felt him sit next to me again.

"If the Chiefs win, this would be the first time to the Super Bowl in years, right?"

"Yes."

"This is an exciting time to be in Kansas City."

I only gave a one word response again.

The room erupted into cheering as our team scored a touchdown. Tom nearly threw his wife off of his lap, Sean jumped two feet, and Dad was fist bumping emphatically. Max and I just sat. He commented about the play, but I said nothing. This was the longest game of my life.

Once things settled down, I did turn to talk to Max. "Thanks for last Sunday. I've never seen Dad so happy. He took a one-two punch with Conor and Mom's deaths."

Max nodded as though he understood. "Why did he retire? Was it for health reasons?"

"No. I think he was just done. He keeps himself busy with Mickey."

"Mickey?"

"The dog."

Max looked around. "I haven't seen a dog."

I looked toward the television quickly at the second down play. "The dog doesn't do well with a lot of people. He's kind of neurotic."

"Now that I won't be living in the city, I would love to have a dog."

I touched his leg. "Now that's another item that should be on your list. You need room for a dog."

He flashed that smile. "I suppose I do." He was looking past me at the game, but that smile was meant for only me. Stop it. He is the devil, and he is tempting me. Temptation needed to be discussed privately with myself when I could think. I needed to get away from him.

My musings in my head were interrupted by another celebration. Meg and Tom were hugging each other. Sean and Dad were high-fiving, and I was sure I saw tears in my father's eyes. And Max pulled me close as one arm wrapped around my shoulders.

"They're headed to the Super Bowl. Just a couple of minutes, and it will be official."

He kissed me on the cheek, and we both pulled away sharply. "Sorry, I got carried away," Max said quickly.

I nervously smiled. "No problem." Why could I not be more articulate in his presence? I never had trouble when I was a little girl. I had no problem yelling at him and following after him. Hmm, I did follow after him. When the boys did take me with them to walk down to the grocery store for candy, he always held my hand.

Our celebration was short-lived. Within two minutes our opposition scored and ended the game. We watched in disbelief at the celebration on the field. The season and the party were over quickly. Meg and Tom decided they needed to head home.

"Are you ready, Charlie?" Tom asked as he grabbed our coats.

"Of course, you're my ride."

Max grabbed his own coat. "I'll drop her off."

Meg was yawning way too much as she leaned against the wall.

"Besides, it looks like your wife is going to fall over," Max kidded. "I'll take Charlie home."

Now what was he up to? I always speculated that he had something up his sleeve. Perhaps this nice gesture was a magic trick to make me disappear?

"If you don't mind, that would be appreciated." Tom

looked at me and winked. "Charlotte, don't bite the nice man." He grabbed his wife's hand and fled, leaving me to the devil.

Sean kissed Dad goodnight. "Max, don't try anything with our little sister." He used his police sergeant voice, and Max saluted him.

"I wouldn't think of it, Sean."

Why had that sentence stung my heart? Was I still just the little sister? Am I just a nuisance or an object of his verbal abuse? Dad must've seen something. He slipped his arm around me.

"Your face just fell. Don't take it personally. Put your chin up. Keep your wits about you," he whispered.

I nodded and left to pick up my purse and coat. I could hear Max and Dad's murmurs as they had some sort of conversation about me. I heard my name a few times.

They stopped as soon as I announced I was ready to go.

I kissed my Dad. "I'll call you when I get home. Don't stay up too late."

"Yes, Mother. Now, get out of here." He patted Max on the back. "Drive safely please."

"Yes, Judge. Thanks for this evening." Max held the door open for me as we left the home. "I forgot how cold it is here in the winter." He was parked on the street. He ran ahead of me, opening the passenger door. The car was already on with the heat blowing through the vents. He ran in front of the car and took his place behind the wheel.

As Max drove slowly down the block, he suddenly stopped the car. "How do I get to your place from here?" His fingers were on the screen ready to enter the address.

"May I do it?" With his permission, I programmed in my address. I watched the directions come up on the screen, with my name and phone number. That was chilling more than the cold outside. "I've never ridden in a Jaguar. This is lovely." I was particularly enjoying the heated seat, warm on my backside and my back.

"I like it." He looked over at me while we were stopped at a traffic light. "I hope you don't mind me asking, but did they ever figure out who killed your brother?"

I wasn't expecting that question. "No. In fact, we all think we'll find a piece of evidence some day. Some days more than others we so desperately want to know."

"I can't imagine. I've apologized to Tom for not being able to be here, and I'm sorry to you too. Conor was a great little guy."

He was. Conor was the closest to my age and always acted as my protector. He was my hero. It remained difficult to hear his name spoken.

"A little more than a year later, Mom was gone." My voice trailed off as I looked off into the darkness. I felt his hand on my coat sleeve.

The silence was deafening between us, yet I sensed his words of comfort. Finally, he said something.

"Charlotte, you do know everything will be okay, right? I mean, you have nothing to hide. It's not like you're keeping some big secret from me."

I felt nauseous. I shouldn't have eaten those last two meatballs. No, I was a miserable human being. With my silence I allowed his statement to become the truth, rather than refuting it.

When we arrived at my house, I quickly scrambled out of the car. "There's no need for you to get out. Thank you for the ride. Good night." I shut the door and literally ran up to my house. I fumbled with my keys in the lock, entered my home, turning to wave before I shut the door. I never did look at him. I wasn't sure I could ever look him in the eyes again. I was a liar.

I called Dad before I had even removed my coat. "I'm home."

"Good. You sleep well."

"Dad, he knows."

The judge cleared his throat. "Charlotte, what does he know?"

"He knows I have a secret."

"Honey, everyone has secrets," he said calmly. "Max has his too. I warned him about that. Don't worry, but you need to know this can be fixed, but you must tell him about that key. As old as it is, it could be nothing, but as long as you hold out this information, the more guilt he will place on you. He's not here to put you away."

Usually, I appreciated my father's logic. Tonight was not one of those times. "It has something to do with Atlanta."

"Really? That's interesting."

"Max came from Atlanta and so did the Martins."

My father chuckled. "Charlotte, what does that

matter?"

"Why is Max here, Dad?" Our sparring questions could go on forever, but my father had no witty answer. Instead, he told me to sleep well. Fat chance.

I turned on the television. I had no idea what was on the screen, but I didn't care. The white noise was the distraction I needed. "Mom?" There was no answer.

"Fine." I turned off the television and headed upstairs to bed. "When I need help I never hear you."

"*Not true.*" I smiled when I heard her voice.

"What is Max up to? There's way more to his story, Mom."

"*He's finding his home. Have patience.*"

I chuckled. "Do you know me?"

"*Yes, Charlotte.*"

By the time I slipped under the covers, my thoughts were racing and most of them were speeding on the Max track. God, help me!

Chapter Thirteen

I worked in the office all day Monday, choosing to allow Tom to contact Max with the two addresses I had for him. I wanted him to see the houses before he even toured them. I didn't want to waste his time if he didn't even like the area or the look of the homes. Besides, the more distance between Max Shaw and me the better.

By Wednesday, Tom alerted me to Max's dislike of both properties. One of them looked too boxy, and the other house looked like all the others. He might be my only client right now, but he was also my pickiest.

The remainder of the week went by quickly, filled with cleaning my office and completing any paperwork that was on my desk and computer. We shut things down around six Friday night. I began to drive home, but I realized I had nothing to go home for. I turned right instead of left.

I headed into the Plaza area. Traffic seemed heavy with everyone meeting at bars, or heading out to dinner. I remained on my tour until I turned down the street of the Taylor Club. With only my low beam lights on, I pulled into the parking area.

Once I turned my car off, I made my decision to go in. I reached into the glove compartment and grabbed my flashlight. I stuck my phone in one pocket, and the old key in the other. Taking a deep breath, I left the car and walked toward the door.

There were a couple of floodlights around the exterior of the house, and it appeared that a couple of timer lights were on inside the room where Mr. Martin was found.

"Here we go." I placed the key into the old lock and turned. The door opened smoothly. Any new owners would be warned to change that lock. Heaven only knew how many keys were out there.

The house was not as cold as that Monday morning when I entered. My flashlight lit my way through the receiving area until I made my way to **that** room.

"Rose? I'm here to talk to you."

I looked around the room. Nothing had changed since the last time I was here. I looked up at her portrait. "Rose, this is you, isn't it?" She was a beautiful young woman.

"Yes."

The whispered word caught me off guard. "I brought the key. It was stuck in the wood by the window over there. Why did I need to keep it a secret?" I pointed as though she could see me. After all these years, I still didn't understand how all of this worked. How could you talk to some people who had passed, and then others you desperately wanted to speak to were mute?

"Rose's key. Important."

I nodded knowingly. "It was your key, but who put it in the window seat?"

My skin crawled. The room was freezing now. That usually wasn't a good sign. I heard the front door open and close. I heard real footsteps heading toward my location.

"Show yourself," I yelled as I held the flashlight in that direction. It lit the face, the real air-breathing face of an elderly man.

"It's only me." He pointed at my hand. "That is my key."

"Your key?"

He removed his hat. Dad wore a hat now and then, but this was a classic black fedora with a gray band on the brim. "I've had it for many years, but the other morning--"

"Don't come any closer." This man could be Mr. Martin's killer. What was I going to do? Throw the flashlight at him? I removed my phone from my pocket and began to press the buttons for 9-1-1.

"I won't hurt you, Miss."

He looked harmless enough in his long cashmere wool coat and plaid muffler. Actually, he looked like he stepped out of an old gangster movie. But there was a softness in his eyes. Despite his weathered and wrinkled skin, he was an attractive man with a smile that could light the sun. It was a familiar smile.

"Love." I heard the woman say just that one word. He didn't flinch, nor did I. It was said in love.

He curled his body a bit and slapped his leg in delight. "You heard her, didn't you? I thought I was the only one who could do that."

I felt completely naked in his realization. No one knew about my special talent, well no one except for my parents. Mom had always said it was our secret, and not to tell anyone, not the nuns, not the priests, or the doctors.

"What are you doing here?" I asked a question quickly to distract him.

"What are you doing here?" he asked back.

"I'm the real estate agent for this property."

He pointed to the key again. "Yet, you have my key."

"Mr.--"

"Campano, Gio."

"Mr. Campano, I'll have to ask you to leave." I raised my voice a bit for emphasis. I didn't want to beat up a little old man, but my brothers had trained me well. I could do it.

He removed his hat and held it in his hands. "I just need to talk to her for a minute or two. Surely, you won't begrudge an old man to speak with his sweetheart." He smiled again. I couldn't, and I didn't, say no. This man was my ghost's secret.

"Sure, but then we both need to go. Rose was your sweetheart?"

"Love." We heard her again. He made the sign of the cross.

"She was my love, my greatest love. Of course, her family didn't approve. I was just a, a working man." His stammer made me think there was more to his story. "I have had that key for decades. I used to be able to just walk into the club, but then when they shut it down, I would come in the early morning, and we would talk. I believe she has stayed for me."

Finally, I lowered the flashlight and turned it off. I looked down at the key, and I made a judgment call. Dad always said to go with your gut. I was doing exactly that.

He began to reach into his coat. "I want to show you something."

I steeled myself in case of an attack, but he removed an old photograph.

"We have one beautiful photo of us. It was taken outside of an old jazz club. We attended the dances there, when Rose could get away. Please, look at how beautiful my Rosie was." He held the photograph in front of him. His hand shook.

I tentatively took a couple of steps and took it. The happy couple were in each other's arms. He looked so very familiar. His dark hair was wavy and full, and his eyes were intense. He definitely appeared to be a stylish man of his time, but he also looked like a mob figure. My eyes moved to Rose. She was stunning in a sheath dress, a jeweled choker necklace around her neck, and a gardenia in her hair. There was no doubt they were in love.

"Wasn't she beautiful?" He took a couple of steps back and headed to the window seat. He clutched the left front of his coat.

My defenses vanished as I ran toward him and crouched down in front of him.

"Are you okay? What can I do for you?"

He patted my shoulder. "I'm just old. I need to sit down. I have a little heart problem."

I laughed slightly. "I've never heard of just a little heart problem."

His breath became even, and he lowered both arms to lean on his legs. "You have a point there."

"This is your key." We both focused on my hand as I gave it to him. "If you really are okay, I'll leave you to talk to Rose."

The key was securely in his left hand, but he reached out with his right, grabbing mine. "How long have you been blessed to be able to hear them?"

I stood up. My knees were killing me, and he noticed. He patted the area next to him, and I took it.

"Well, I wouldn't always say it's been a blessing, but it began when I was very little."

"Ah, well, it is a subject that receives some doubt from so many. I could always hear my mother. She was the only one. She died in New York City right after the boat she was on docked. They were coming from Sicily. Then, after Rose passed, I could feel she was still around. One day, I came up here. I had been right. She was here."

"She talked to me the morning of that murder."

He nodded. "Yes, we had been visiting."

I held my finger up to stop him. "You brought the rose. A rose for Rose, right?" With his nod, I clapped. "I knew it! That makes complete sense. The police didn't even pay attention to it."

"The police see what they want to see," he murmured. His tone was sad and angry.

I thought about my own brothers, and he did have a point. They did seem to go down a rabbit hole on occasion. Even Dad had his problems over the years with a lazy or an ambitious detective wanting to sway a case one way or the other to clear his desk. Some had even decided who was guilty before they gathered evidence, but that was years ago when part of the force was as corrupt as the criminals.

"I really should be leaving." I stood up quickly, still holding the photograph in my hand. I directed it in his direction, but he pushed it back.

"I want you to have it. I don't know how many more years I have on this earth, and you've talked to Rose so maybe you'll remember us. Do you have a great love like ours?"

My face warmed. "Um, no. I've been in love, but as far as it being a great love, I'm not sure that it exists anymore." Sadly, I was being more honest with this man than I had been with myself in a very long time.

"Do not settle for less, even if you have to be alone. Alone isn't so bad; lonely is a death sentence. When you find that great love, do me a favor. Make sure you fight for it if you must, and you hang onto it until the day you die. That's what Gio says!"

I smiled. "Thanks, Gio. I will try to remember that."

He nodded. "You are welcome, Miss--"

"O'Donohue, Charlotte O'Donohue."

His back became straighter, his head less relaxed. "Judge O'Donohue? Are you his daughter?"

Everyone really did know my father. "Yes. Do you know him?"

"Our paths have crossed. He is a fair man. Your mother was a saint. I am sorry about her death, oh, and your brother. That was a shame. Give your father my regards."

I nodded. Death could be a shame, on many occasions. "Goodnight, Gio. Take care."

I turned to leave and heard Rose's voice one more time.

"Max."

I quickly returned to Gio's side. "Did she just say Max?"

Gio nodded yes. "Does he mean something to you?"

I had no answer. Did he mean something to me? "I know Max."

Gio looked up at me with piercing eyes. "Whatever you do, you have to be honest, Miss O'Donohue. Truth is the key." He smiled as he raised the door's key up to his face. "The key is Rose. You need to tell him. It may be important."

By the time I made my way down to the car and sat behind the wheel, I was shaking from the cold and what

I'd just experienced. As I drove out, I noticed that Gio's car was nowhere to be found. If he didn't drive, how did he get here? Once out on the street, I saw the bus stop at the corner. Of course!

Despite the heat on high in the car, I continued to shake. Gio was real, right? I wasn't seeing an apparition, was I? I had only seen a spirit a few times, besides he took the key, and he gave me a photograph. No, he was definitely alive, and he was familiar to me.

I knew one thing for certain. I needed to speak to Max. Now, Rose's Max. What did this all have to do with nailing me for murder? Maybe Gio had been a hitman in his prior life?

Chapter Fourteen

"Dad," I called out as I came through the front door. "Where are you? I brought apple fritters."

"I'm in the kitchen, honey."

Mickey greeted me as I was halfway through the dining room and followed me to meet up with my father. Dad sat at the kitchen table, his eyeglasses perched on his nose. He looked over them as I entered.

"You know, apple fritters aren't good for you or me."

"Good morning to you too, Dad. I won't tell Janie if you don't." My sister was the food warden of the family. She was extremely healthy, running marathons for no apparent reason. At least we didn't think there was a real reason to run that far to nowhere.

I looked over on the counter as I dropped my package and purse and removed my coat. Dad already had the coffee made, and it smelled like the old coffee plant on Broadway when it roasted its beans. That building now housed lofts; everyone missed the wake-up aroma.

Pouring two cups of hot coffee, I sat down at the table and unwrapped the pastries.

Dad removed his glasses and grabbed a fritter. "You only bring these when you need something. Do you realize that?"

"I do not."

His left brow rose, and I had no response. Of course, he was right again.

"This time I just need some information. Do you know Gio Cambana?"

Dad dropped his fritter onto the napkin on the table. "Where did you get that name?"

I should lie to him. I seemed to be getting pretty good at it. Perhaps, with a little more practice I could become a professional liar? But I couldn't lie to him, especially when he was staring through my soul.

"I met him last night, and he said to give you his regards."

He leaned back in his chair and folded his judgelike arms. He would pass judgment on me, and this time wouldn't be pretty. I couldn't skip this ticket.

"At the Taylor Club."

He remained silent. He pulled back to the table and

began to eat his fritter again. He completely ignored my question. Heck, he was ignoring me.

"Dad, come on, please. The key was his."

"Charlotte, do not tell me you gave it back to him."

I took a bite and chewed and chewed.

He strung three obscenities into a sentence. I didn't know that could be done until today. "What were you thinking?"

"Let's just take one thing at a time, shall we?" I could act like an adult. It was definitely hard in the presence of one's father, especially if he was Judge William Padric O'Donohue, Sr.

He took a drink of coffee and began. "Gio, Giovani Cambana eventually became part of a crime family that had its birth in Kansas City. He began to make his name bootlegging tires. You weren't even born when the River Quay was blown up in a mob war in the 1970's. That area is part of the River Market now. Cambana turned to the feds for protection. He gave them quite a bit of information as a confidential informant. He didn't serve a day in prison that time. He should've."

"He seemed nice." I got in three words before he began again.

"Gio was always charming. His sins were his job. It was never personal for him. He never pledged allegiance to one family over the other. I knew him, and I knew about him and Rose Taylor."

My mouth fell open. Thankfully there was no fritter in there. "You knew about him and Rose?"

"What do you know about them?" The sparring had begun. I needed to take my time with my answers to slow down this interrogation. The questioning of the witness was to begin, but I needed to object.

"Rose spoke to me in the house. I told you. But Rose and he were very much in love." I rummaged through my purse. "He gave me this."

Dad took the photo in his hand. His smile was comforting. "Yes, they were very much in love. I was just a young kid when we all heard the rumors. Rose's husband was such a piece of--" Dad stopped. "Well, he wasn't the nicest man. He was a ruthless businessman, just as his father was before him. He married Rose because she was beautiful. He met her at a debutante ball in New York City, and they married in less than three months. I guess she is what you would now call a trophy wife. She had breeding, pedigree, and money. He brought her here to Kansas City, and in the beginning my parents said she was always in the city helping this charity, or making this donation. She was an angel."

"Then something changed?" I asked quickly when I had the opportunity.

"My mother said it was about five years into the Taylors' marriage. They still had no children. Rose didn't come out anymore. She canceled social engagements at the drop of a hat. There were rumors that he abused her. You know how gossip spreads in this small town, big city. One woman swore she saw her with a black eye. A doctor treated her for a broken arm. Rose fell here; Rose fell there. Rose was clumsy, and her stairs were too steep."

"That's awful." It was disheartening to think of that beautiful woman being treated as a thrown away possession.

"I'm not sure when Gio entered the picture, but they were quite the couple. Everyone in town knew Rose was stepping out on her husband. But that was it. I certainly don't know all the details. What I do know is I was a young attorney when I met Gio. Years later, during the River Quay incident I helped him with the information he gave to the federal government. I can't say any more about my interaction with him, not even to you."

Or won't say, I thought to myself. I bet he could and would talk to Max. Sharing legal information with another legal mind was probably within the rules.

I moved the photo toward me and placed my finger on Gio's face?

"Why does he look so familiar to me? I didn't feel threatened by him; it was as though I knew him," I admitted.

Dad rose to refill his coffee. "Well, there could be a couple of reasons for that feeling. I do have a photo of Cabana and me in my office here at the house. You kids were always coming in there to play, even if I was working. But you were usually the quiet one. You used to come in there all the time. You just sat in the big comfy chair near the bookcase and read your books. That photo is placed just above that chair."

I motioned for a refill of my coffee. He pulled the pot and poured. Why did Dad still brew his coffee? We'd have to insist he get one of those one-cup machines. It would change his life.

"Don't tell me you still have that chair in there?"

"Oh no. Your mother made me donate that big old thing to charity about ten years ago. Did you know you had a small doll wedged into the cushion?"

I thought for a second. "Bitsy! That's where I hid her. Sean wanted to see if he could eat her, and then poop her out. I had to protect her."

Dad just shook his head. "I'm surprised I have lasted this long. Your brothers should have been the death of me."

"Dad, why else could I possibly know Gio besides that photo? I mean, he took away my fear almost immediately. It was something in his smile."

Dad reached for my hand. "Are you sure it doesn't have something to do with your talent?" He was never very comfortable discussing the afterlife voices.

The first twenty years of my life, Dad never knew I could talk to those who had passed. Mom and I held that secret. Mom made me hold that secret. But two days after my twentieth birthday, I awoke screaming. I was home from college on winter break. Dad ran into my room with a gun in his hand.

"Charlotte, stay there. I'll check the room." He hit the lights and searched the room as well as the windows. "Who was in here?"

"My man," I answered plainly. "It was just a bad visit." I placed my hand to my mouth in realization of the secret I had revealed. He just looked at me as though I had grown two heads. By the time Mom arrived, Sean and Conor had spilled into the room. Mom shooed them out, and made Dad drop the gun.

"She had a man in here, Rosemarie."

"No, my love, she didn't. Now, go back to the bedroom. I'll explain it all. Let me get Charlotte settled down. Now go." Mom literally pushed him out of my room and shut the door.

I was wiping the tears from my face as she sat down on my bed and held the covers up. She always made the demons fly away. "Now, slide back in here."

I did as I was told. She grabbed a tissue and wiped off my face.

"I had hoped that once you were away all of this might stop. Do you have it when you're at college?"

"Yes. I have headaches too. They seem to be getting worse."

She soothed me. Her soft voice and gentle hands petted my head and wiped away the fear with the tears. "What happened this time?"

"My man, my guide told me Uncle Patrick is passing away on Friday. That will hurt Dad."

"Friday? Your father's birthday? Oh my. That will be rough."

Mom kissed me on the forehead. "Do you need something for your headache?"

I shut my eyes. "No. I just need to get back to sleep."

She seemed to understand. She nodded and began to leave my room. "I'll turn the lights out, dear. Now get some sleep."

"Mom, are you going to tell him?"

She nodded. "I think it is past time. It'll be okay. I remember him talking about his mother and her dreams. They never acknowledged that they were anything but dreams, but she knew when events were coming just like you do. I've told you I had it when I was a little girl, so you do come by it naturally."

"I don't think there's anything natural about this. Mom, is that why you never thought I was going crazy?"

She giggled. "I'm sorry, but I've always known all of my children are crazy, just to different degrees. You just happen to have the most exotic form of crazy."

I'd never thought of myself as exotic.

That next morning Dad peered over his glasses at me as I ate my cereal. Nothing was said, but I knew deep down that he thought of me differently. Maybe he didn't think I was a freak, but he definitely thought of me as unusual. After Conor and Sean left the table, Dad stood up. I could feel his eyes on me. My mother noticed it too. She continued to do the dishes at the sink.

"Charlotte," he said as I dropped my spoon. "I love you."

He reached over and took me into his arms. Just as quickly, he released me and walked out of the kitchen. That was it. After that, we had subtle discussions now and then. After Conor and then Mom died, we had several conversations. He became my confidant.

My thoughts had carried me away, but Dad remained silent, waiting for an answer to his delicate question.

"I don't think Gio Campano was an apparition. At one point last night, I thought that maybe he wasn't really there, but he gave me this photo. He is alive. I'm sure of that. No, it was his smile. I've seen it before. His entire face lit up when he looked at me. His smile is like the cherry on top of whipped cream. I felt better with him than I have in a long time."

Dad pulled his hand away quickly. "Gio? Gio made you feel good? An octogenarian with a criminal past made you feel better?"

I shook my head. "No, I'm confused. He reminded me of someone. He made me feel safe. Whoever he reminds me of is the one who makes me feel better. Does any of this make sense?"

He smiled. "I think in your head it makes sense. You do seem happy this morning. Any word from your mother on all this?"

"Yes, but I don't want to talk about it just yet. Dad, would Rose be Max's grandmother?" The wheels in my brain were spinning. I wasn't sure where this ride was going, but it was open, and I was clearly a passenger on it.

He blinked a couple of times. Maybe he was searching for a name? "Why, yes. Max's mother Olivia is the only child of the Taylors."

"They did have a child?" I was incredulous. Why would she have a baby with her terrible husband?

Dad sipped his coffee. "Ah, well, there's a story. We

all think she might not be their child. You see, several years into the Taylors' marriage, Rose left town. She was absent for about a year, maybe two. When she triumphantly returned, she was carrying a beautiful baby girl. When asked, if anyone dared, Rose apparently said she found the little girl in an orphanage in Florida. She fell in love and adopted her."

"Why was she in Florida?" The entire story of Rose was beginning to go south, literally.

"Her family was very close to the family who built the railroads into Florida, connected the Florida Keys, and on and on. Supposedly, she went down there to recuperate and regenerate. I'd say it was to get away from her husband."

My thoughts went into a different direction. "Or to get away with someone else?"

Dad dropped his mug onto the table. "Charlotte, what are you thinking? I know that look. Your mother used to have that same face when she was plotting how she was going to purchase a very expensive pair of shoes."

"I'm just thinking, not buying a pair of shoes."

"Charlotte," he said as he touched my hand. "I'd

rather you forget all about this and just go buy the shoes."

I nodded as though I was listening. It would be hard to walk away from this mystery. I had a connection with Rose and now with Gio. There had to be a reason. Oh, and I didn't need a new pair of shoes! Maybe another purse would be nice.

Chapter Fifteen

Over the weekend, I made sure I looked at every piece of information about Gio Campano my father had in his study. The photo still hung in the same location it always had, and Dad offered several newspaper clippings he had kept over the years. In every photo, I saw something. I still didn't know what it was though.

Monday morning I dragged myself into the office. Meg stopped me at her desk.

"Cynthia Martin is in Tom's office, and she's going forward on the purchase of the Taylor Club."

I was shocked and speechless. Thankfully, Meg continued to offer me information.

"She called late Friday night and said she wanted to meet this morning. She was here at the door when we arrived at eight. I went out and brought back coffee and danish for all of us. The closing is today, and she'll go over there next."

I looked toward the closed door and began my own speculation. Why on earth did she want to purchase the house now? After all she said to me at the funeral home, how did she dare come in here again? Why was my brother talking to her? Oh, yes, it would be an amazing commission on a two million dollar house. It would probably take another couple to make it a home.

When my sudden thoughts went to Gio, I stopped being a real estate agent looking at a chunk of money. How would Gio talk to Rose again if Cynthia Martin and her family lived there? That woman wouldn't understand how he needed to be there. It was strangely his family home, the only family he had.

I scrambled to my office to avoid her, but I failed. As I rounded the corner, Cynthia Martin and Tom exited his office. We, she and I, stood there like idiots. I was surprised when she smiled.

"Charlotte, thank you for finding that house for us. It meant so much to my husband. I hope there's no hard feelings for my outburst at his funeral." She stuck her hand out for me to take. Thankfully, I still had my hands full with a coffee, purse, coat, bag, and laptop.

I managed a weak smile and lied. "I understand."

"Do you? Thank you. You see, my husband was having an affair, it just wasn't with you." She looked me up and down. Mondays were not a good day for me, but today I looked particularly more frazzled than usual. "I don't know why I thought he'd ever have something for someone like you."

I almost opened my mouth, but Tom stood behind her with his finger up to his lips.

"Thank you, Tom," she smiled nicely at him. "You too, Charlotte. I need to get to that closing appointment."

"When will you be moving in? Will you begin remodeling?" I stammered.

"Soon and soon. Goodbye." She stopped short of the door. "By the way, I just want you to know that I'll be starting my own business here in Kansas City."

Tom clapped his hands. "That's wonderful. Maybe we can send business your way? What will you be doing?"

"I doubt you'll be sending me business, and I certainly won't be sending you any. I'll be opening my own real estate agency. So get ready, O'Donohues."

Tom's face fell as the door closed behind her. "She's a real--"

"Nothing," Meg added. "Come on. We still have this sale." She kissed him on the cheek and his face softened.

"You're right. We will worry about her later, or never. There's enough business to go around. Honey, make reservations at our place. We need to have a celebratory lunch."

Finally, I was able to throw all of my items onto my desk and returned up front.

"You gave her the only key, or did you find yours?"

Tom was kissing Meg. He sighed as he faced me. "Must you ruin this?"

"I must." I placed my hands on my hips for emphasis.

"If you must know, the other one is still missing. We aren't going to worry about it. I dropped the one key to the closing attorney before daylight this morning. "

"Did you make a copy for Max?"

Tom became perturbed with my questions. "What does it matter now? You should be happy with this commission, sister."

But I insisted. "But does Max have a copy?"

"He took the key down to that detective, but he brought it back saying they didn't need it. They had everything they needed from inside the house. What does it matter, Charlotte?"

Somehow it mattered to me. If Max didn't make a copy, it meant that Cynthia and Gio had the only remaining keys. It meant we still had a missing key out there.

I worried about Gio. What would he do without Rose? If he couldn't speak to her now and then, the man wouldn't have anything to live for.

"Be happy," my brother instructed.

I turned and headed to my office. I just couldn't be happy knowing that a great love would be ending no matter how much would soon be in my bank account. Gio's open door to Rose would be locked by Cynthia Martin.

I ate with Tom and Meg and tried to put on a brave face. Tom even ordered champagne, well a sort of champagne. My brother was too cheap to order the real bubbly. I was lifting my glass to my lips when I saw Max Shaw smiling at me from across the room. He was sitting at the bar surrounded by other men in suits. He waved. I just lifted my glass to him. He began to walk over to us.

"Max is coming over to us," I warned. Tom turned around at the same time Max reached the table.

"Max, come celebrate with us."

He looked over at me and saw my glare. He didn't sit, rather he leaned on the empty chair next to me."What are you all celebrating?"

"Cynthia Martin bought the house. The sale ended up being over two million."

I noticed the pensive look on the attorney's face. "Really? I'm very surprised that she went ahead and bought a house where her husband was killed."

Tom gulped down his drink. "I never thought about that. I'm not sure I could do it, but she'll be doing so much renovation, maybe that room won't exist."

"**No**," Max and I both said at the same time.

Meg and Tom seemed shocked at our concurrent answer. "What would be so wrong with that?" Meg finally questioned.

Max waved his hand for me to go first. "It's such a lovely old home. I mean, you can renovate, but still keep the ambience of the place. I just don't think she'll care about that."

"I agree. I'm afraid she just won't appreciate it, like someone, well like Charlotte might." Max's composure was a little unhinged. I noticed his clenched jaw.

What had gotten into him? He surely didn't want Cynthia Martin living in that house. And why was he complimenting me? He didn't know that I would relish preserving the history of the place. But he suspected. He thought he knew me.

"I'll let you all get back to celebrating," Max stated. "I have lunch guests. Congratulations."

As long as he seemed to be off his game, I upped mine. I softly placed my hand on his to stop him from going. He looked down at our physical interaction. He smiled that smile. Ah, there it was.

"Max, did the police ever find out about that rose on the mantle?"

"No. Forget about it, Charlie." His tone was sharp and concise. He pulled his hand from beneath mine. "You all have a good day." He turned and left as quickly as he had arrived.

"What the hell was that about, Charlotte?"

I took a drink from my glass and winked. We all did have our secrets, didn't we?

Tom and Meg didn't go back to the office, and he suggested I go do something, maybe see a movie. I dropped by Dad's instead. I had work to do. It was way past time to wrestle as much information as I could out of my father.

"Dad, where are you?" I let myself into a quiet, empty house. Mickey greeted me as I dropped all of my things into one of the large chairs in the living room. "Dad? Where is he, Mickey?" In the quiet I heard machinery in the garage. Dad was woodworking.

Our father wasn't a woodworker, but it wasn't the first thing he attempted as a hobby once he retired. It wasn't that he particularly enjoyed the activity, but it allowed him the time to think. So Dad was trying to think today?

I flicked the light switch on and off and then on again to gain his attention. He turned around quickly, pushing his goggles upon his head and removing his ear plugs.

"What are you doing here in the middle of the day? Not that I'm not happy to see my youngest." He continued to remove his gloves and turn off the machinery. "I was due for a break. Let's go make a hot cup of something."

He started following me before I even agreed. We ended up in the kitchen, and I took my favorite place at the table while he searched through the cabinets. "I know I have good tea somewhere. Here it is. Does a spiced one sound good, Charlie?"

"Yes. It's kind of cold today." We were heading into February. Even though the sun was out today, the wind was blowing to bring the temperature down. "You know, Dad, you're the second person to call me that today."

"We all call you Charlie now and then."

I flipped through a magazine as Dad set the kettle on the stove. "But you didn't add O to the name."

He faced me. "Ah, so that's what this visit is all about? What do you need?"

"I need some assurance that Max Shaw is a good one."

I gathered my father wasn't expecting that because he looked as though he'd seen an actual ghost.

He nodded. "Max is a good one. He's had his ups and downs like any normal human being."

"Why would he care if Cynthia Martin bought the Taylor Club? His family hasn't lived there for a long time. In fact, it was their family's attorney who was in charge of the sale through some family estate trust fund."

"Won't you be sad when I sell this place?" He looked around at the large kitchen that used to hold us all in its flavorful embrace.

"I guess so, but he seemed off his game today."

Dad held his hand up. "Wait just a minute. Are you telling me Mrs. Martin went ahead and bought the house where her husband was killed?"

"Bingo, give that man a prize," I cheered. "Now you see my dilemma."

I remembered when mom was in her last days, and she had finally been transferred to the hospital. Dad couldn't bear to sleep in their room. I would find him on the couch every morning. When she died, it took him a month and moving around the furniture a little before he slept alone in their bed.

The kettle whistled, and he went about the work of making our teas and pulling out his favorite cookies. We sat across from one another as was our routine. He was quiet, and I could see he was thinking. Perhaps he was finishing the thinking he had begun while woodworking?

"Dad, United States Attorneys don't get involved in a single murder like Mr. Martin."

He was biting the inside of his mouth. "We've talked about that before." Now, he seemed irritated. "You should've come clean about that key."

I decided I'd use my own tactic and ignore him. "I asked Max about that rose. He blew me off. Supposedly, the police didn't think it was important. The good news is that because of their laziness, they know nothing about Gio."

"Stop mentioning him." Dad's hand pounded the table. "No good will come from you researching him, talking about him, unearthing things that should be buried. I told you to be honest with Max. If you had, maybe you would've made his job a little easier."

"Why should I do that for him? He cost me a lot of tears when I was little. I hated him." My voice was now as loud as Dad's.

"Don't say such a thing. You didn't hate him. You idolized Maxwell Shaw. He was your first crush. He pointed a finger right at me. "You still have a crush on him. I see it on your face when he smiles at you. He has one of those crooked smiles that make a woman swoon. You aren't immune."

I grabbed his hand. "What are you really worried about, Dad? I'm not the murderer, and you've told me in so many words that Max doesn't think so either. Gio won't hurt me. He seems to respect you, and besides he is an old man with a broken heart. That's all. So, Dad, what is it?"

I saw the tears well up in his eyes. "I'm worried," he began as his voice caught. "I'm losing you." I reached for him, but he turned away to wipe the tears. "I want you to be happy. If you want to be single all your life, and you're happy, that will be grand with me. But when I walk you down that aisle and hand you off to Max, it will be the happiest and the saddest day of my life."

I rose from my chair quickly and hugged him from the back. We both cried big ugly tears that couldn't be forgotten. "You silly man! You're not going to be marrying me off to *Poop Head*. What are you thinking? Have you been in the brandy too much? You know what Mom would say about that. What is really going on with all of this?"

He began to laugh, and I sat down again. "Fine. I'll tell you a little. I'll tell you what I can. Max was assigned to Kansas City to specialize in some high value cases. The Martins came from Atlanta. Your clients were involved in some real estate schemes of their own. They were both licensed agents. I know they told you Mr. Martin was in finance, but there seems to be a lot more to their story. He was involved with a lot of very powerful people. This is just my opinion, but I think Max is on their trail with some hidden agenda of his own."

"Well, that would be interesting. Mrs. Martin just announced to us today that she will be our competitor."

"That would make sense," Dad answered thoughtfully. "I talked to Max's dad last week."

"When were you going to tell me?"

"Never," he joked. "It seems as though this is a special assignment for Max, and he asked to return to Kansas City. He'll be working with the FBI closely so his dad was thrilled. Ed always wanted Max to be an agent."

I chuckled. "Kind of like you wanted me to be an attorney?"

"I never said that," he answered defiantly.

"Nope, but you thought it. Mom told me. I was your last hope for a lawyer."

He acted sheepishly, turning on his charm and his smile. "Would I do that? Your mother wasn't feeling well when she said that."

"That's your story?" I eyed him suspiciously.

"And I'm sticking to it, Charlotte."

"So, Max has his secrets," I murmured. The more I thought about it, it was possible that he had more than one secret. "Why would you marry me off to him? He's way beyond my pay grade!"

"You sell yourself short, but I know, and I suspect, my dear baby girl," he said softly as he flicked my nose, "that you are a little more than fond of the devil."

"But you're never supposed to dance with the devil," I reprimanded in my best Irish accent.

"Who said anything about dancing with him? Love can be a very strange thing. Besides, Max almost grew up here. Frankly, I thought he was my son until he moved away to college." We both shared a good laugh.

"Well then. I can't marry my brother!"

Dad continued to laugh. "I'm not sure how Paddy or Tom found women to marry them. Sean will have a problem too, but Max isn't really your brother. I wouldn't mind a son-in-law, if it comes to that. You couldn't do any better than him."

I stood up suddenly.

"And where are you going in such a hurry?" he asked as he stood up too.

"I'm going to check the brandy. Obviously, you've been drinking way too much."

Dad placed his arms around me, but the hug was short-lived when the doorbell rang.

"Wow, I never get visitors during the day."

As Dad headed to the door, I led Mickey to his crate. He didn't like unexpected guests either. The dog was already whining when he heard the door open. I heard muffled words as I headed into the living room.

Shocked to my core, I rocked back on my short heels. Gio Campano sat in my mother's chair. He stood as I entered the room.

"There she is. Miss O'Donohue, it is so good to see you."

My dad and I exchanged knowing glances. That certainly didn't take him a long time to make his way to our home. I continued to remain silent, allowing my father to take the lead. I sat across from them.

"Well, Gio, I am surprised to see you after all of these years. You are looking well." My father's tone was that of a judge, monotone with a touch of consternation and authoritarianism.

"It's like this, Judge. I'm sure your daughter told you

we met. The Taylor place is more than just a house to me."

"I understand completely, Gio," Dad said knowingly. "That was many years ago."

"It was. I need to tell you something about the morning that man was killed. Judge, I know you'll be fair, and you'll get the information to the proper authority. They have this detective, but I don't think he's any good."

I stifled a laugh. Gio and I had the same opinion of Detective Marino. Too bad Max hadn't expressed his lack of confidence in the man.

"Gio, before you tell me, is this information that is going to result in a crime, one that you committed?"

The once powerful gangster laughed loudly. "Oh no. I haven't done anything in years, Judge. On the soul of my mother, I haven't committed any crime."

Dad nodded. "Well then, let's hear what you have to say."

"Wait," I interrupted. "Would you like something to drink?"

Dad's eyes were shooting darts at me. It wasn't good being the target in the O'Donohue household, but my parents had taught me to have good manners.

Gio laughed again. "Oh no, not right now. I need to tell you both this first. Then, if you let me stay, I might take a little drink."

All three of us stared at each other. Gio cleared his throat. He unbuttoned his overcoat, and loosened his tie. Finally, he began as Dad and I waited patiently.

"I take the bus all over the city. I gave up my car about ten years ago. My eyes just aren't up to it, I have a bum knee, and a cranky heart now and then. I took the bus that day to the house. I usually get there before the sun is up, so it's dark when I arrive."

"Excuse me, Gio, but why do you go to that house? It's been empty for years," Dad wondered.

"I visit. Judge, you need to just listen to this." Gio looked over at me. I knew he would probably remove the entire part of how he spoke to Rose, and I understood omitting that information.

"Now Judge, don't get angry, but I have my own key." He removed the vintage item from his pocket and showed it to my dad. "Rose gave me that key years ago when we were close just for emergencies. I opened the door that day and went in. Usually there's a light or two on here and there, but I have a small flashlight I use in the dark part of the house."

Gio began to cough in an attempt to clear his throat. I jumped up and ran to the kitchen for a glass of water for our guest. When I returned, I was surprised to see my Dad and Gio huddled. They both looked up quickly and smiled at me as I handed him the glass.

"Thank you. So, I went in. I always leave a red rose on the mantle, and then I usually stay in that one room where Rose's portrait is hung. I talk to her. I tell her what is going on in the world, and how everything has changed so much. I look at her, and hopefully she is looking at me." He glanced over at me and continued.

"I was there for just a little bit when I saw a form walk in front of the window. I've become sloppy in my old age. I remembered that I hadn't locked the door after I came in. I panicked, Judge. I had left the key in the window seat, and I guess I sat on it during my visit. Your lovely daughter found it. This one." He waved the key. "I escaped out the back door, but I heard a man, you know heavy steps. I know the difference between a man and a dame. That's it. I hightailed it out of there and went down to the bus stop."

My dad remained motionless. His head was leaning in his hand, supported by the chair's arm. "Gio, are you going to tell me the rest of it?"

Gio made the sign of the cross. "So help me, Judge, that's all I have to tell you today."

I squinted as I looked at him. I saw a remnant of a once powerful man, one who was not stupid, one who knew the nuances of his words. That's all he had to tell my dad today. So there was more. Had he seen the murderer?

Dad took in a deep breath and sat back in his chair, his head against the cushion.

"When the man came in, you went out the back door. Gio, that door has been sealed off ever since the house has been vacant. I saw the police report. I can check the bus schedules, but I have this feeling that you didn't go down the block. Then, why did Rose give you a key all those years ago?"

Gio looked over to me. "Your father has always been a very smart man, and a fair one. I don't want any trouble, Judge."

Dad moved to the edge of his chair and pointed his finger at our guest. "You came to my house, Mr. Campano. Now, you tell me, or you tell the police, understand?"

I remembered that tone from the time that Tom and Sean took all their friends down to Judge Rochester's lake house and trashed the place. I had been playing in my room, and I could have sworn the roof of the house actually shook. Suddenly, I wished I had popcorn to watch this drama.

"Calm down, Judge. Fine. I locked the door. The man had a key. It was Mr. Martin. I saw his photo in the newspaper. He brought in a young redhead. She was a looker, Judge. She reminded me of Hayworth with that flowing hair. She was giggling a lot, and they were talking about pulling one over on his wife. I was watching from a hiding place when someone else opened that front door. That Martin fellow was kissing that redhead. She was trying to lean against the hall wall and one of her heels stuck in the floor. The parquet pattern needs to be refinished in the hallway, and with her little heels she began to topple over. About that time, that Martin fellow starts laughing, but it's not at the redhead."

Gio stopped to take a drink of water and cleared his throat. "The redhead gasped. She began to scream, but I put my hand over her mouth. I pulled her into my hiding place, and we waited. The back door I used was open. Servants used to use the one on the north side of the house, and I was able to pry the one board over the missing doorknob. That's how we got out. Her car was parked in the back. I had her drop me off at a bus stop down by one of the hotels. That's it. We didn't exchange names or numbers."

Gio smiled as he ended his tale. Even I realized he wasn't telling the entire story. What I didn't understand is why he felt the need to come to the house to tell that tale. Dad grasped his hands. He looked over to me with a blank face. I could never tell what he was thinking when he was like this. I was only grateful that I had never been a lawyer in his court.

I'll forward it on and say that I received it from an anonymous source. Now, how about some dinner? As I recall, you said I made a mean carbonara."

Gio looked toward me. "Well, I'm staying if you're cooking."

The judge stood. "I better get cooking. Daughter, I'm going to need some help in the kitchen. Gio, you look through my wine fridge and pick something out. And take that coat off and get comfortable."

Chapter Sixteen

All I did was toss the salad. I sat at the table, and they handed me a bowl of lettuce, sliced tomatoes, green and red peppers with a few onion slices. They asked me to toss. I tossed. They stood around the stove sharing stories, wine, and ingredients.

My father was in bliss. It was funny how the man could be surrounded by his family for these last two years, and the sublime happiness that he actually was finally enjoying was given by Max, and now by an ex-mobster.

In an hour, the three of us were seated around a table, eating carbonara, salad, bread, and drinking lots of wine. We laughed. I supported my head in my hands as the wine muddled my brain, but I smiled. I smiled so much my face began to hurt. They told stories that never had reached the newspaper, and Gio shared a few that the police had never even known about.

"Whatever happened to Rose's daughter?" Gio asked.

My father's wine glass landed on the table with a thud. Gio took the wine bottle and filled it slowly. "I asked about Rose's daughter. How is she?"

"She moved away. She got married and had two children."

As if on cue, Max was knocking at the kitchen door. I ran to open it.

"Sorry, but no one came to the front door, but I saw your car. I wanted to talk to your dad." He swept in before I could stop him. He halted as he saw our company.

"Dad, Max needs to talk to you," I announced. I scooted behind him to take my seat. My head and the room were beginning to spin.

"I'm sorry, I didn't know you had company," Max said slowly as he looked at our guest, studying his face, seemingly memorizing each feature. His usual beautiful crooked smile faded slowly and his caramel eyes darkened.

Dad motioned to the open seat next to me. "Max, please, sit down. You're not interrupting. I'm just visiting with an old friend."

Max quickly removed his leather jacket and took

his place. He looked different. He was dressed in jeans and a sweater, much different attire than I had seen him dressed in just a few hours ago.

"Max Shaw, this is--"

"Giovani Campano," Max added before my dad could finish his sentence.

Gio's head dodged back and forth as though he was attempting to remember another time. "You look familiar, but I'm sorry. My memory isn't the best anymore."

I was shocked. The two men had just shared years of memories without one lapse. Now, Gio couldn't remember?

The usually quick witted, articulate Max stuttered. Then he remained silent, looking to my dad for answers.

"Max is Rose Taylor's grandson, Gio." Dad and I watched for some reaction, but Gio was good. He just smiled that smile. I glanced at Max's face. He seemed to be in a stupor.

I stood up during the silence and grabbed another wine glass and another bottle. I placed the glass in front of Max, and filled it with what was left in the bottle on the table. He picked it up and drank it down.

"Okay, then," I muttered as I grabbed him a plate and filled it with food. "Here, eat." He looked down at the plate and then at me.

"What's the boy doing for a living? He sure doesn't talk much," Gio joked.

"He's a United States Attorney," I happily answered.

Gio only said one word. "Jesus."

It took Max three glasses of wine before I saw the vein in his neck stop pulsing. He also ate two plates of food. Dad was sharing a story about Judge Morrisey when Max interrupted the conversation.

"You knew my grandmother."

Gio nodded. "I knew her very well, many years ago."

"You were the reason she left my grandfather," Max stated plainly.

Gio smiled. "Who told you that? Your mother?"

Max didn't answer. Of course his mother had told him that. Who else? If Max could talk to Rose, he would know the truth.

"Well, your grandmother left your grandfather because she wanted to leave. She came back though, didn't she?" Gio filled his glass with more wine, as did my father.

"Yes," Max answered slowly as if he was deep in thought. "My grandfather was an awful man."

My dad touched Gio's arm before he could answer. "Max, your grandfather was a difficult, hard man. That's what made him such a success."

Max shook his head. "That and my grandmother's family money. She brought dollars into that marriage, and he only brought her pain. I've heard the stories. Hell, I've read the stories. She was in love with you, Mr. Campano."

Gio nodded. "And I loved her."

Max smiled. Gio smiled. It was as though each one were looking at a mirror image. I looked like a fish gasping for air. Dad tapped my arm and motioned with a finger to his mouth to be quiet. At that moment, I realized my father had known all along, possibly for years. Perhaps Max had even had his speculations?

"My mother wasn't some little girl my grandmother found at an orphanage, was she?"

"Max, maybe you two could use some privacy. Charlotte and I can give you some space," Dad suggested, but Max held my hand as I stood.

"No, please, stay. You all are more of a family to me than my own. Mr. Campano, are you my biological grandfather?" Max's plain question left nothing to the imagination. It was finally time for all the lies to fade away.

Gio only could manage a nod. The tears filled his eyes. His head hung in embarrassment. Dad stood up and placed his hands upon his shoulders. "Max, you need to know that Gio, for whatever bad he has done in the past, was his best self when he was with Rose Taylor. He loved her. He still does this very moment. He also loved your mother very much. I hope you give him a chance to get to know you."

"I came back here to do a job, but it seems I'm solving a mystery, and discovering that my family really doesn't exist." Max's sentence dripped with sadness. My heart was beating quicker, but it was for the sorrow in his own.

Gio's one large hand reached up in thanks to my father. "Judge, you have been a good friend. The boy doesn't owe me a chance, but thanks for what you said."

Nervously, I began to clean the plates off the table and collect the silverware. All three men watched me. I also pulled out another bottle of wine. It thumped when I placed it on the table. I could feel their eyes on me as I went to the refrigerator and looked for something, anything. We needed dessert.

"I know you have cheesecake in here. Where the hell did you put it?"

With my head stuck in the refrigerator, the laughter was muted. "Ah, there it is." I reappeared with the dessert in my hands. "Got it. Now who wants a piece?"

We all had cheesecake, the great equalizer. Mom always believed that you could take on anything with a little bit of sweet. In this case, she had no idea how right she had been all those years.

At first, the conversation was frenetic and filled with question after question. I learned more about Rose. She wasn't just a voice I heard; she was now someone I knew, and was beginning to like very much. The stories became longer, and Max had to tell his new grandfather how he used to make my life a living hell. He also shared how our family had saved his life when his father was so busy as he headed up the FBI ladder, and his mother was traveling with friends all over the world. She had taken his younger sister with her to Paris, Cannes, Milan, Rome, and all of the other fashion spots as she toured Europe.

Hours later, I began to yawn. I looked up at the kitchen clock, the chicken one that Conor had bought Mom for Christmas one year, and saw that it was almost midnight. We'd lost track of time in memories and way too much wine.

"I'm not sure I can drive," I admitted.

"I'm not sure any of you should drive," Dad announced.

Gio stood awkwardly, hanging onto the edge of the table. "I can take the bus, Judge."

"You will not. It's too late, Gio. There's a guest room down this other hall. You won't even have to climb the stairs. Max, you can have Tom's room, just like always. Honey, you have your room. Now, let's all get to bed before we can't make it."

We followed his authoritarian tone out of the kitchen. Dad began to turn off the lights. I ran back into the kitchen to make sure the stove was off, and the back door was locked. Mickey popped out and stayed by his master. Dad turned on the lights in the guest room and showed Gio the bathroom. He made him promise he would be there in the morning for a good Irish breakfast.

"Gio," Max called. "I'll see you in the morning, right?"

I could see the nervous twitch in Gio's hands. He seemed desperate to touch his newly found family member. Max took all the doubts away as he suddenly embraced the old man.

Gio rested his head on Max's shoulder. "I'll be here. I promise you, and I always keep my promises."

The next morning, my eyes opened slowly, first one eye and then the other. Thankfully, it seemed to be another gloomy winter day. I didn't need the sun. Correction, I didn't want the sun streaming into my room. I sat up slowly on the edge of the bed. Quickly, I grabbed my head.

"Oh my gosh. Why?" But I remembered the reason quickly. My stomach was churning. I drank like a fish, a fish who drank too much wine. Last night I listened to story after story, and kept drinking everything that was poured into my glass.

"Bacon?" Was I completely out of it?

"Charlotte."

I heard my mother's voice. "Yes?"

"Forgive."

Who did I need to forgive? "Mom, what?"

"Forgive."

I shook my head in a losing attempt to seek reality. Sometimes the messages were cryptic for me to figure out. Sometimes, they were in my face with information I needed to know. That had always been the case when a relative was going to be passing over. I called it that because it was a movement, not a finality as the word "death" implied. They were still there, just in another form of energy.

I stood slowly, hoping the room wouldn't spin. It didn't, but its color was off. Everything looked blah in gray tones. Had I drunk so much I lost my sight? Closing my eyes one more time, I opened them slowly. I'd have to think about Mom's comment later, much later when the color came back to my sight and my cheeks. I saw my face in the mirror and almost threw up.

I rushed out of my room to the bathroom and opened the door. Max was already there.

"Charlie!" he yelled as he turned toward me. Thankfully, it looked as though he had just finished shaving.

Holding my hand over my mouth, I motioned toward the toilet and barely made it before I became sick. At this point, I didn't care what he called me. I knelt in front of the bowl and hung onto the side. Heck, I was holding onto the earth.

Soon, my hair was away from my face. Two tanned hands brushed my face in an attempt to keep my loose strands out of my mess. I waved him off, but one of the hands remained. Soon I heard water running. A cool cloth was placed on my forehead. I was sick just a couple more times until I turned to sit on my backside on the cold tiled floor.

Max crouched in front of me. I finally looked up to see his concerned face and his bare chest. He was only wearing his jeans. One of my dreams was coming true, and I was too sick to touch or even to stand.

"I'm so sorry," I mumbled.

"There's nothing to be sorry about." He collected the towel and stood up to run it under the water then wring it. He returned it to my forehead and came down to my level to sit next to me on the floor with his legs out in front of him. Even his bare feet were tanned.

We sat shoulder to shoulder not saying one word. I was finally able to spread my own legs out and noticed the differences in length.

"Your height is all in your legs," I commented. Now our legs were touching, denim jeans to my fleece pajama bottoms.

"Yep. You stopped growing along the way."

"Dad used to say I filled out," I mumbled. Why the heck were we sitting on a cold bathroom floor having a very ridiculous conversation?

He softly shoved my arm. "You filled out nicely and added curves." His head was closer to mine now.

I suppose I would have blushed if I wasn't so sick. "I still need some work. I hate to exercise. I loved tennis, until I broke my ankle. And I love a good dessert like that cheesecake last night." Suddenly, the thought of cheesecake was nauseating. The taste in my mouth was indescribable.

"Um, could you reach up in the cabinet and get the toothpaste?"

Max didn't ask why, he just moved. He handed me the tube and watched me rub the paste on my teeth and tongue. In an unlady-like action, I spit into the toilet bowl beside me. It wasn't perfect, but it was better than feeling as though cheese had rotted in my mouth.

I looked up and smiled half-heartedly. "Much better. Thank you."

He joined me down on the floor again. "Why do you call me *Poop Head?*"

That's what he wanted to know right now when we were sitting on the floor?

"Because you called me *Melon Head.*"

He crossed his arms in front of him. "We have grown so much." He looked at me and smiled, then laughed. "Just look at us."

"We look like we're in college." I began to laugh uncontrollably, pointing at him.

"What? What's so funny?"

"And you're a United States Attorney! You don't look like one this morning."

Max unfolded his arms and looked up at the ceiling. "I haven't drunk that much in years."

I pointed at the toilet bowl. "Obviously, I haven't either."

He smiled that smile that I now knew he had inherited honestly. I followed his hand as it raised and wiped away errant hair from my face.

I was unnerved. As much as I hated him when I was little, he and my brother Conor were the only two who had watched out for me when all of us walked across the street or into a store to get candy. Once, when we went to the cheap afternoon movies one hot summer day, he had raised me in his arms so I could pick out which candy I wanted on the counter. Here he was taking care of me, again?

"So, Charlie, what did you learn last night?"

I focused on his hand as he pulled it back slowly. "I learned never to drink with two old men."

"There is that," he murmured.

"What did you learn?" Of course, he had discovered a grandfather.

"Um, nothing very earth shattering except this morning I used a disposable razor that apparently someone stole from a hotel." He laughed as I gave him a shot on his arm. His muscles were rigid. What kind of workout did he do? "Seriously, besides that big DNA discovery, I learned that somehow you got into the house again. I've known for awhile, but this is a good time to talk about it, don't you think? You want to tell me about how you got in?"

Really? Now? "Off the record, right?"

Max nodded. "Agreed. What happens in the bathroom, stays in the bathroom."

"First, do you have a copy of the key you returned to Tom?"

"You're supposed to answer, but fine, yes. I did make a copy before returning the key to the agency. I'm assuming you gave that key to Cynthia Martin."

"Well." I tried to continue. I tried to gather my thoughts, but I just kept looking at his feet. "Fine, well, here's the thing. We are still missing that key Tom told you about."

"So what key did you use?" His brown eyes seemed to be getting darker in preparation for bad news. But maybe it was my problem with my eyesight today.

My stomach rumbled, and we both heard it. "The day of the murder, the police, Sean, made me get out of the way. I sat in the window seat at the back of the room. That would be the east side of the room I think. I found something stuck in the wood, and it was an old key."

"When were you planning on telling the police about this?" Yes, the eyes definitely did get darker with anger. Yet, his voice was chillingly low.

"I'm telling you now. Please, understand that Dad wanted me to tell you, but I needed to go back into the house to see if I'd missed something. That's when I met Gio." I shut my eyes and cringed at the oncoming onslaught of verbal attacks. But they didn't come.

Slowly, I opened my eyes and looked at him. His face was blank. I couldn't read anything. Of course! Dad said he was a good lawyer.

"Of course you did," Max said quietly. "Are you and Gio investigating this murder on your own?" Max stopped. "Wait a minute, you met Gio there? Are you going to tell me he was there the morning of the murder?"

"I didn't know he was there that day, but he was. He can tell you the rest, but we have some theories we developed before you arrived yesterday."

"You have some theories?" Max's voice raised in volume, and he quickly removed himself from my side. "What do you two think you're doing? You're not the private detective and the gangster solving the crime of the old Taylor Home with some antique key."

"Taylor Club."

"It was a home before it was a club."

"Fine. Whatever you want. You're apparently used to getting your way, and I'm not going to argue with you."

"Good. You won't win. I always win." Max looked at his face in the mirror and used a towel to wipe off the imaginary shaving cream. He looked down at me as he opened the bathroom door.

Max really was a sanctimonious ass.

"Do you need anything before I leave? I can get your father for you." His tone was dispassionate. I guess I shouldn't expect anything less from the devil.

I did my best to place some sort of adult resolve on my face as I looked up at him defiantly. "I don't need my father, *Poop Head*. I am a grown woman. I can take care of myself."

He chuckled. "You keep telling yourself that, Charlie O. It is comforting to know that some things never change. You are still just an annoying little sister."

I slapped the tile floor in anger. How dare he? We were having a moment, and he had to ruin it. Well, I actually ruined it by not telling him the truth, but that was beside the point. How dare he just leave me sitting here, wallowing in my hangover! I smelled bacon again. With my stomach rumbling, it was time to make my way downstairs.

If Max got out of hand down there, Gio and my Dad would save me. I didn't need Max Shaw to do anything for me. I never wanted him to touch my hair again.

Chapter Seventeen

By the time I made it into the kitchen, Max was eating his breakfast, and Gio and Dad were drinking coffee and talking about the time Max's father arrested a certain mob figure.

"Good morning," I said quietly as I sat down at the other end of the table, away from Max Shaw.

"Let me get you something, honey. How about a muffin and an egg, maybe some bacon?" Dad was already turning to the stove to fix me breakfast. Now, that's what a man did.

"Fine."

Max didn't look up from his plate. I knew what he was doing. All my brothers "stewed". They went over the entire conversation in their head, and then elaborated on it. When they did that it always ended up being my fault. My oldest sister had always been immune, but they blamed it on the baby. I was responsible for most of the bad times in their childhood. At this very moment, in Max's mind, I was probably responsible for Mr. Martin's murder, the decay of the Taylor Club, his grandmother fooling around with a gangster, and possibly the downfall of the Roman Empire.

I felt Gio's eyes on me and watched as his gaze centered on Max, and back to me again. He knew something was wrong. Of course it was! There was complete silence.

Soon, Dad had a plate of food in front of me along with a cup of coffee. Gio motioned him to look at us, the guests who weren't communicating.

"That was some night," Dad commented. Max and I remained silent.

"It sure was," Gio added. Again, Max and I remained silent. The two of them exchanged glances and some whispered words.

Slowly, I ate my food, stopping in between bites to make sure it would stay down.

I sighed. I looked over at Max. To gain his attention, I picked up my fork and dropped it onto my plate. All three men looked in my direction. Dad and Gio smiled, Max glared.

"You know, not everyone is perfect," I began. "Human beings have been making mistakes for centuries. They make wrong decisions. They fall in love with the wrong person. Some people only tell certain people certain things when those people are ready to hear it. Some people even forgive people who have called them names over the years. And believe it or not, winning isn't everything."

The realization hit me like a brick. Mom said to forgive. I needed to forgive Max for all those years of name calling, and he needed to forgive me for omitting just a little piece of evidence, a key piece.

"And certain people should have the sense to know when to tell the truth," Max answered.

"You really are a *Poop Head*." I could see Dad and Gio watching us vent our wrath upon each other.

Max stood up from the table. "Judge, Gio thank you both for last night and breakfast this morning. I'll be in touch. Maybe the three of us could do dinner out, and it'll be my treat."

He stopped and turned to face me. "Name calling? You really still are the obnoxious, needy little sister who is always trailing behind. If you were practicing law, I'd have you disbarred. Grow up Charlie before it's too late."

He didn't allow me any response and made his way quickly out of the kitchen, followed by Gio. My father sat down at the other end of the table and took a drink from his coffee.

I didn't know where to begin, so maybe I should just stay silent? I took a slow drink of caffeine. Dad continued to stare at me. I hated it when he did that.

"I am assuming you finally told him about the discovery of the key."

"You would be correct," I answered. "He is impossible. He really is like a brother, a nasty brother who still thinks you're a child when you're a capable grown woman who is very successful in her career."

Dad studied my face. His smile made me wonder what he was up to. "What was he upset about?"

"Obviously, because I hadn't told the police about the key."

"Ah. You hadn't told the police. Think about it, honey. He said to the police, not him."

My head was already splitting. I didn't need my father making me work a word problem right now. "What's your point, Dad? I'm not up for this."

Dad got up to go to the coffee pot. "What I'm telling you is he already knew you had another key. He was just upset that you put yourself in jeopardy going back to the house."

Now the confusion in my head became even greater. "Dad, how could he know?"

Dad slowly poured his cup full and returned to the table. "Because he's been following you. I told you not to underestimate him. I know what kind of a shark he is in court. Honey, I saw him in action three years ago when I went down to Atlanta for that conference. He was formidable then and was only an assistant. Now he has that much more experience. I warned you. Don't play with fire."

I felt singed. I felt as though the fire had burnt my heart. It was almost like the time Sean said he hated me. Almost. This felt different for some reason. I didn't really know Max Shaw anymore. Heck, I didn't even recognize him. We hadn't seen each other since childhood, and that had been over two decades ago. But why did this hurt so much? Even his threat of disbarment should've meant nothing, but it had done the opposite. I wanted to fight him, for something.

I stood up, probably too quickly, as I felt my stomach rumble. "He has messed with the wrong girl."

As I began to walk out, Gio stopped me. "Max has a temper, doesn't he?"

"You think that's a temper? Well, he hasn't seen anything yet. I like to win too." I briefly saw Gio and my father smile and nod, almost like some private club greeting. Who knew what they were thinking? I rudely fled up to my room to grab the rest of my things. I was going home, to my house. I paid mortgage payments just like a responsible adult. I needed a shower. Then, I needed a plan. I needed to show Max that I wasn't a meddling little sister anymore. I was going to do something that the police, and not even the great prosecuting attorney had done yet. It was time to solve a murder, and I was the woman to do it, yes, the woman!

Chapter Eighteen

I called Tom and said I wouldn't be coming into the office. I began to draw up a timeline and pulled up notes on my laptop of anything relative to the Martins. I usually did a full description of each client, including their wants and needs, and a background check. I realized very quickly that the Martins hadn't been very forthcoming with their details. One of my notes stated I felt like I was pulling teeth. They never mentioned a real estate connection. Cynthia Martin said she worked in sales, her husband in finances and investments. I found a couple of phone numbers for them. I also had the name of the business that was transferring him to our area. I'd line up the calls for tomorrow.

As I made my plans for attack, the nagging thought of Max Shaw following me, or having someone follow me just wasn't acceptable. I needed to get back into that house, but I didn't have a key. Tom didn't have a key. Gio did, but I had no way to contact him. Of course, the devil had a key. I would die before I'd ask him to borrow the duplicate to go back into that house. But, somehow, I knew the answers were in there. Maybe Rose could even tell me?

I paced back and forth from the living room to the kitchen. My mind raced with different thoughts including how Cynthia Martin had treated me at the funeral, as if she intentionally was trying to set me up. If she was being truthful, she did know her husband was having an affair. If both of the Martins were involved in some sort of criminal activity involving real estate, had they begun to turn on each other? Obviously, their trust of one another had begun to deteriorate. It was one thing when they cheated strangers out of their money and property, but when they began to cheat each other would and could they resort to murder?

There was no legal way to get my hands on their financial reports. Max had power to do that; I had nothing but speculation. It seemed that Max had all the power. He had a key. Max had a new grandfather, and I needed to borrow Gio for more details. There had to be more to this story, and more to this murder.

After a lost afternoon of pacing and nursing a headache, I noticed the sun was setting. I disliked how early it became dark in the winter, and today was no exception. That darkness fueled my foul mood. But I couldn't feel sorry for myself. I'd brought this on my own head, but I refused to admit that to anyone. My phone rang and for a second I thought for some reason that it might be Max calling to apologize. No, it was Paddy.

"Charlie, get over here. We're having pizza and beginning to assemble the float. I messaged you last week about it, but you never answered me."

"I've been busy being a murder suspect."

"Well, we could use one of those. Get your tush over here. Sean, Jane, Tom, and Meg are already here. Linda demands you come to protect her from the O'Donohue clan. You're one of us, but she seems to think you are always on her side. I don't get it."

I got it. Linda and I had bonded from the moment she had walked through our front door. That, and she had me in her wedding as a flower girl. I always sided with her on everything, even those things I didn't really agree with just to irritate the others. These days, Linda was the one person who reminded me the most of our own mother. She was calm in a storm and bitey when needed.

"Fine, but I'm not doing anything on the float tonight. I'll eat pizza."

"Whatever, just get over here. We aren't waiting on you to eat."

"I wouldn't have it any other way," I answered as he hung up. He was in the process of yelling at Sean about some pot of gold and where it should go. Only in my family would that make sense.

Some of my first memories were of the annual Kansas City St. Patrick's Day Parade. The O'Donohue family always participated, and Dad was one of the most public personalities. We even won a few awards over the years. I changed my sweatshirt, throwing on a warmer sweater. Paddy's large garage wasn't the warmest. I had no plans to be out there the entire time nailing chicken wire in place.

I parked my car behind Tom's and headed into the house, but something caught my eye at the end of the driveway. It was a blue Jaguar. What the bloody--

I stopped at the door. With as much noise that was being made, they'd never hear me come or go. I could just turn around and drive away. I'd grab something to eat, take a nice warm bubble bath, and be in bed by nine. But it was too late.

"Go on in," Dad yelled from the driveway. He had just pulled up and was walking toward me. "He won't bite, you know."

"But he may suck my blood," I answered. "Wait, the devil doesn't do that."

"Charlotte," he muttered as he shook his head. "Have faith."

"And Mom tells me to forgive," I added. "I don't do either very well."

Dad caught up to me at the door. "Well, this is what you do. You turn the door's knob like this. You push, and you are in. Easy. Now, walk into the house."

"He was mean to me."

Dad shut his eyes as if in prayer. "As I recall, he was always mean to you, just like a brother. Unless--"

"Unless, what?"

"Unless you don't see Max as an obnoxious brother anymore?" Dad winked at me.

I had no words. Charlotte O'Donohue was remarkably and unbelievably speechless. "Arrrggghhh," I yelled, sounding distinctly like a melon headed cartoon character.

Linda greeted us as we were taking off our coats.

"I thought I heard you two. The pizza is in the kitchen, and we're all in the garage as usual. I think this float may be a winner this year. Oh, and there's beer in the refrigerator."

Dad and I both grimaced. Neither one of us would be drinking anything that was alcoholic for a few days, if then. We ate our pizza and drank some much needed water. We could hear the laughter, the yelling from the garage. Dad quickly ate and headed out. After a great roar at his arrival, it quieted down. Linda came to join me.

"So, what's new?"

I placed my pizza down on the plate. "Nothing much."

Linda studied me for some reason. "Really?"

I briefly picked up my food. Now, I threw it back down. "Why, what have you heard?"

"Nothing." She looked like she swallowed something disagreeable.

"Linda, I can go home. I really don't need this tonight. I'm only here for you." It seemed like I was irritated by just about everything. I couldn't manage a smile. In fact, I hadn't smiled since this morning with Max. I was absolutely wonderful until he came to town.

"We need help, ladies. Meg thinks you'll agree with her." Paddy yelled rather loudly from the float project.

"We better get out there," Linda admitted. "You know what happens when all those men are in charge."

"I know. No one is in charge then. Mom always said not to let them design the float."

The phone rang, and Linda headed to answer it while I entered the garage. I took one step down when glitter rained down on me. I was completely covered by the stuff in a matter of seconds. My hair was as gold as a leprechaun's pot. I brushed it away from my eyes and looked to find the attacker.

"I'm so sorry. I grabbed the bag, and it broke when I lifted it." Max stood there motionless as my brothers, Dad, and even Meg laughed hysterically. Paddy was crying. Dad leaned over in an attempt to breathe. Meg turned away, and Sean and Tom had fallen to the floor.

I stood motionless. I had glitter on my eyelashes, and perhaps up my nose. It was definitely in my mouth. I said nothing. I stood with my arms out, immobile.

"Oh my goodness! What happened to you, Charlotte?" Linda asked as she joined us.

I pointed at the offender. "Max happened to me. It's always been Max."

Max tried not to laugh. To his credit, he did remain concerned. "I'm so sorry. Seriously, the bag broke when I lifted it up."

I heard Linda chuckle behind me. "Charlotte, come on, honey. Let's try to clean you up." She turned me around and led me carefully to the guest bathroom by the den. "I'll go upstairs and get you another shirt. I'll be right back."

I stood in the bathroom and got my first look at the damage. No wonder they were laughing so hard. I looked like a ridiculous gold human pompom. I didn't laugh; I didn't cry. I just didn't.

"I am so sorry, Charlotte." Max stood just inside the door. "We really do need to stop meeting in bathrooms." He smiled that smile.

I began to wonder what sort of items were available inside the cabinet that could wound him. Death would be too good for him.

"Max Shaw, get the hell out of here," I shouted.

"Let me help."

"You've done quite enough for one day."

"Here, let me get this clump off your neck," he suggested as he began to reach toward me.

"I said to leave me alone. Don't touch me." I made the mistake of pushing out as he stood aside. As I began to fall, he did what he did best. He held me up. He caught me. I ended up against his sweatshirt adorned chest. He held me in his arms briefly, looking down at me as I looked up at him through glitter laden eyelashes.

I couldn't move out of his arms, and he didn't release me. Is this what it felt like to be burned by the devil? It was warm, and it didn't hurt much at all. In fact, I liked it.

"Are you okay? Did you twist an ankle?" He lowered his eyes down to my feet for some odd reason.

"I'm fine," I said as I pulled out of his arms. It was then that I smiled. I pointed at his shirt. "Look, you've got it all over you now, even your jeans. Now that's funny."

Max came to look in the mirror and shrugged. "I suppose I deserve this. It seems you really do grow on a person, kind of like fungus, gold glitter fungus."

"What on earth happened while I was gone?" Linda asked loudly as she arrived with a new sweater for me. "Max, Charlotte, what have you two been doing?"

"Max caught me again, and this time I left a little

reminder." My laughing made Linda laugh. Max was stoic. "You owe me."

"I don't see it that way. It was an accident. I said I was sorry. What more do you want?" His serious tone put a damper on the levity that Linda and I were sharing. He stormed out of the bathroom, leaving us wondering.

"And that was Tom's best friend for years?" Linda asked. "I don't see it. I mean, he seems nice, but wow. I don't think he fits into the family at all."

She handed me one of her sweaters and towels to wash this stuff off. I wasn't going to stay anyway. I would do what I could and then take a vacuum cleaner to my body. I would really need a shower. Goodbye bubble bath!

"It's my fault. I sort of didn't tell him something very important, but he was having me followed, and then there was this large secret that I uncovered, and he's mad because I began figuring out this murder thing, but I'm pretty sure he knows some stuff he's not telling me." I stopped as I looked at the confusion on Linda's face. "Well, he started doing that stewing thing they all do."

Suddenly, Linda understood. "Oh, I hate it when they do that, and they all do it, except for your father. What is that all about?"

"I don't know. I'd say it was a family trait, but like you said Dad doesn't do it."

Linda began to brush the glitter out of my hair. "I'll vacuum this up. Did Mom do it?"

I thought about it. Hmm, maybe she did. "I do believe they got it from her. She did stew. It took her days sometimes to decide what to say to you, and in the meantime, you just stayed away. Yes, she was the culprit who passed it onto the boys. Thankfully, Jane and I didn't inherit that behavior."

Linda looked at me strangely. "Considering what's going on with you and Max, I'm pretty sure you've been stewing for quite awhile."

Had I been stewing about Max all these years? I'd completely forgotten him. It would have been silly to waste time on him. I wouldn't admit it to Linda, but she was right. I was stewing, but I preferred to label it as analytic behavior.

After I changed my shirt, I was finished for the night. I headed out to the group and stood on the edge of the steps just in case an errant bag of glitter flew past me a second time. Actually, I wouldn't put it past him.

"Goodnight everyone. I've had quite enough for one day."

Tom held up a jar of glitter. "Are you sure you don't need some more?"

I stuck my tongue out at him. "I'll be up to helping on this later this week."

Paddy came over to me. I saw Max behind him, wiping his hands with a towel.

"Charlotte, are you okay? I mean, beside the glitter bomb. You're looking, well different."

I appreciated his concern, but not right now. "I look gold, Paddy. I need a hot shower and to go to bed. I promise I'll be over this weekend to work with you and my wonderful nieces and nephews."

Paddy blew me a kiss and went back to the base of the float. Max headed toward me.

"I'll walk you out."

"That's not necessary." I turned to leave, but I could hear his footsteps on the wood kitchen floor. He was directly behind me.

"And yet, I'm still going to do it."

He helped me with my coat and followed me out to my car. We walked in silence. I unlocked the car, but was stopped by his arm leaning against my vehicle and near my head.

"Do you ever take no for an answer?"

He held me at the elbow, supposedly making sure I made it to the car safely?

"Nope," I answered.

"What is with you?"

"Seriously?" I snapped back. "You're the one that turned toleration into hatred."

"Really? You're the one who calls me the devil."

I opened my mouth and then shut it quickly. I wasn't going to lie, or omit anymore. He wasn't worth it. "You and I have never gotten along."

"That's not true, and you know it. I took care of you when your brothers forgot about you."

"And you were mean to me. Do you know what it's like for a little girl's confidence to be likened to a cartoon character who has a large head and an even larger body?" I tried to open my car door, but he shut it with his hand.

"I meant it nicely. You were cute and chubby."

I laughed at that answer. "You did not mean it nicely. You were a jerk who only looked at the cheerleaders, like Tracy Winters. Remember her? You saw her at the pool, and you said she was a real babe. She had long thin legs, and longer hair that was so blonde it was sun-kissed. Oh wait, it was sun-kissed from the hair color she used. She was so fake, but you thought she was a babe."

His brow rose. He smiled that smile. I was beginning to hate that grin. "Wow, you really remembered that even though you didn't realize who I was the day I saved you from the ice? In fact, that's another thing. It seems as though I'm always catching you. Have you noticed that?"

"You owe me for this glitter." I ignored everything he was saying as I tried to open my door.

"Yes, I do. How about a truce? Why don't you meet me at the mansion Friday night? I'll call Cynthia Martin tomorrow and tell her I need one more look before I feel comfortable releasing the house. After that, she can do anything she wants. She can bulldoze it for all I care. She's already said she'll pack up any of my family portraits or items she finds in the house and attic, so she won't think anything of it. Maybe she'll think I just need one more visit to say goodbye."

I noticed his tone had changed. His voice was softer, nicer. He was actually attempting to make amends. "What about Rose's portrait? You have to save it."

"For Gio, I know." Max seemed to lack any emotion when it came to that house and anything within it. He reached down and opened my door. "Friday, at seven? I won't be out of court until five or six, so that'll give me enough time to change and get there. Wear clothes that don't matter so we can check out a few of the hiding places."

I nodded as I got into the car. "That's perfect. I just need to get in there one more time. I just have this nagging feeling that I'm missing something."

"Yeah, I feel the same way, but I know a little more about that house than you do. Just like you know about that trap door in Paddy's room, I had my own secret hiding places. Then we'll be even. It'll make up for the glitter. As for all the rest, you'll just have to learn to forgive because obviously you never forget."

I felt like he stabbed me in the heart. Was I really like that, or was it just with him? Forgive, that's what I had to do.

"I'll see you Friday at seven." He shut my door, and I drove slowly down the street. He remained standing in the street, watching me leave. I didn't know what he was thinking, but I knew we wouldn't ever be even, especially when he discovered Gio and I hadn't told him everything. Actually, we hadn't told him much at all. And Rose hadn't told him anything, at least Max hadn't told anyone if she did. Maybe that was another of his secrets my father said he had?

Chapter Nineteen

Friday didn't arrive fast enough for me. We shut down the business for the weekend around two, and I headed over to Dad's for an early dinner then home to change into jeans, a flannel shirt, and sneakers. When Dad heard what the great outing was for the evening, he wasn't particularly receptive to my plans.

"I don't think the two of you should be going over there, especially at night. I don't feel good about this," he complained.

"Is it because I'm going with Max? Do you think he'll lead me into a perjury trap or something like that?"

"No, that's not it." Dad filled the dishwasher as we talked. He sincerely seemed worried for some reason.

"Dad, it's just a house." I patted him on the back to comfort him.

"No, it's not. You don't know what went on there." He turned to me and grabbed my hands. "Charlotte, I don't want you to go."

My father's hands were shaking. "I told Max I'd be there tonight."

"Now you're going to do what he says?" Dad pulled me into his arms. "Max will take care of you, but I'm worried about both of you. You know that house is haunted, and it is for a very good reason."

I looked up at my dad and felt very small. Yes, I was the baby, but I was still his little girl. He was always larger than life, not just in height. "Dad, Rose won't let anything happen to us. She spoke to me, and she's Max's grandmother. She'll protect us."

He let loose after he kissed me on the head. I gathered up my things and headed to the front door.

"Charlotte, you need to remember that some awful things happened there. Rose Taylor was abused, and Max's own grandfather died under suspicious circumstances. Gio may have murdered him, and got away with it. If pushed, if you and Max find out something Gio doesn't want you to know, I wouldn't trust that he wouldn't make sure you both were silent, even after all of these years. Do you understand me? Don't trust anyone but yourself, not a charming ex-gangster, nor a ruthless United States attorney. Gio was a killer. Max, well I've noticed that he doesn't look at you like a little sister anymore."

I ran back from the door and kissed him on the

cheek. He held me tightly one more time, and then he let me go. "You're running into trouble either way. Protect yourself, Charlotte."

"Dad, I'll be here tomorrow morning for breakfast. I love you for caring though."

Dad walked me to the door and yelled at me as I walked to the car.

"I love you, and I'm making blueberry pancakes tomorrow. I'll see you then."

Later, I stayed in the darkened parking lot, sitting in my car until Max arrived. At seven, I saw the headlights of the luxury car pull into the lot and park beside me. He exited the car, and I met him on the sidewalk.

I kept my distance from him, taking Dad's advice to heart. Something was changing in our relationship. Wait, did we have a relationship? He was like an older brother to me, wasn't he? Well, he acted like a brother most of the time, obnoxious and difficult to read.

He smiled as he came closer. "Do you know you are absolutely glowing?"

Wait, what? "Excuse me?" I was totally caught off guard.

He came closer and touched my hair. "In the light, I can still see some of the gold glitter. You're glowing."

"Can we just get inside? It's cold out here." I turned away from him and headed up to the front door. Was this his attempt at charm? I just needed to keep my head on straight and get in that house for a final time.

Max followed and reached around me to put the key into the lock. He opened the door, and I followed.

"The rose was on the mantle. Gio told me he brought the rose for Rose."

Max turned on his flashlight. "Gio and you are pretty tight, huh?"

"He can be very charming." It must be a family trait. I managed a forced smile.

"Exactly what did you do the morning of the murder?" Max seemed distracted by tapping on one of the walls.

"Well, first I noticed Mr. Martin's car, and it looked like it had been there for a while. The windows were frosted over and snow was sticking to the vehicle. I didn't see his footsteps in the snow on the sidewalk. I unlocked the door. I saw the rose on the mantle. I checked a few of the rooms, and then--"

I stopped short before I told him Rose had directed me into the sitting room. Max noticed that something was wrong. He stopped tapping.

"Then what, Charlotte? What aren't you saying?"

I had to lie. I had to protect my secret. The devil would use it against me. He was charming right now, but all that could and would change if he knew.

"I guess I didn't realize how it bothered me. Sorry. I headed into the sitting room to look for him and saw the body. Oh, wait, that window was open and the cold air was blowing in. I shut it." The window had been opened. Is that how the murderer left the building?

I turned on my own flashlight and headed toward that window. I looked outside and down from the structure. Someone could step out from that window right onto an elevated part of the lawn. "Max, look." I pointed out. "Someone could just slip out of here and walk away down that back road. No one would notice them unless a neighbor saw them climb out of the window. It would've been early on a Monday morning so the likelihood of that happening would've been minimal."

"I know the police interviewed the neighbors, and no one saw anything, but a car that was parked there briefly."

I headed into the sitting room and turned on one of the lights that I knew had been on that day. "A car? Did they get a look at who got into that car?"

"Why are you so sure someone got into the car, and not out of the car?" Max looked at me, raising one of those charming brows.

I decided to lie again. "Just a turn of a sentence. It's nothing else." I turned on the other lamp and turned to see Max looking up at the portrait of his grandmother.

"She was so beautiful," Max said softly. "I wish I had known her."

"You never met her?"

"I don't remember her. She saw me when I was a baby. We moved into this house after she passed away. My grandfather had died before I was born. As nasty as he was, I'm beginning to feel grateful about that. If Gio did kill him, I would completely understand."

"Really?" I was shocked to hear that from a United States Attorney. "Would you forgive him?"

Max took the portrait off the wall and walked it into the hallway, placing it on the floor. When he returned, he gave me his answer.

"As mean as the man was, I'd probably buy Gio whatever he wanted if he admitted he murdered my grandfather, well old man Taylor. Have you remembered anything or found anything?"

After seeing his face while he was looking up at Rose, it was going to be increasingly more difficult to lie to his face. I could hear Rose, but Max was immune.

"Tell him. He'll know."

As I listened to her, Max searched my face. "Charlie, are you okay? You have a funny look on your face."

"Um, yes. I need to tell you something. I know a little more now. Mr. Martin came here to rendezvous with a woman."

Max's face became dark and disapproving. "So, you were carrying on with a client?"

"Max Shaw, do you always have to think the worst of me? No, *Poop Head*, I was not. He was meeting some young woman, well younger than me. Just listen for a minute, and do not judge."

"Fine. Go ahead. I'm listening."

I could hear the disdain in his tone. "Gio had been here. He heard Martin coming in so he hid. He said he went down the hallway by the kitchen. He stayed, at least long enough to see the woman. I don't know all the details, but the woman and Martin were startled by someone else entering. Gio grabbed and pulled Martin's lady further into the darkness for protection. I don't know the timing, but eventually, Gio and the woman escaped. It was probably her car parked on the backstreet. He said they left through one of the back doors, the old servant entrance. I'm not sure about all that."

"I need to get this all down. I'll want Gio and you to give me the timeline. You two seem to be very good at keeping secrets. Are you sure you aren't the one who is related to him?"

"I wouldn't mind it. Maybe I could tan better than I do," I answered blandly. Max managed to chuckle at my comment.

"Charlie, why did Gio come here? Why the rose on the mantle?" Max's face had softened suddenly, and I didn't feel as though he was going to handcuff me to the interrogation table.

"Gio came here to remember. He would just sit in that window seat and look at Rose. That old key was his. She had given him that key years ago. They love each other so much, Max."

"You mean they loved, past tense."

I thought about agreeing with him, but when it came to love I just had to be truthful.

"No, I mean present tense. I know she passed on many years ago, but their love is alive. It's alive in his heart, and I can even feel it here in this house. Her love remains, and so does the love your parents had while you were growing up here."

Max smiled. "You don't know my parents very well, and you definitely have a romantic view of the world, Charlie. Enjoy your delusion."

He began to investigate the tiles around the area where Martin's body had fallen. I scowled. What was wrong with him that he couldn't believe in love? Sure, Rose had suffered, but she found a great love with Gio. That had been real. I was not living in some fairytale world, but couldn't I hope for just a piece of that magic?

Max kneeled down. He looked up at me with a questioning look on his face.

"Charlotte, you said Gio hid down the hallway by the kitchen. They would've been seen by the murderer, unless--"

He shot up from his position. "Come on. I have an idea."

We walked back out into the main hall. First, Max slid the portrait down into the kitchen by the back door and began thumping on the wall.

"What are you doing?"

"When I was a kid, I had this hiding place. I just

don't remember how I accessed the entry, but it was on this wall, where Gio might have been. He may be just omitting that detail. Maybe years ago when he'd sneak in to see Rose, he came from that back street? He could come in from the secret bookcase up into the house, and he might've left that way too."

Max heard something different. He took a fist and wrapped it along the seam of the wall. One piece separated, and Max pulled it apart. "Presto!"

"Oh my heavens." Our flashlights revealed a few books remaining. "Those are really old."

"We need to get these out of here before Cynthia Martin moves in," Max suggested. He handed me a few books, and I stacked them near Rose's painting.

Max waded in, and I joined him. "This used to look a lot bigger."

"Of course," I laughed. "You were a lot smaller. Wow, here's another old book." I checked the date. It had been published before World War I. "You are definitely going to need to get these out of here."

Max flipped through another book. He pulled something out of it. "Look, I hid this comic inside when I was hiding out from everyone."

"It seems as though you perfected hiding out. It

must be in your gangster DNA."

"Charlotte, that's not really that funny."

I chuckled. "Well, I thought it was amusing. Or maybe, you only read comics? Was that your speed then?"

Max glared, but replaced it quickly with that smile. We were only inches apart as he placed an arm over my head. "You know, Charlotte, you irritate me."

His proximity was unbearable. "What?"

He smiled again. "Oh, not in a bad way. You have a lovely neck."

I shook my head. "Excuse me? I really don't understand what you are talking about, Max."

"Well then let me show you." He began to lean down, slowly. I watched his forehead, his eyes, his nose, and then his mouth come dangerously closer to mine. I usually didn't look at his lips, but they were right in front of me. I was the one who had just lectured him about love and romance. Obviously, he didn't believe in either so why was he tormenting me this way? Was it just to make fun of me?

He was within an inch of kissing me when we both heard the front door open slowly. Max pressed a finger up to my lips. We listened in silence. I could hear my heart. Max listened intently, confusion etched on his face. If Gio was visiting, he would've yelled out. He had to have seen our cars parked in the driveway. We couldn't discern the next noises. In a few minutes, the door closed and surprisingly was locked. We waited. We couldn't take the chance to walk out and straight into the arms of a murderer. We were breathing hard in the confined space. I didn't know about Max, but I was scared to death. I wasn't hearing Rose. I felt evil, a strange darkness that chilled me to my core. Dad warned me about this house, but I thought I would be protected. Now, I realized if anything was going to happen, we were going to have to solve it on our own.

I didn't know what Max was thinking, but I was going over in my mind who would have opened that door. I figured Gio wouldn't be here at this time of night. Max had the duplicate key in his pocket. Cynthia Martin had one key, the key I had used. There was still one missing. Had Mr. Martin removed it off of Tom's desk? Is that how he entered the house before I arrived? The police hadn't found one on his body.

Did the murderer have that key? Did that woman have it? Or, and I really didn't want to think this way, had Gio concocted a tale this entire time? I would never hear the end of it if Max ended up with the upper hand. That would open me up to Max's condemnations and ridicule every time he saw me. If he didn't mention it, I would see it in his eyes.

Max motioned me to stay put as he pushed past me in the tight space. He crept out into the hallway. I heard him yell out a string of profanity.

"Charlotte, come out. There's a damn fire by the front door. We can't get through there."

Max reached for me, pulling me out of our hiding place. "It's too bad to even try to go near the front door." We headed into the sitting room, looking out to the front terrace. "Those doors in the sunroom and the back doors are boarded up and chained now."

"Look, Max," I yelled. I pointed to another fire that roared in the bushes in front of the house.

Max quickly gathered me in his arms and looked around at the house. I prayed, and then I heard Rose's voice.

"Trust my grandson. He knows a way. I knew it too. It saved me."

"Max, you know a way out."

Max grabbed my head in his hands. "What?"

"You're Rose's grandson. You know the way out.

She used to get out when she escaped. Think. How could you get out?"

I saw his eyes change from confusion to confidence. He knew. He remembered.

He grabbed my hand, and we ran. "Come on. Follow me back into the bookcase. Just keep holding my hand."

I trusted the boy who used to grab my hand and usher me safely across the street. The narrow passageway seemed to be growing smaller, but I trusted in Rose. She had been a petite woman, but we would have to make it. It was harder on Max and his over six feet frame. At one point we took a right turn and kept moving.

"We should almost be under the kitchen. There was a root cellar that my parents used for wine."

The darkness enveloped us. Cobwebs clung to my hair. It seemed to be getting colder, if that was possible.

"Here it is. They left wine bottles."

What if we couldn't get out? What if we died down here? They would never find us.

"Max, are you sure about this?" Fear dripped from my voice. I felt his hand grow tighter around mine.

"Charlie, it's just a few more steps. The door should be here." He pushed on what appeared to be a trap door of some kind. It wouldn't budge. "Ah, there's latches over here. I'll pop them." Max placed his small flashlight into his mouth. He pushed again, but the door didn't give way.

"Max." He turned to me, dropping his light in the process. He picked it up quickly and lit my face.

"Keep breathing, Charlotte. Here, you hold my flashlight. I have a Swiss knife. I'll get it open." Max took out his knife and went to work on the edges. He brought over a wine box to stand on. He loosened two of the latches and shoved them with his shoulders. The old cellar door creaked, but the movement was only in inches.

I began to beseech God, the Blessed Virgin, Mom, my brother, and Rose. I heard no voices in this hidden space. I figured if we didn't get out, I'd be speaking to all of them face to face very soon.

Max battered the door two more times with his broad shoulders. The door was moving, but not enough to allow us an exit. I prayed harder, and Max worked on the latches one more time. He stopped and looked down at me and into the light.

"I will get this open, Charlotte. I promise. I never quit."

"I know. That's what Dad said about you. I trust you."

"Right. I might fall off of the box this time, but I'm going to really heave my entire body up against it. Don't worry if I fall," Max explained.

I watched as he used his weight. The exit popped slightly. Max did fall off the small box, landing next to my feet. He stood up quickly and looked up at the door.

The door moved all on its own. We felt the cold air flow down on us as, slowly, ever slowly, the door was removed. We saw the darkness, one of the street lights on the road, and Gio's smiling face.

"I knew it. Let's get you out."

Max piled three boxes up in a pyramid and had me climb onto the top one. He pushed me up, and Gio pulled at me as I crawled as best as I could. During Max's turn, he was a better climber, and Gio and I pulled him up and out.

Gio and Max ended up in each other's arms. "That's my grandson," Gio said proudly. He reached over to gather me in. "And you! I knew Rose wouldn't let you down."

"Why are you here?" Max quizzed.

"Judge O'Donohue called me. He didn't feel right.

He had a feeling so he picked me up, and we headed over here. Your Dad drives like there's a house on fire."

"Oh my, Lord, there is. The house is on fire," I yelled.

"We have that under control. The fire department and the police have already been called and are arriving. Let's get back to your father, Charlotte."

Gio and I walked slowly toward the front of the house as Max ran on ahead. Gio held me. "Did Rose help you?"

I leaned my head into him. "She did. She said her grandson knew the way. She used to escape through that bookcase and out through that cellar?"

He grinned. "Yes, and I would wait for her at that door to help her out. We used to have a rope ladder that she could use just in case she had an emergency. In the old days, I was thin enough to come through there, but I only came into the house a couple of times. I don't like close spaces. They remind me of jails."

"And that would definitely scare you!" We shared a laugh as we slowly made our way to the front of the property.

Chapter Twenty

The lights from the firetrucks and police cars lit up the entire neighborhood. People flooded the streets to see what was going on. I noticed Dad and Max as Gio and I made our way through all of the news trucks already onsite.

As though he could sense me, my father turned around. I ran to him. I hadn't done that in a long time. "Daddy." Trembling, I fell into his arms and began to cry my heart out. He held me tightly, soothing me with his hand, and softly stroking my hair. Finally, I pulled out of his arms to wipe away my tears.

He held me on both of my upper arms. "Are you okay? Are you sure?" He seemed to be looking me over in some sort of unusual examination of my body parts. I still had all of them.

"I'm fine. I'm scared, and I have cobwebs all over me, but I'm safe now. I can't believe you came."

My father grabbed me in his arms again, bringing his head down to my ear. "She told me. Your mom told me. Charlotte, I could hear her." I alone heard what he was saying; only I could understand it.

"Dad, really?" When he released me, we were both in tears. I was speechless but so happy for him. Mom watched over us one more time.

"I couldn't believe it, but I did what she told me to do. I called Gio on the way over to him, and I called Sean. I admitted to him I didn't know what the heck was going on, but I said I had a feeling. Now, I understand why you say what you do."

"I know," I admitted. "It takes too long to explain it to people, and even then they'd think you were losing your mind."

Even though my father had tears in his eyes, I saw a genuine smile, one that I truly hadn't seen in a long time. "I blocked the culprit's car in when we drove up." He pointed over to our vehicles.

I stretched my neck to see who the police had taken into custody. There were so many people, and neighbors were walking into the street to watch the show. The fire department had most of the exterior fire out by now, but they were fighting the flames at the front of the house. I saw Max talking to Sean and several other police officers.

As I came closer, Max turned toward me. We just looked at each other at first. Then he flashed his smile. I answered weakly with one of my own, and he turned back to answer questions coming from someone who looked like a detective.

Dad and Gio were at my side as I stopped near our parked cars. Looking over to where Dad's car was parked parallel, I saw the car, but I didn't recognize it. But, the two men who had been speaking with Max rushed over to the police. That's when I saw the back of their jackets, and the huge FBI letters. The agents talked briefly, and then stood on either side of the suspect in custody. They were taking over as the other officers backed away, gaining me a better view.

They turned the dark clothed person around. I was able to see the arsonist for the first time. It was Cynthia Martin!

"Mrs. Martin?" My shock raised the level of my voice.

"What the heck? Why would she set fire to a house she'd just purchased?" Dad said out loud the same question I was wondering.

"She set the fire, and obviously, she knew someone was in the house because I told her I wanted one more look at the house," Max commented as he joined our group of three. "What we'll need to discover is if she meant to kill Charlotte and me, and in addition to arson, is she her own husband's killer?"

"You've been tracking the Martins. Max, do you think she's capable of all of this?" Dad asked. He stood on one side of me, and Max was on the other.

"Of course she is," Gio answered quickly. "She's a real piece of pecan pie."

All three of us looked toward him. He shrugged and smiled. "Fine, she's a real nut. Is that better?"

We all laughed, and Max went over to his grandfather. He said nothing. He only raised his hands to Gio's shoulder, but the old man pulled at him for an embrace. It seemed as though Max softened in his hold.

"I don't know how to thank you and the judge," Max admitted.

"We're family. That's what we do." Gio brushed it off, but I could see how moved he was by Max's gesture.

Max shook his head. "Well, I've never had much of a family who would do that." He looked toward Dad and me. "I guess that's why I found another."

"I'm just relieved you two are okay," Dad said.

Max's attention was drawn to the FBI agents.

"I need to go. I'll probably be busy way into the early morning, but I'll check in." He began to walk away from Gio and stopped abruptly. He pointed at the man who now had a part in his life. "I'll see you as soon as I can, you too, Judge O. Thanks again."

As he rushed away, he stopped one more time and returned to face me. Our eyes met, but he didn't say a word. He just kissed me on the forehead and ran off. From the corner of my eye I thought I saw my father and Gio share a handshake, but that gesture could've been for any reason, foremost, that a grandson and daughter were safe from a murderer.

I might have thought something of it, but Paddy always kissed me on the forehead. Max was just acting out of brotherly love, and out of relief. I figured it would be days, maybe weeks before I saw him again. I fixed my attention on the remaining fire. A house could be rebuilt and renovated, but once a portrait was destroyed it was ashes.

"Let's get you home." Dad placed his arm around me. "You're coming with me tonight." He looked back at Gio. "You too. I'll fix you a huge breakfast in the morning, Gio."

"Sounds good, Judge." We walked to Dad's car. He almost pushed me into the backseat as Gio took his place as the passenger upfront.

"Sean," Dad called. "I'm taking Charlotte home, to our house. Gio too. If anyone needs us, like the attorney over there, tell him where we'll be. May I move my car?"

Once Sean had walked over, he peered into the backseat at me. "Sure, Dad, you can get out of here. Thanks for what you did. I don't know how or why you figured out that something was up, but I'm sure glad you did." My brother placed his hand on the window's glass and winked. "Is she going to be okay?"

"Of course she is. All of you kids are tough. Come over around nine tomorrow morning. I'm making breakfast."

"If I can, I will, Dad. I love you," Sean added.

"I love you too, son."

As we drove away, I looked back at the job the fire department was undertaking. The damage could be massive and that would be the end of that. Before we headed out onto the street, I saw Max's eyes look up from something a police officer was showing him. He waved and returned his attention to the matter at hand.

"What do you want when we get home?" Dad asked as he drove through the Plaza. We passed more police vehicles on their way up to the Taylor Club.

"A nice bubble bath, and anything you have to eat."

"Gio and I were thinking about pizza. I can order it while you're in the tub."

Tonight, he didn't want to cook? Fine, that was what I usually ate on a lonely Friday night.

"Sure, Dad. Whatever you want is fine." I was sure there was some joke that included a judge, a mobster, and a real estate agent eating pizza. Right now I had so many thoughts in my head, I just wanted peace and quiet. And yes, pizza.

I woke on Saturday morning to the smell of something wonderful. Was it sausage, eggs, and maybe cheese? What was he fixing? Definitely, Dad had coffee brewing. I threw on a robe I found in my closet and headed downstairs. Gio and Dad were sitting at the kitchen table.

As I entered the kitchen, they both rose from the

table. "What are you two doing? You don't need to get up when I come into the room." They didn't need to, but it was wonderful to receive the special treatment.

"Honey, the timer went off. I'm getting something out of the oven," Dad admitted.

Gio added his comment. "I'm getting you a cup of coffee. Black, right?"

"Oh, well, yes, black is fine." I sat in my usual place. My hair probably looked like a bird's nest, but I really didn't care what I looked like. I was alive. I survived.

Dad and Gio were very busy doing this dance of food and drink. Gio had a pitcher of orange juice in his hand, and Dad was removing a casserole of some kind from the oven.

"This is a pitcher of mimosas, Charlotte. Would you like a glass?"

I nodded exuberantly at Gio. "Oh, yes, please."

I was served like a queen. I could definitely get used to this. "Is Sean coming?"

"I texted him, but he must be sleeping in," Dad answered. "I bet he had a long night. Paddy was probably brought in too because they'd been there the day of the murder."

"Do they really think she murdered her husband?" I asked as I served myself more of the casserole. I'd only eaten one piece of pizza last night. I guess having a near death experience cuts off your appetite?

"I think she did it," Gio announced. "I know things like that. In fact, you could say I'm a professional. Maybe I can become a consultant for the police department?" He was joking, but Dad's glare quickly stopped the laughing that Gio and I shared.

"They definitely have her on arson, and I suspect Max will have his federal case all wrapped up with a tight little bow when he gets done with the questioning and pulling together the financials on that couple," Dad answered.

I lifted my fork in the air for emphasis. "I knew it. I wanted to get my hands on their history, but of course, I couldn't. It all began when she accused me of the murder and of having an affair with her husband. I knew it." I was so proud of myself. If I'd only had the integral pieces of information, I could've solved the case, and we wouldn't have almost lost our lives. Max. What was he doing right now?

"Has anyone heard from Max?" I asked shyly as I

placed another bite of food into my mouth. My father and Gio shared winks. "What? I just wondered if he was okay. Someone needs to worry about him!"

"And that someone is you?" Dad asked.

Gio and he shared another knowing look. As I placed my fork on the plate, I threw it a little too hard creating a noise of frustration. "We were almost killed. We shared a huge event."

"It was that," Dad admitted. "I'm not sure I've been that scared in a long time. I told you not to go to that house."

I rolled my eyes. "Oh, here it comes." I picked up my fork and waved it at Gio. "You never knew that my father is not only a judge, he's a preacher too."

"Charlotte, this is serious. I almost lost you." I saw the concern in his eyes, and I hated that I had caused him such distress when I foolheartedly ran full throttle into danger. But Max did that too, and it seemed I enjoyed following him into the adventure.

I was saved from any more sermons by the rapping at the backdoor. Dad moved from the table and let the visitor in.

"Good morning, everyone," Max greeted as he came in and removed his coat. He seemed to have changed his clothes, but it looked as though his head hadn't hit a pillow yet.

"Well, sit down, son. It looks like you need coffee," Dad said as he gathered up a cup and sat it down in front of Max. My partner in peril sat next to me, and across from Gio.

He lifted the cup up to his mouth and took a healthy drink. "I really needed that. It's been a long, long night."

"Did you get her to talk?" Gio asked.

Dad continued to grab another plate and cutlery, handing it off to Max.

"Well, yes and no. She's admitted to the arson. She said she was out of her mind with grief after her husband was killed." Max served himself a healthy piece of the casserole. "But, I do have some other charges ready to bring to a grand jury, just not for the murder. I can't really talk about it yet. Sorry."

"Well, I know she did it," Gio reiterated.

Max ate for a few minutes and then wielded his own fork in Gio's direction. "By the way, you're coming in for a statement with Detective O'Donohue Monday morning, nine sharp. I will personally pick you up and deliver you to him. You need to tell us about Martin's girlfriend in a formal statement, Gio."

Gio looked as though he was a deer caught in the headlights of a very big truck.

"I'll take him," Dad volunteered. "Besides, I'll be his legal counsel."

Max laughed out loud. "I wouldn't expect anything less from you, Judge. Gio, you're not in trouble, but we need to refine our information, and we need to know about that woman. Do you have her name?"

"No, but I have her license plate number. Will that do?"

Max winked at his new grandfather. "Yes. Write it down for me."

Gio reached into his pants pocket and displayed an old billfold. He pulled out a piece of paper and handed it to Max. "Here you go. I'm always happy to do my civic duty."

We all laughed at that statement.

"And how are you today, Charlie?" Max finally directed his attention to me. He touched the back of my head. "Um, what happened to your hair?" His focus turned to my attire.

What Max was seeing was what I really looked like. I hadn't even taken a brush through my hair, and

I wore not one bit of makeup. I was wearing a raggedy robe that I'd left behind years ago, and my pajamas and slippers. I looked like I did the day I was experiencing the hangover effects of drinking with two retirees. I was sick that morning.

"I had a bad night, okay?" I moved away from his touch and his smirk. Returning the favor, I eyed him. "You don't look the best either, you know."

"At least I have an excuse. You got a good night's sleep. I haven't been to bed yet. I've been working."

On second look, he did look like he'd been out all night. His hair was a bit unruly, but his five o'clock shadow was from two days ago. His eyes were bloodshot.

"Judge, this is really good. Do you mind if I have another serving?" Max asked.

"Be my guest. You deserve it. Have you been by the house yet today?" My dad managed to ask the one question I wanted answered.

Max looked up from the serving he was placing on his plate. "No. I'll go over there next."

For all of us talkers, it was ironic that the silence invaded the kitchen and lingered. A judge and attorney

who specialize in speaking were quiet. The charming
mobster had nothing to add, and I just sat looking
inside my coffee cup as if some answer would appear. I
suppose each one of us were in our own thoughts. Dad
still looked at me as though I would never leave his
sight again. I had always felt his protection since the
day he hung onto the side of my first attempt at riding
a two-wheeler. Gio looked at peace, glancing at Max as
though he was an unearthed buried treasure. Max was
in his own world. He ate in peace, probably thinking of
what had been found and lost.

I had nothing to add. But I couldn't stand the
awkward silence. "I'd like to go with you, over to the
house."

I gained the table's attention with one sentence.
"What? I want to see what it looks like."

Max's heavy sigh precipitated his answer. "Sure."

"No," Dad muttered.

"I agree. No," Gio added. "Max, don't you have
people who could go do that for you?"

"No, Gio, I do not have people. I want to see what
kind of damage has been incurred. I'll be careful."

"I'll get dressed." I stood up quickly before Dad

could argue against it. As I headed upstairs, I heard him yell Max's name. It was better for Max to receive Dad's wrath rather than me.

Chapter Twenty-One

"It doesn't look that bad." I reviewed the front of the house, the black singed markings all over the entrance. The stench from the fire lingered. "It smells like a campfire gone bad."

Max touched the door frame. He examined the now non-existent wood frame. "After all of these years, the door is completely gone. Let's go in, but please be careful. If you get hurt now, your father will never forgive me."

Max stretched out his arm to offer a hand as I stepped over the debris that used to be the mammoth solid wooden door. The burning smell was worse inside the house. "I won't be able to stay here very long. I'm allergic to smoke."

Max dropped my hand quickly. "You need to stay outside then. Don't get sick. I just need to look around for just a few minutes."

I nodded in agreement as Max strode down the

hallway, stepping over broken glass. I watched as he headed to the secret bookcase.

"This damage is fairly minimal." He touched the wood, but then his focus turned to the portrait of Rose, just where we had left it.

"Is she okay?" I asked as I slowly made my way to him.

The portrait was in his hands. "It's fine. There's a little black here and there, but the portrait itself is untouched."

Of course, it was! Max continued in his search for whatever he was searching for, but I headed into Rose's sitting room.

I whispered softly. "Rose? Rose? Are you here?"

I heard nothing. This room had been damaged significantly. Structurally, it was probably safe, but the smoke had ruined the tile and the walls. All the glass windows were broken, and the doors were shattered.

"Love."

I whipped my head around. I heard her. "Rose?" I had to keep my voice low. I didn't need to try to explain this to Max. Besides, I didn't enjoy his interrogation techniques.

"Love."

I had heard her. "Max, your grandson is safe. Oh, and Gio is fine. I don't know what's going to happen to the house though, so he may not be able to come and visit."

"Family."

"Yes. And Max knows about Gio. Gio and Dad saved us."

"I know."

Really? She knew? "Did you tell him where we were?"

"Yes. Your mother and I protect family."

I smiled. Yes, you always had to protect your family. "I better go now. Thank you for all you did. I wish I had known you. God bless."

"Love, Charlotte. Max is family."

I was about to answer her when Max rounded the corner.

"Are you talking to yourself?" He began to touch the walls.

"No, just upset at how this room looks." My eyesight followed his continued surveying of the damage. He ran a hand down the wall, stopping, seemingly contemplating a large dilemma.

I couldn't understand what he was doing, and I was becoming frustrated. "Max, what are you looking for?"

He moved on to look over the window seat where I had discovered the key.

"Hmm? What?"

Obviously, he was in another world. "What are you looking for?"

"Ah." He turned to face me. "Metaphorically or physically?"

The question was odd. "I'm not sure. You keep looking at the walls, but then you seem to be in some sort of contemplative trance."

He didn't answer me at all, instead he continued his quest for whatever. I watched quietly, eventually walking toward the front hallway.

"I can't take the smoke anymore. I'll be outside."

He said nothing. I looked back one more time to see him standing in the middle of the room. This would be the final time I would walk inside this house. That last look and Rose's words would have to do. As I walked away, I noticed Max had moved Rose's portrait near the entrance of the house.

In a few minutes he joined me, the portrait in his hands. "I'm ready. Sorry about that. Are you feeling okay?"

"Oh sure. Are you?" Again, he didn't answer. He walked in front of me and headed to the car, placing the framed portrait in the trunk of his car. We didn't talk until we sat inside the car.

"You didn't answer me back there, so let me rephrase the question. Max, what brought you to Kansas City after all these years?

Max leaned back and shut his eyes. "Why did I come back here? I suppose there were a combination of reasons." Max glanced back at the house. "I'm learning it's not the house that matters, but who is in that home with you. Let's get some lunch."

There was way too much silence between us. I did enjoy witty and constant conversation. If idle talk filled up the airspace, I couldn't hear anyone else. It wasn't as though I didn't want to hear those whispered voices, I just didn't always know what they were attempting to tell me. During this ride, I glanced over at Max and remembered Rose's last words. There was more to the *Poop Head* than just being an arrogant, egotistical pseudo brother. I just didn't know what it was yet.

He took me to a restaurant on the Plaza, one that I usually couldn't afford. I wondered how much money I had in my purse. I did have my credit card, but now that the Martin sale would be falling through, I needed to watch my finances until spring brought more home sales. I hated that cyclical aspect of the real estate industry.

After we ordered, I confronted him again. "Max, you never answered me." If I was the irritating little sister then why not act like one? But he had said I irritated him in a good way. He liked my neck? What was that all about? Had he almost kissed me?

"I know. I've been trying to formulate an answer. It all began with a case in Georgia, one that the Martins were involved in. The FBI was investigating, and I actually had a friend who was a financial victim of one of their schemes. The Prescotts vanished. Imagine my surprise when they ended up being the Martins here in Kansas City. At that point I was offered an assignment I can't discuss."

Realization crossed my face. "So that's why you were at the funeral!" And here I thought it had just been to irritate me. Hmm, that word again. Now, I just needed to accept his explanation that he had an assignment he couldn't discuss.

"The president assigned me to the Western Division, and you don't say no to the president. Besides, the only good times of my childhood were spent here, with your family."

Fortunately, our food came, and I just let that comment linger in the air. My curiosity seemed to have a life of its own. It was pushing me to know more, and why.

"I know Dad still talks to your father," I said. "He seems like a wonderful man. Isn't he?"

Max wiped his face with the napkin, and smiled that smile. "Of course he is. You have to understand that when I was growing up he was just so busy. He rose to the top of the FBI here in Kansas City while I was still in high school. My senior year he was sent to Washington, D.C. He just wasn't at home, or for that matter, in our lives. He wanted to be, and he did everything he could, but he wasn't like your dad. Our relationship was different."

"No, you're wrong, Max." I shook my head negatively. "Dad was just as ambitious as your father, and he was just as busy. He was gone for long hours, and we didn't always see him, or be able to share our lives with him. You should talk to Paddy and Jane. They don't have many childhood memories that include Dad."

Max pierced my heart with the sad look in his eyes. "Then what was the difference? I'll tell you. Your mother kept him present in your lives even if he wasn't there. My mother was less active and less committed."

I guess I never realized what Max's homelife was or wasn't. At my young age, I just figured a boy like him had the same life we all had. Apparently, I was incorrect, so much so that no one realized just how bruised Max was. He found safety at our home. Frankly, I would've selected a home where they didn't have six children.

"Mom did hold us all together," I answered. "I'm sure your mom tried, right?"

His awkward laugh didn't assure me that Mrs. Shaw was the greatest role model for mother of the year. "You would think she would, but she was too busy with all her social commitments. She felt as though she had a certain station to live up to. That's what she did. She never shared any good stories about my father when he was gone either. I remember your mother telling us at the dinner table one night what an important job your father had. I never heard that."

There was so much more to Max Shaw than his *Poop Head* demeanor revealed. I found myself watching his mouth as he told me about lost Christmas celebrations and non-existent birthday parties. As his sister and he became older, his mother left him and his father to their own devices and hustled to Europe with his sister, Taylor. I only vaguely remembered him talking about her once. To me, a trip with my mother would've been a treat, especially to escape from the rambunctious brothers, and a sister who locked her door to me. To be honest, there was that time when I used all the makeup she owned in the world to freshen up my dolls and stuffed animals. They needed to look good. I was throwing them a tea party!

"And I guess I'm ready to make someplace a home, rather than just having a closet," Max admitted softly. "That's why I need to find a place. I wouldn't mind having a family, a real family in a few years. I just don't know if I'll be any good at domesticity."

Yes, we still needed to find him a home. "You know, after all of this calms down, we can start that search."

The mercenary in me knew we needed to gain back the commission we lost.

The server brought our check, and I began to dig in my purse.

"No, Charlotte, I've been eating off of your family since I arrived back in town. Besides, I owe you. I should never have put you in such jeopardy."

I noticed our server returned quickly and gathered up Max's credit card. She winked at him and said she'd be right back. He shot her a slight smile. My heart began to beat faster. He was sitting here with me. I wasn't invisible today, was I? Besides, what was Max Shaw's appeal? He was fairly normal in build, well for someone who looked like him. He did have those slightly darker features, but his tan was beginning to fade. His eyes were dark and brooding. Perhaps the server enjoyed a bad boy look? He did have that, but my opinion was skewed from years of verbal abuse. He didn't seem to be that way anymore. But did he still see me as the little sister who had no place in any of his adventures?

"Max, I wanted to go. I always appreciate my father's concern and yours now too, but no one tells me no if I want to do something. I'm not the same little girl that was shut out of the fun, or led around by someone."

Our server returned. She handed Max a card, no doubt with her phone number written on it. How rude! Max read the card as she walked away and placed it under the water glass.

"Charlotte, I think we both know neither one of us backs down. Besides, we're adults now. The past is in the past."

I chuckled. "That's very adult of you, but it seems as though your past is haunting you. You might have to settle for living with those ghosts." I know I did.

He stood up from the table and quickly came over to help me with my chair. As we left the restaurant, I turned back to see the server's card had been left behind. I relished some sort of weird satisfaction in that.

As we walked to the car, Max bumped my arm playfully. "So, I know you have a secret. Tell me."

I stopped walking. "What?" My face had probably drained from any color.

"Why so serious? Your secret, how do you put the past in the past and not live with those ghosts?"

I had been holding my breath, but now I released what little air I had in my mouth. "Oh, that."

His brows furrowed in wonder. "What did you think I was talking about? I mean, sometimes, you do seem to know information before all of us mere mortals, but then you'd have to be psychic, and you're just Charlie!"

At least he hadn't added any derogatory usual Max remarks, but he was touching on a very taboo subject. I couldn't tell Max, not now, maybe not ever.

I began walking again, and he joined me at my side. "I forgive, Max. I've heard that's what you're supposed to do. And, I suppose, sometimes you do have to live with the ghosts. You can learn from those voices, and then just make your own way. You especially have to forgive, not forget, everytime you find another piece of glitter."

He leaned over, throwing an arm around me as we continued to walk. "You're still finding that stuff? I really am sorry."

"Yes, and you should be. I swear when I die, they'll have a large Irish wake, and one of my brothers will look down in the casket and say 'doesn't she just glow' as he drinks a shot of whiskey."

"Sean?" Max suggested.

"Sean." Our shared laugh continued as we got in the car. He hadn't removed his arm. When he finally did, I could still feel his warmth even over my coat.

"Let's get you home. Your house or your dad's?"

"Dad's. We need to have a little talk."

Max winced. "By your tone, I have the feeling it's not going to be fun for him."

I let Max think what he wanted. No, I wanted to hear about my father's experience of hearing Mom's voice. We hadn't talked about it since last night in the frantic embrace of fear.

Chapter Twenty-Two

"I was worried about you when you left with Max. I sat down to watch the usual Friday night shows, but something was nagging me."

Dad and I sat in the living room after Max dropped me off. I could tell he was nervous, yet happy talking about his experience last night. He kept rubbing the arms of his large chair and looking toward the photo of my mother that was on the mantle.

"I finally turned off the television and began to walk through the house. Mickey kept following me, but we were coming back from a tour of the kitchen when the dog began to whimper as he looked up the stairs. I thought I'd go up and see if anything was wrong, but the dog didn't follow. Mickey hid under my chair."

"The dog knew something was up," I whispered.

"I went up to your room, and that's when I heard your name. Someone was calling your name, and it was your mother. I yelled her name, and I heard her as clear as a bell. She told me to go. She said you were in danger. I just about lost it."

My father's eyes filled with tears. His emotion was raw. I quickly went near him and sat on the ottoman as I held his hand. "It's okay, Dad. I'm here."

His warm smile comforted me. "I know. It's just that, and I hate to say this, but I so wanted to talk to her more, but you were in danger. Please don't think badly of me."

My tears flowed freely. I held tightly onto the very large hand of the man who held me up through so many difficult situations. "I completely understand. I heard Rose Taylor for the last time today. There's such a loss sometimes. I've learned that over the years."

"Well, I'll never forget it. Gio was calling me. He felt something, and we both knew you two were in trouble. He was already at a bus stop by one of the hotels so I said I'd pick him up. I ran out of this house calling Sean while I drove. I've never sped through the Plaza like I did last night. Heck, I'm not sure I ever have gone beyond the speed limit." He wiped away some of his tears and began to grin. "You know, your mother had a heavy foot. She gave me hell when I wouldn't speed getting her to the hospital when she was having you."

"I've heard the story. You two were a great couple. Max and I were talking about that today."

My father's eyes perked up. "Were you now?"

I playfully hit his hand. "What are you thinking? I've seen you and Gio plotting something. Well, forget it. Max is like a brother to me. He always will be."

Dad tipped my nose. "But he's not. Now, tell me why your mother and I were so wonderful. I like to hear things like that."

"Dad, you do know all of us kids know how much you tried to give us attention when you were so busy, right?" Mickey walked into the room and spread out on Dad's feet. "Max said he didn't have much of a family life, and he found one with all of us. His dad was busy, and his mother was not very attentive, but he mentioned it didn't feel like that here."

"Charlotte, that's nice to hear. Your mother and I tried so hard. It was tough when Paddy and Jane were growing up. We weren't married a year when your brother was born, and then Jane came another year later. I was just beginning my practice. I took everything I could get. Then when Sean and Tom were little I was still working a high volume of hours, but we were better off financially. By the time Conor and you came along, I was already a judge making my way up."

"But you always made it for church on Sunday," I added.

"Your mom swore she'd kill me if I ever missed Mass with the family. She said she had a place picked out in the park where she was going to plant me. And I already told you about her devious plans for my demise many times over. God, I love her."

I patted his hand and stood up. "Present tense is what I like to hear. She loves us, and we love her. Did Conor talk to you?"

"Wait, you hear Conor too?" Dad's face had turned very quickly to a lovely shade of white.

"Yes," I answered truthfully. I probably should've kept that one to myself.

"Good God." He grabbed his head in his hands. "Charlotte, is he--"

"Dad, he's happy. He's with Mom."

As his head was uncovered, the color had returned. "So that's why you keep saying he was killed. He told you."

I said nothing. I saw him search my face, but I couldn't say anything.

"Charlotte, answer me." He used that tone, the tone that made you think he knew everything you'd ever done wrong in your lifetime.

"Dad, where is my car? I didn't see it at the Taylor mansion today."

"Your brother drove it to your house this morning. Charlotte, answer me, please."

Adding 'please' was a nice touch, especially for one of the toughest judges in the country, even if he was retired.

"Dad, all I can tell you is I **know** Conor was killed. You told me to stop looking into it, but one day we will find out the truth. Tom and Sean agree with me, and they don't talk to dead people."

"Then we'll talk about this another time." Dad stood and along came Mickey. "Let's get you home. Should we stop for burgers? I bet you're hungry."

I grabbed my coat and headed for the door. "Actually, Max took me to lunch so I'm not really hungry."

As we made our way outside, Dad locked the door and placed his arm around my shoulders. "If your brothers were here, Tom would think that was nice of

Max, and Sean and Paddy would be wondering what was going on. Ooh, lunch with Max."

"That's enough out of you, old man. It was just lunch."

"With Max," he added. His joke was falling on deaf ears.

"By the way, we have to work on the float after church tomorrow," I mentioned. It was almost St. Patrick's Day. "Do you know if Paddy signed us up for more than one parade? We were in the one up north last year."

"If he did it's the Brookside one."

As we pulled out of the driveway, I began to think of what day it was. "Dad, if he did, then we have to have it ready by next week."

"We better get to it, but I don't think he did. So, over at Paddy's after church, and let's hope this time you don't end up glowing like a leprechaun's pot of gold." His laughter filled the car, and his attempt at an Irish brogue only made my eyes roll.

I only wondered if Max would be there. He'd be busy now with all of this craziness wrapping up, and the court cases just beginning. But I had lunch. With Max.

By the next morning, I'd forgotten all about what was behind me. I decided to take my own advice, and look forward to the week ahead. Tom and I needed to sell a few houses to make back the lost commission. After a few weeks of murder and mayhem, it would be good to go back to slow and mediocre.

Jane had a great lunch for all of us float creators after church services on Sunday. We all changed out of our nice clothes and into our work clothes and began to finish painting the float, if not the world, green.

"So, let me get this right. Max is now part Italian?" Paddy pondered Max's lineage while attaching the moving arms of our leprechaun. We had named the little elf O' Toole.

"Yes," Dad answered. "Watch where you're putting that extra arm, Paddy."

Paddy swung the second arm over Dad's head. "And his biological grandfather is Giovani Campano."

"Ouch. I haven't heard of a US Attorney being related to the mob."

"Gio is a lovely man," I added. That comment elicited groans throughout the garage.

"He was a killer, a hit man," Sean interjected.

"He's very charming." I knew I wasn't going to win this battle, nor should I, but someone had to stand up for the man who saved me.

"Dad, you worked with him when he rolled over on that Mafia guy, right?" Paddy had both arms in place and was gathering his electronic contraption to see if they would move correctly.

"Yes, and Gio was very well-mannered. We now know where Max gets his charm," Dad answered. He winked at me. I stuck my tongue out.

"I like Max's dad," Tom added. "His mom was a real witch."

"Was she?" My head shot up. "I didn't ever meet her. Why? Was she mean?"

Tom came to my side to help paint another layer of green. "I guess you could say she was very cold. We had to stay outside if we ever went over to that house. That's going to be a mess with Cynthia Martin. I'll have a headache next week with all of that."

"What do you think will happen with the property?" If we could get someone else to purchase it, maybe the mansion could be renovated. Maybe Rose's place would be safe.

"I'll have to check with her attorneys. In all likelihood, the bank will back out due to the criminality of the events. I'm not sure how we can put it on the market again with all the damage sustained in the fire."

I shook my head. "It would be such a shame to have it taken down." Of course, Rose wasn't really there, but Gio wouldn't have anywhere to go to be with her, to remember. "It's a magnificent house, if someone would take the care to make it a home."

"I told you before, Charlotte, that house has had bad things happen in it." Dad shook his finger at me. "Don't make it out to be a fairy tale castle."

"The dragon woman used to live there," Tom laughed. "Max would agree with me."

"Would I, Tommy?" Max's arrival seemed to always be about drama. He stood in the doorway, holding a can of beer.

Everyone cheered upon his arrival. Since when did he become an integral part of float production? I guess years ago he may have helped, but I never remembered any talk of how much we missed Max as we worked into the wee hours of St. Patrick's Day to finish before parade time.

"I was disparaging your mother," Tom admitted frankly. "Charlotte was delusional for a bit. She sees your old family home as some magical castle. We all don't believe in fairy tales, but your house used to have a dragon living in it."

Max joined us in the garage. "Sadly, Tom is correct. My mother was like a dragon, foul tempered and spitting fire. She still is, but happily she is miles away. Besides, I don't remember any happily-ever-afters coming out of that place. Now, if Charlotte had said the old place was haunted, I'd agree with her."

Dad and I looked at each other. Our faces drained, fearful that someone had discovered my secret.

"Did you ever come across a ghost when you were living there?" Tom directed his question at Max as he came around to his side.

"What do you need me to do?" I watched as Max completely ignored his former best friend. Had Max encountered Rose or some other spirit years ago? Maybe Gio had said something to him?

"We need help on the green paint, or maybe you'd like to continue that glittering project from the other night?" Sean was being so funny. I'd have to hurt him later.

I saw Linda elbow Dad in his ribs lightly. I thought I saw her lips form my name and Max's in the same sentence. My father nodded and smiled.

Of course, my loving family laughed at my expense about the glitter bomb incident. I noticed the only one not laughing besides me was Max. I also noticed that my dear sister-in-law and my father were looking at Max and I as though, well, I didn't know what their silly smiles meant.

"I'll do whatever is needed to get this float ready so I can watch all you crazy people in that parade. It's been years, and I can't wait," Max joked.

"Well, and you'll have to come to the after party," Dad suggested. "I make a mean corned beef and cabbage."

"No matter what, I'll be there for dinner." Max picked up a brush. "Now, let's do this people so you all can make fools of yourself."

"Do you have any Irish in you, Max?" Linda asked from across the room. She was adding a large green hat on top of the leprechaun's head.

"Apparently not. Right now, I'm not sure what I am. Next week I may discover that the mayor is my cousin."

No one said anything. "So, what is the theme this year? I remember you all used to have one every year."

"Well, since Dad was a judge, and Sean and I are in the police department, we've got a good one this year." Paddy smiled widely. "Our theme this year is 'Greenbloods', you know, like that cop show on television. The family in that one are all in law enforcement of some kind. Except for our two weirdos, the real estate agents, we're almost the same."

"I wouldn't say, almost. There's only the three of you. That's only half of the family," Max stated. "Greenbloods? Seriously, Paddy?"

"We need another member of the family in law enforcement to break the tie." Paddy didn't realize that his statement caused our Dad to wink over at me. I knew what he was thinking. I still had my law degree, and a license hidden in my bedroom closet. I was sure that's what he was thinking. That had to be it. We just weren't going to add another member of the family, unless Sean married a cop. Or unless Dad adopted Max.

Chapter Twenty-Three

The week of St. Patrick's Day, we received a registered letter at the agency. Meg signed for it and ripped it open. "Oh my dear Lord, Tom," she yelled. "Charlotte, get out here."

Tom came running. Meg shoved a check in his hands. "Look, it's our commission."

Tom continued to look at the numbers on the check. I couldn't wait all day.

"What is it?" He handed it to me, and my eyes searched for the numbers. "Oh my--"

"There's a letter too from some New York lawyer." Meg handed it over to her husband.

I was too busy, and in shock, looking at that amount of money. This would replace the money we lost on the Martin debacle. "Tom, what does the letter say?"

"It's from the Taylor Foundation. The Foundation was selling the house, well, they are removing it from the market, but they wanted us to have our commission. Wow, this is more than fair. They didn't have to do this."

"I'm happy they did," Meg admitted.

I handed the check back to Tom and quietly walked back to my office. I sat down at my desk and did absolutely nothing. The Foundation had taken the house off the market. They didn't have to pay us anything. Would the house now be destroyed?

"Charlotte, are you okay?" Meg's head popped around the open door. "Why aren't you celebrating?"

I managed a smile. "I wonder what's going to happen to the house."

"As much pain and suffering that happened there, maybe it should be torn down."

I nodded, but inside I felt a loss. Forgiveness was a powerful thing; maybe the house just needed a little tender loving care to become whole again.

"You've really become fond of that place despite the fact you almost died in it, haven't you?" Meg asked.

"Yes. There's something about it. It needs to be saved." It would take a heroic effort from someone. I didn't have the money to do it, and now it was all in the hands of some lawyer and a foundation who didn't feel passionately about it.

After work, I headed over to the house. All sales signs had been removed. As I pulled into the parking area, I saw Max's car. Maybe he was having an additional one last look around.

It was still daylight, with the sun barely beginning to set. The blown and broken windows and doors were boarded up, and a temporary door had been placed on the exterior. I carefully walked up to and turned the knob. Slowly, I opened the door and stepped inside.

"Max? Where are you?" I headed into the sitting room. As I entered, the room felt cold not just in temperature, but probably because Rose's portrait wasn't hanging on the wall. I heard footsteps upstairs. "Rose, what is he doing?"

"Family for you. Max and Charlotte."

I was almost giddy hearing her voice, and she'd said my name, and Max's.

"Rose, everything will be okay," I whispered. I didn't need Max realizing that I had a special exotic skill. "Max is a good one."

"Yours, Charlotte."

I didn't understand that, but maybe I hadn't heard correctly. I heard more noise upstairs and the creaking of the front stairs. Max was running down them.

"Charlotte? What are you doing here?" He was dressed in well worn jeans and sneakers and wore a sweatshirt that had seen better days.

"I just needed to see the house one more time. I guess the Taylor Foundation took it off the market, and I'm worried they'll tear it down." I sat down in the window seat. I'd had a client meeting that afternoon, and I was wearing heels for the first time in weeks. My feet were tired, and my calves were aching.

"They won't tear it down."

I laughed. "You are always so certain about everything, aren't you? Do you ever have any doubts?"

He came over to sit next to me. "Um, let me think, do I ever have doubts? No." He smiled that crooked smile with his very kissable lips. My heart began to do that extra beating thing it did sometimes when Max was near.

My laughter was louder than usual, especially in the vacant house. "The attorney sent us a letter today, and we ended up with more of a commission than what we lost with the Martins. By the way, how's your case going?"

"Oh, it's going. It'll be awhile. Three more victims have come forward. The FBI is taking the lead while we pull it all together. When we impanel the grand jury for the indictments, you, Tom, your father, and maybe even Gio will have to testify, but I'll have a staffer do that. We'll worry about that in the future. Does the commission help all of you out?"

The relief was in my voice. "Of course. That was a big loss to take. They had been my clients since November. And when are we going to get you a place?"

Max stood up quickly and walked to the wall where Rose's portrait had been featured. "I think this wall is empty without her portrait up here, don't you?"

I pulled my coat tighter around me. It was so cold, almost as if Rose was sitting next to me. I'd experienced that before when someone who had passed wanted to talk, and I wasn't listening. "The entire room is cold without her."

"She was a good old girl," Max muttered. "Do you know I found a photo of her holding me when I was a baby?"

"I'd love to see it." I really would take great delight in seeing a little Max, but more than that, I would love to see Rose, a happy Rose. I watched Max. He was lost in his own world, touching the plaster and bricks. "I should be going home."

Max looked back at me. "It is getting dark. I need to turn off the light upstairs, and then I'll walk you out. Just stay here. Don't go wandering. There's a lot of damage to the dining room."

Before I could agree, he ran out of the room and up the stairs. I moved to where he had touched the wall. I touched it too. "Rose, you take care."

I heard nothing. After all these years, I still didn't understand how this beyond life thing worked. I patted the wall and headed to the front door as Max galloped down the steps.

"Max, did you ever find that extra key?"

Max reached around to turn off the light in the hallway. "Martin took it from Tom so he could have his little tryst without his wife discovering. Cynthia claims to know nothing so we haven't found the key yet. We'll keep searching for the truth, but we may never know. It won't matter now that there will be a new front door on this place because of the fire."

I understood and nodded. "Did you find an area of town you want to live in?" I asked. We needed to find him a place to settle down.

"Here." Max pulled out the key from his pocket. "I need Gio to look at this staircase and see if the wood carving can be restored. There's a lot of paint and varnish on it. Maybe your dad could look at it too."

"I wouldn't worry about it. So, you want to purchase a place around here? Great. I'll start looking tomorrow."

Max joined me at the front door. "No, Charlotte. Here. I own the house. I got a good deal since I knew the family."

I blinked a few times. Maybe if I opened my eyes after a series of incredulous blinking I would see a different form of reality? "Excuse me?"

"I own the house. I was checking upstairs to see how bad it was so I could move in as soon as possible." Max's face was light. His smile was comforting. My realization began to show in my face.

"You bought the house. That's wonderful." I threw my arms around him without thinking. It felt so natural to hold him around his neck. His arms grasped my waist. It was nice. In just less than a minute, my life changed. I pulled back quickly, realizing the inappropriateness and contrasting contentment. It felt so right.

We pulled apart and shared blank looks before Max shrugged. "It seems you're very happy about this."

"I am. How could you tell?" We shared a nervous laugh. "I just think this is great. Wait--" He tilted his head attempting to anticipate what I was going to say next. "Did you give us that commission? You did, didn't you?"

"The Taylor Foundation did. It was only fair. You did a lot of work."

I shrugged playfully. "Oh sure. I almost sold the house to a couple of con artists. I found a dead body here, and the man's wife possibly became a killer and an arsonist. I'm great."

The crooked smile diminished, and those dark brown eyes became deep and soulful. "You are great," he murmured. Max coughed as if he was clearing his throat. "I'm happy you're happy. Now, let's get you home."

He stood in the same place he had caught me only weeks ago when he shut my car door and watched me pull away. I looked in the rearview mirror and didn't see anyone who remotely looked like an obnoxious brother. My heart was going to jump out of my chest if I didn't do something quickly.

"He used to call you *Melon Head*," I said out loud. The beating slowed, but it was still at a faster pace, almost as if I was falling. I was falling. But I was afraid I'd end up getting hurt, again. The devil used to be an angel.

I was questioning my sanity, especially when it seemed like my car turned on its own and rested in my father's driveway instead of my own. Linda's car was already parked there.

I entered through the front door and heard them in the kitchen. The two of them seemed to be thicker than a pair of thieves plotting a jewelry heist.

"You know, if you don't lock the door, anyone can just walk in," I announced as I kicked off my shoes and headed into the kitchen.

"Charlie, get in here and eat your dad's lasagna. It's the best I've ever had," Linda yelled.

I hugged Dad's back as I entered. "If you keep cooking like this, you'll have to open your own restaurant. Hey, Linda."

"I feed all of you. This house is my restaurant. Grab yourself a plate. There's salad on the counter too."

I filled my plate with the pasta dish, salad, and bread. "What's up with you, Linda? Where's my brother?"

"He's working. He took a night shift so he can be off for the parade and the day after."

I sat down and dug in. "Oh my gosh, Dad. This is so good. Seriously good. Did you make it from scratch?"

He proudly nodded. "Even the noodles. I've been practicing with that pasta maker Meg and Tom gave me for Christmas. I've been developing that recipe."

I made every bite count. Linda and Dad were unusually quiet which was very disturbing. Linda had been in this family for so long she was just like another sister to me. Like this family, she was never this quiet. Dad and she seemed to be doing some form of code with their eyes.

I chewed slowly before I finally exploded. "What? What is going on?"

"We've been wondering the same thing," Dad answered coyly.

"What?" I bit into my bread in frustration.

"Your Dad has been developing that recipe, but what have you been developing, Charlie?" Linda nudged my arm.

"Have you two lost your minds? What are you talking about?" I took another bite. I didn't want to stop eating even if they were acting like relatives who should be locked up in the attic.

"You and Max," Linda finally answered.

Dad nodded, and I closed my eyes. "Have you two been hitting the whiskey again?"

"No," Dad answered. "We've been watching and evaluating. Our observations have concluded that you and Max have something going on."

I finished the last bite on my plate and stood up to take my plate to the sink. I turned and leaned on the kitchen counter. My arms crossed in front of me as some sort of defense. My heart heard a suggestion of a connection with Max, and it was doing that weird fluttering again. Oh my gosh! How old was I? I was old enough to know better. But lumping me with Max, teaming us, observing that something was going on, made my heart feel some expectation that had been placed on the back burner for many years.

As I looked at the two of them, I knew they were serious. "What do you two see? I don't feel anything." So, I would lie.

Linda folded her own arms in defiance. "You two are flirting. You like him, and he definitely likes you, and not in a brotherly fashion. I was telling Paddy last night--"

I pushed back off the counter and leaned on the chair. "Oh my dear heavens! You talked to Paddy about this?"

"Well, he didn't see it, and I was telling him about how Max rushed to help you when you were glitter bombed, and then he worked beside you on the float last night. He didn't work with Tom, his former best friend. Of course, then there's the incident when you two almost died in his family's old house."

I pointed at my father. "And you! Did you know he is going to fix up his old childhood home? He said something about you and Gio working on some of the wood. What is that all about?"

"I knew. He told me, in fact, in full disclosure, he calls me almost every day. Yes, Gio and I thought we could do some of the detailed work. Some of that could cost a small fortune."

My head leaned back. I didn't dare tell these two that we had received a very large check, definitely without a doubt, spurred by Max Shaw. "You didn't think to tell me? I felt like an idiot tonight when I'm asking him about where he wanted to live--"

Linda's brow rose. "You saw Max again tonight?"

I shut my mouth. Seriously, Charlotte, can you not be quiet? You are only adding to their delusion. "I stopped by the house after work. I wanted to make sure that the sale signs were down. Max was there checking out the upstairs to see if he can stay there while he renovates the house."

"Ah, so Max isn't the devil anymore?" My father's eyes were glistening in delight, absolutely glistening.

"Well, I don't want to talk about that. Besides, the devil was a fallen angel, so maybe he has some positive attributes." I tried to sound as dispassionate as possible.

"And it doesn't hurt that the man is extremely good looking," Linda added. "He has a lot of positive attributes, if that's what we're calling it now."

My face flushed. What could I say to get me out of this? "He's Tommy's friend. He's like a brother to me." I was going to hell for lying but practice makes perfect.

Linda and my father burst out laughing. Dad was having a hard time catching his breath. Linda's face was as red as the wine in her glass. I gave up. I sat down and threw myself on the mercy of the court.

"Fine. Are you two happy? I do feel something for him, but it's ridiculous. First, he's Tom's old friend.

Second, he used to treat me terribly, and he still sees me as the little obnoxious, whiny sister. Third, we have nothing in common. Fourth--"

Dad threw his hands up in the air. "This isn't a trial summation, Charlotte. Look, all of that was years ago. You are all grown up, and believe me, I've seen how he looks at you. If I didn't like the man, I would be warning him away. I told you, I may not be clairvoyant, but I know for sure, I'll be walking you down the aisle and handing you over to him."

I couldn't look at Dad anymore so I turned my attention to my sister-in-law. She had tears in her eyes.

"What your Dad said was beautiful. He's right. I've seen it too. I didn't tell you that Paddy woke up this morning, turned to me and said that I was right. He'd thought about it all night long and agreed that Max sees you much differently than just as our Charlie. Paddy realized Max called you Charlotte last night, and it was the way he said your name. I'm not sure your brother is happy or mad about it."

"But there is no **it**!" I yelled. "Don't you two get it? I don't think he'll ever see me like **that**. He's looking for a family, that's all."

"There's always room for one more at the table," Dad said quietly. He grabbed my hand. "Honey, Linda and I will say nothing more. Maybe we have it all wrong, maybe we don't. Either way, you and Max will work it out, or you won't."

"Great, Dad. Now, you sound like Mom when she'd give her own spin on that old song. I hated when she'd say if it's meant to happen it will. But, she was right. If it's meant to be, then it will happen. I have my doubts, and I'm not sure how I feel about it anyway. That's the truth."

Linda grabbed my other hand. "Now, who's lying? We'll leave you alone to figure this out. It won't be easy for us, or for you. Because if you two do get together, you'll have worse things to face than doubt. You'll have to face your brothers. God help Max if it comes to that."

"Linda does have a point," my father acknowledged. "Tom will find it especially difficult thinking that Max and his sister are having a romantic relationship. I suppose I will have to provide legal representation when your brother kills your lover."

Hearing my father say that word was cringe-worthy, but thinking about my brothers' response **if** we did become a couple was frightening, for me, and especially for Max. Thinking about making love with Max might make it all worth it. No.

"You are right. Then, no on Max. It's probably just some kind of weird holdover crush from the days when he held my hand as we crossed the street. It's over before it even begins."

A burst of laughter filled the room once more.

"Oh, Charlotte. You've got it bad," Linda said.

"Yes, and you don't even really know it, honey." Dad's soft comment made my heart beat faster. I knew it, and I was concerned. This was bad.

Chapter Twenty-Four

The float was completed two days ahead of the parade date, and by the morning of St. Patrick's Day the O'Donohue family was in fine Irish form. We rose early and attended the annual Mass, followed by a traditional Irish breakfast at Browne's. That marketplace had been an Irish meeting place for decades. Some of my first memories were of their scones. Although I was unsure about my future, I knew that if I did have a family we would gather there every St. Patrick's Day for food and conversation before we headed to the parade line.

Tom and Sean were working on the final touches, making certain that the leprechaun's pot of gold actually poured out the wrapped chocolate coins. Children were going to love it along the route, and I was thankful to have a go-to snack on the float.

Our family produced one of the most green creations in the entire parade. It was probably due to all of those layers of paint Max and I had put on it. Ironically, the glitter on the float was a work of art. Thankfully, Meg had completed that task without any more mishaps. She had painstakingly glittered every fake gold coin spilling out of the leprechaun's pot of gold. We didn't allow Max even near it.

We were passing one of the great Catholic churches in Kansas City on Broadway when Tom began to yell at someone in the crowd.

"We'll be at Dad's for dinner. Make sure you're there."

Our float stopped to allow for one of the bands to perform for the throng of people lining the street. Dad touched my shoulder.

"Max is standing over there." My eyes followed his hand.

Paddy and Sean yelled for Max, almost beginning their own chant. Luckily, he was laughing at the two already drunk O'Donohue brothers. Sure, his smile was charming, perhaps even intoxicating, but his laugh warmed my heart. He unsuccessfully attempted to ignore them.

I waved, but he was still speaking with my idiot brothers. Sometimes, it was hard to believe that two of them were in law enforcement, and the third was a highly regarded realtor.

This time Dad tapped my shoulder. "Charlotte, it's now or never. The boys are drunk, and they'll never realize what's going on. It's your play."

This was a dangerous game. I wanted to shake my head and tell my father how ridiculous he was, but I couldn't. It was time to offer Max something he wanted and needed.

"Max, Max," I screamed over the throng. He was looking over the float. "Hey *Poop Head*!" His head turned immediately in my direction. I extended my arm down to him.

"*Poop Head*? Really?"

"It got your attention, didn't it? Max, get on up here. If you're looking for a family, I can offer you one." My heart was pounding. I searched his eyes as he remained silent in all of this noise. As if in slow motion, his arm raised up, and he took my hand as he propelled himself onto the float.

"Max, we always have room for one more in this family," Dad said as he patted him on the back. Dad looked down and winked at me. He was looking at our hands. Max hadn't pulled away as we were still holding on to each other. The float lurched as it started up, and I fell against him.

"It seems like I'm always falling for you."

Max ended our hold and was supporting me with his arms.

"I'm just happy to be here to catch you, Charlotte." His mouth was right by my ear so I could hear him over the din. He looked at me and kissed my cheek.

He hadn't kissed me on the forehead this time. I leaned over and in the only irresponsible action I have ever taken in my entire life, I decided to gamble. I took both my hands and cupped his face. If this went wrong, I could always say I was drunk.

"I can't believe I'm going to do this so if I've got this all wrong, just call me Charlie, and I'll just go back to being Tom's little sister." I took a deep breath and placed my lips on his. I kissed Max Shaw. He pulled me into his arms, and the kiss deepened. All thoughts of childhood bullying swirled away in a green haze, or perhaps a glitter gold cloud. My heart beat quickly, and I could feel his own doing the same.

When we finally pulled apart, out of the corner of my eye, my father was clapping and my sister and two sisters-in-law were smiling. Gratefully, the boys were busy, well, being the boys.

"You aren't just Tom's little sister," Max yelled.

"Oh," I yelled back and nodded. I stared ahead and waved, but I wanted to cry. He hadn't called me Charlie, but he certainly hadn't said he was happy or excited that I had made a move, and made a fool of myself. In fact, he was quiet, on a float at a St. Patrick's Day parade watched by thousands of people. I knew I had really messed things up. What had I been thinking? Oh, I knew what I had been thinking. Pushed on by my father and sister-in-law, I believed I just made the mistake of my life.

As if he were reading my mind, Max grasped my elbow. "Charlie, remember, I don't doubt anything I do?"

"Yeah," I shouted. "So are you finally unsure about something?" Could Max suddenly be just a mere mortal like the rest of us sinners? I still didn't want to look him in the eye. Besides, I was wiping away a tear.

"Hey, look at me." He turned my chin with his hand until I was facing him again. "I never doubt anything. I'm here to stay."

I had to get myself out of this. I touched his arm. "Did I just kiss you? Sorry, I've had a few drinks." I shrugged in feigned embarrassment. I needed to sell this act.

Max smiled and leaned down to my ear again. "I'm not sorry, Charlie."

Before I could hear any other words from my failed mission, Tom was playfully grabbing Max from behind, adding strings of green beads around his neck. "Hey, buddy. You need to pretend to be Irish today. Everyone does it."

Max entered into the fun, but he looked at me a couple of times through shielded glances before heading back to Paddy and Sean. I stood alone with a fake smile plastered on my face. This was worse than New Year's Eve when you didn't have someone to kiss at midnight, and you'd stand in the middle of the ballroom taking a sip of champagne. I had been there, and I had done that several times, for years.

I felt an arm around me and looked up to see my father. "That was an awful idea," I shouted.

"Honey, I saw it as a first step. It will be a delicate dance with that one."

I looked up into those very kind eyes. "Dad, I'm not sure I want to dance with the devil, remember?"

My father patted my arm. Despite the party around us, my father and I were quiet. Dad turned around to look at the back of the float where all of the men had congregated. He waved.

"What are you doing?"

Dad hugged me again. "I was just waving at Max. He's looking at you. He has no idea that he is in the middle of a parade. He's thinking, and it isn't about whether or not Sean will fall off the float this year."

But he had called me Charlie. This dance with the devil wasn't worth losing my heart.

Chapter Twenty-Five

By the time we made it back to the house, Dad was already in the kitchen cooking away. He prepared most of the food the day before, but he had every pot on the stove boiling. As soon as you entered the house, you knew it was St. Patrick's Day at the O'Donohues. The fragrance alone would turn your blood to green. Mom would be so proud that we still had our traditions, and they hadn't died when she did.

Obviously, my mood was blue despite all the green around me. I dropped down into Dad's chair in the living room. Surprisingly, Mickey headed toward me and placed his head in my lap.

"Thanks, boy. I need companionship." I petted him slowly as I watched all of my family congregate in the kitchen. No one saw me sitting there alone. "Wow, this has to be the crappiest St. Pat's day ever. What about you, Mickey?" I resorted to talking to the dog. Actually, it was probably the best decision I had made all day.

Sean was screaming something about Greenbloods

being the best name ever. He also held the trophy we had won for best humor. A few other people, some of Dad's former staffers, and friends of the married couples of our family filtered through the house. A couple of them waved at me as they headed in the opposite direction. My nephews and nieces greeted their Aunt Charlie. I'm sure I looked like a lost puppy, or a pissed off elf. If I left now no one would realize I was gone until tomorrow. I could probably fake it and make them feel like I'd been sitting there the entire time.

Linda walked into my space of doom and sat in Mom's chair. "Charlotte, I am so proud of you. You finally put yourself out there for love."

I continued to smooth Mickey's hair in different directions. "For what, acting like the biggest fool in the world? You and Dad really set me up."

"Charlotte," she murmured dismissively. "We did not."

"You did. You both made me believe there was something that wasn't there. I'm feeling like an idiot, or at least like a ridiculous lovestruck teenager. I left those years behind a long time ago, but that's what I feel like right now. I took a chance. The risk didn't pay off. I really don't want to talk about Max ever again."

Linda took a gulp from her wine glass. Her eyes peaked over the rim. She knew I was angry. Usually, everyone messed with the little sister unless the little sister talked in a monotone fashion, with absolutely no emotion. Then they knew to leave me alone. I was surprised she was still sitting there, but her attention had turned to the hallway.

"Linda, have I made myself clear? I never want to talk about him again."

"Wow, who stole your pot of gold?"

There he was, the subject of my angst. I said nothing. Linda said nothing. How much more stupid looking could I get?

"Well? Who don't you want to talk about again?" Max smiled. Of course, he did! The devil was always humored by misery.

"Mr. Martin. I never want to talk about that man again." I could now lie and not blink, nor show any expression of any kind. Repetition honed your skills.

Max removed his jacket and sat on the arm of the sofa. "But you'll have to when you testify." He folded his arms over in front of his broad chest and smiled again. "It won't be that hard. I'm sure your dad and I can coach you so you won't be nervous. Didn't you participate in mock trials in law school?"

Mickey's head popped off of my lap, and the dog sulked slowly to hide behind Dad's chair. I should've done the same thing. I nodded. Law school seemed years in the past, yet I was beginning to think that maybe I needed a career change.

"I won't be nervous. I know what I saw, and what I did. Besides, I'll be coached by a regular prosecuting attorney, not you. He'll be the one asking the questions, right?"

Max nodded. "You sobered up quickly."

His statement went unanswered. Linda stood up with her now empty glass. As she walked past Max, Linda smiled. "I think Judge O has the food ready."

Max arched one brow. He stood up slowly and looked down at me. "Did I do something?"

"No, of course not. You never do." I stopped. As I stood up, I finally removed my coat and headed into the hallway. "Wait a minute." I stopped and turned to face him. "Yes, you did, again."

"What? How could I have possibly done something to you, again? What the hell?"

"That's funny you should mention hell. Nevermind."
I turned once more, but was caught by a long arm
spinning me around.

Max nodded toward the kitchen. "You know, of all
of them, you are the most normal."

I rolled my eyes. If he only knew how wrong he
was. His dead grandmother could tell him a thing or two
about me.

"And you're the one who can push my buttons
unlike any of your brothers. All you have to do is look
at me, and I, well, I--" Strangely, Max's stammering
made me feel more confident.

"I remember what happened on the float. I was an
idiot, and I apologize again, but you! You called me
Charlie. I'm forever Tom's little sister. That gets really
old."

"I didn't call you Charlie O or *Melon Head*, and you
are Tom's little sister!" His voice raised to meet my "I
told you the conditions, and you called me Charlie."
This conversation was obviously going nowhere.

"But I didn't add anything else!" His final yell
brought Dad into the hallway.

"Go to hell, Max. I've been waiting almost my entire
life to tell you that." I smiled smugly and turned on my

heel, nearly running into my father. I never looked back.

I heard Max though. "Judge, what did I do?"

"It's what you didn't do, Max. Let's get you something to eat. You'll feel better."

I lifted my head high as I placed too much cabbage on my plate. I'd suffer from the gas later, but I was going to enjoy something today. I completely ignored Max as he fell in line behind me to serve his own food. Neither one of us said a word.

I ate, I had my first beer of the day, and I laughed at all of the bad jokes and the antics of my crazy Irish family. Max enjoyed himself too, but we ignored each other. My life would return to pre-Max starting tonight. Oh, we'd see each other socially now and then and at court during the trial. But Max was just a bad memory of my childhood and for a few months during adulthood after I found my client murdered in a house I was selling.

I smiled at Max later and realized my dance with the devil had ended, and it was time to change partners and tempo.

Chapter Twenty-Six

O'Donohue Residence

"Max, get in here before you get soaked," Judge O'Donohue said as he greeted the United States Attorney for the Western Division. His guest immediately removed his rain-soaked overcoat and brushed a hand through his hair.

"Wow, this would've been miserable at the parade last week," Max commented as the Judge took his outerwear. "It's wet and still cold." Max blew on his hands.

The retired judge hung up the coat and eyed the man standing before him. Max had called and asked if he could come over. Of course, he was thrilled to hear from him. "I have a warm fire in the living room, and Gio brought me a good bottle of Irish whiskey. Do you care to open it with me?"

"Of course. After you, sir." Max extended his hand and followed his host into the living room. The judge opened the bottle and smelled it.

"Your new grandfather has good taste." The judge winked at Max and poured two full glasses. "Let's sit down." The judge took his own chair, but Max remained standing. He was dressed for work, not a social meeting. His dark navy suit was impeccable and was accented by a tan and navy tie, and a light pin-striped button down shirt. Max paced over to the fire and back to stand in front of the judge.

"Max, sit down before you make me dizzy. Please." Judge O'Donohue had never seen Max this way. He suspected he knew the reason, but it was so much more entertaining to wait until his guest admitted what was going on. He extended his hand toward his wife's chair, but Max sat across from him on one of the ottomans.

"Judge, I believe I can speak freely to you, right?" Max's eyes finally held the judge's gaze.

"Of course, Max."

Max took a drink and watched Mickey enter the room and lay by the fire. He took another drink and watched the fire.

"Max, do you have a legal problem? Have you finalized the charges on that Martin woman?"

Max nodded. "No legal problem, and we've already

obtained one indictment of arson on her, but frankly, I don't think she killed her husband. I think someone else was in that house that day, maybe hiding on the third floor and disappearing down the back staircase. We've talked to Martin's girlfriend. Her statement matches Gio's. Unless those two, perfect strangers, conspired together to take out Martin, we have a murderer who may just have gotten away with it. I suspect it was the Martins' other partner, or maybe even a past victim."

"Marino should still be looking into the murder and that suspect. Maybe he can drum up something."

"Yes. The FBI continues their larger scale investigation that could last for years. We know their former partner flew into Kansas City one week prior to the murder. We have no record of him ever getting back on a plane to Atlanta, or anywhere for that matter. Marino's case is still open," Max admitted. "But, finally, I have enough to put her away in several states for fraud, illegal wire transfers, embezzlement, etc. Judge, there may be some very important, very powerful people involved in all of this so I need to tread carefully."

Judge O'Donohue nodded. "Then be very careful. People like that are powerful for a reason, and they're used to getting their own way." Silence filled the room as Max stared into the fire, and Judge O'Donohue stared at Max. "Max, will you be staying?"

"Yes, dammit." Max startled himself. "I'm so sorry, Judge. I didn't mean to growl at you. I'm feeling a bit overwhelmed, and I never admit that to anyone. My life here isn't going as I planned. I came here with a purpose to discover a few things, and instead I have a new grandfather. This job is more challenging than I thought; the city has completely changed, and I have a new home with so many projects I don't know where to begin. Nothing is going as planned."

The judge leaned over and touched Max's arm. "Gio and I are coming over tomorrow to look at that wood, and he said you wanted us to meet with the contractor about the kitchen."

"Yes, I would be grateful if you two could do that. Heck, visit with him about the entire first level. I drew up some plans, and I have them on the table in the kitchen. Gio says the contractor is a good guy, but Gio's idea of a good guy--"

"I'll check on him. Tommy should know."

Max smiled. "Tommy recommended the man too. We went over my ideas, and Tom feels like it can be done. I want a guest suite on the first floor, and please make sure Gio likes it. I'd like him to be able to live there with his own entrance but connected to the house down the hallway near the sitting and sun rooms. I also want a small patio near that wing with privacy for him to sit or to grow his tomatoes he's always talking about.."

Judge O'Donohue rubbed his unshaven face. Max was one of the best men he knew, but he knew the attorney hadn't come here to talk about a renovation project. "Gio used to grow the best tomatoes I've ever eaten." He took another drink and leaned forward. "Max, what is really wrong?"

"Judge, I've had a rebirth here. I tried for so many years to escape my past, all of my past except for this house and your family. I hope I can always think of all of you as my family." Max's voice was low and faltering. He looked down into his drink. His eyes filled with tears when he finally looked up at the man he admired even more than his own father.

The judge placed his glass on the table and reached over to place his hand on Max's jacket. "Why don't you get comfortable? Get that jacket off and get rid of that tie. And for heaven's sake, when you get up to do that, grab that bottle and bring it over here."

Max wiped at his eyes and smiled. "Yes, sir." He did as he was instructed and poured two more full glasses of liquor.

"Son, and yes, I do feel like you are my son, what the heck is going on with you?" The judge asked, but he knew. Charlotte wasn't the only clairvoyant in the family who had a sixth sense. His was known as common sense, and he had it in spades. "Max, no matter what, you will always be part of our family, unless you break our hearts."

The judge could see Max gulp in fear. "That's what I'm here about. I think I've hurt Charlotte, again."

Finally the truth was out, but the O'Donohue patriarch sensed all of this wasn't just about his dear daughter. The judge leaned back in his chair and got comfortable. "You broke her heart."

"I knew she wasn't drunk, but she was quick on her feet and thought that one up to save me, and I suspect to save her heart. I told her I was here to stay. I told her I never doubt anything, and I panicked. You know, I have crash landed twice in an airplane and never felt the fear like I did after she kissed me. I started it. I kissed her on the cheek, and before that at the house I may have led her to believe that there was more between us than there is."

The judge closed his eyes. "No, Max," he whispered. "This will break Charlotte."

"Sir? What?" Max leaned in.

Judge O'Donohue sat straighter as if he was back on the bench. "Max, what are you saying?" Now, even he was confused. Had he been so wrong about the feelings he had seen between Charlotte and Max? If he was wrong, he would tell Charlotte to move on. She said she was done with Max, but she wasn't.

"Max, I just told you that you are part of this family. I ask one thing. Don't lie. Charlotte is my daughter. Now, I want to hear only the truth. Is that clear?"

Max let out a deep breath. "Yes, sir. The truth is I don't think of Charlotte as Tommy's little sister. I don't think I ever will again, and I can't believe I'm saying this to you."

The judge made the sign of the cross before Max glanced up at him. "Max, I feel like I should ask what your intentions are with my daughter? And I don't want to hear some fancy speech you might use before a jury. I'm immune to that kind of rhetoric."

Max smiled. "I goofed it up with her. I didn't call her Charlotte. I didn't realize what she was really asking me, or telling me. I called her Charlie."

"Son, plain and simple is what I want. You came to me, remember?"

Max nodded. "Sorry. Judge, I miss her when I'm not with her. I drove past the real estate agency this afternoon and when I didn't see her car, I drove past her house. She was opening the front door and going inside. Sir, I need to fix this, but I just can't be who she wants or needs. Not right now."

The judge didn't pull any punches. "Okay, but yes, you two have made quite a mess. You're the one who has to fix this. She's so much like my wife, and that means she won't bend, but sadly she will break. It's on you. Max, you've always gone after everything you wanted. Your mother told you not to go out for the football team. You did and became a top conference player. Your dad wanted you to eventually go into the FBI, and you went to Annapolis. Both of them didn't want you to fly, and so you did. You flew jets, planes, and whatever else you could get off the ground. You had that law degree and served at JAG, and you're still serving in that capacity in the reserves. Your mom hates that. You never hung out at the country club. So, God help me, you have to go after my daughter if she's the one you want. This time you may have to lose to win, and maybe you need to tell her the truth that you are a mess, that you care about her, but you need what… to find yourself? And you and I know that after this assignment, you may be gone as quickly as you came."

The shock showed in Max's eyes. He wasn't sure. "My job poses a problem that I can't share with Charlotte, but I will fix this. I'm not sure I want to get married or have a family. I'm not sure it will go that far. I need to discover things about myself first."

The judge smiled. "You don't want a family? You know that can't make me happy. Well, I'll be out of it now. From now on, it's between you and Charlotte. Be honest, be fair. Throw away the past and think about what you want your future to be, just like you look at that house and imagine how you want it to look after it's been renovated and refurbished. Make those plans and make that happen, whatever that is. Maybe you should stop overthinking. Got it?"

"Yes, sir. I guess I have more thinking to do than I

thought when I came in here. I'm not sure I can give up my search though."

Even though the judge detested the answer, Max was still special to him, and he always would be with or without his relationship with Charlotte. "Have you eaten? I've got a roast in the crock pot. I'd love some company at the table." The judge stood up and looked down on his guest.

Max nodded and stood. "It seems like I eat over here all the time."

"All my kids do. Come on." The judge placed his arm around Max. "You will love this. I use just a touch of balsamic glaze with garlic cloves. Oh, I made fresh bread today, and Gio fixed me up with the best butter. He knows a guy."

"Of course he does," Max said as they both laughed. The weight of indecision just minutes ago lifted. All Max had to do now was figure out what he really did want, and what he couldn't live without. Or who.

Chapter Twenty-Seven

Max dropped off an envelope for me at the agency.
Who wrote letters?

Dear Charlotte,

*After speaking with your father, and downing an
entire bottle of Ireland's best, I thought this would be
the best way to express my thoughts. I have many. Most
of them are confusing and ones I never thought I would
have.*

*The judge told me story after story. One that stood
out was how you were named. Your mother had control
of the daughters' naming with Jane and you. Her
favorite authors were Jane Austen and Charlotte Bronte.
Jane's middle name honored her mother, Elizabeth. Your
middle name was in honor of a woman who had helped
save her child. Your father said I could share a little of
the story.*

*My grandmother Rose, along with Gio, found
a doctor to help out a very sick child on a very bad
Christmas day. Your mom had met Rose Taylor by
accident when her small bag of chocolates had ripped
and scattered all over the floor of the candy shop. Your
mother had bought those chocolates with the laundry
money she had saved. They were meant as a present
for your father. Rose stopped and helped pick up every*

*piece. Your mother was in tears that her gift was ruined.
She didn't have the money to purchase any more, but my
grandmother did. Your mom left with the chocolates and
a new friend who offered her number just in case the
young pregnant woman ever needed anything.*

*William, Jr. was born and Christmas was meant to
be the happiest first family holiday, but he soon spiked a
fever. The young attorney called every doctor he could
think of, but no one was willing to come to his aid. They
didn't have the money to just show up at a hospital. With
desperation setting in, your mother called Rose Taylor.
Rose Taylor called Gio Campano. A doctor arrived at
the O'Donohue's small apartment less than an hour
later. The baby was rushed to the hospital and treated
with the best of care for a week. Rose and Gio made
sure all of the bills were paid. No strings were attached.
In fact, your dad didn't realize who Gio was or his
involvement until years later. Gio never mentioned the
event. My grandmother and your mother exchanged
letters over the years, just like your mother's great
authors used to do with their own sisters.*

*My hope is this letter explains our great connection.
I'm afraid that I won't measure up to who you deserve.
I'm afraid I don't know what I want the future to look
like. I came back to this city to find something; I'm just
not sure what I will discover. But what I do know is that
I miss your sarcasm and your humor. I miss the way
you glow, and the way you bite your lip. I miss you,
Charlotte Rose O'Donohue.*

Yours,

Max

Who wrote letters in today's society of technology? Max did, and he wrote them quite well. I missed him too, but now I needed him to just be an older brother. I needed to let him go. My head knew that. Now I needed to convince my heart.

Chapter Twenty-Eight

It was a sunny, beautiful almost spring day in Kansas City. But I was still gloomy. I just couldn't clear the cobwebs out of my head. I hadn't even heard any voices the last couple of weeks. Mom and Conor didn't wake me in the morning, and of course, I hadn't visited the Taylor Club to hear Rose.

I drove by the house a couple of times. One time, Max's car was parked in the lot as were a couple of other trucks, and my own father's car! Later, he explained that Gio and he were helping Max out. Wasn't that nice? Tom, Meg, and he would become best friends again, and Sean and he would probably go to a couple of ball games together. There was no doubt that Dad would feed Max. They enjoyed each other's company, and they could talk about the law like none of us could. The next time I saw him, I planned on being cordial, smiling through clenched teeth until my face fell off. Max Shaw no longer made my heart beat faster or my face flush with warmth. But that letter had given me another ounce of hope, but I didn't want to hang onto that. I needed to let it go. I would keep the letter and look at it lovingly on those days when something reminded me of Max. I did the same thing when I looked at the designer purse my ex had given me as a Christmas gift right before he called off our engagement.

Maybe in a few years, we would all go to Max's wedding. I'd eat the rubber chicken and maybe a piece of cake. I'd dance with Dad and watch as the happy couple shared a kiss. I would get him a pasta maker as a gift. He and Dad could compare recipes. He'd probably marry another lawyer, and they could discuss depositions together in bed. I'd find somebody, or maybe nobody. I would become the top real estate agent in the area and have millions in the bank. I'd buy Dad a home in Florida. He'd become a snowbird and the entire family could vacation there every year. But other thoughts and careers were filling my head. I'd unearthed my law books from my closet, and one afternoon I'd sat looking at my license for almost an hour. I was unsettled and very much wanted to be content.

I sat with my dreams on the park bench at Loose Park. Conor always used to come here to think. Who knew what about, but that was Conor the thinker. Spring was arriving in a week or two. Tiny buds were popping out here and there as the first signs that it would soon be warmer. But not today. I kept my hands in the pockets of my jacket. The wind was blowing cold, but the sun was a little warmer. The few ducks on the pond drew my attention. I could hear someone behind me, probably coming to the sidewalk that wound around the park. A shadow blocked my sunshine. I lifted my head in that direction.

"Max. Max?" What the heck was he doing here? He looked like he'd been working at the house. His attire was a hoodie, jeans, and sneakers. He hadn't shaved, and he looked like he just rolled out of bed. His scruffy appearance was such a contrast to his usual sophistication.

"Your dad told me where you were." He sat down next to me.

I looked back at my ducks and glanced at him. "You look like hell. Rough night?"

He stuck his hands in his pockets too. "Rough nights. Plural."

I nodded. I understood that. Besides, sleeping was highly overrated.

"Why here, Charlie? The guys and I used to come here to find girls."

"My girlfriends and I used to come here to talk about boys," I admitted honestly. "Conor and I used to visit this very bench to discuss dreams about the future. Sometimes, I still hear him."

"That's nice to think you do," Max murmured. "Sort of like Gio when he visits with Rose."

"Yes." Little did he know what truth he had just said.

"I usually go for a long run when I want to clear my head."

"Of course you do." He was almost more attractive in his disheveled state. Darn him! It really wasn't fair, but of course the devil always looked good in any form or shape he morphed into. That's how he could get you to sin. There was no more running away for me.

"Charlie," he said as he turned his head to face me. "I came here for a new start, and boy did I get that. I'm solving a real estate scheme that I've been tracking for two years. I reconnected with all of you, and I've acquired a grandfather."

"At your age? Wow, you are something." I laughed. Finally, he broke into a chuckle too. "Why are you here?

You haven't told me why you tracked me down."

Max shook his head. "Do you ever sugarcoat anything? Must you be so direct?"

"Have you met my family? If you aren't direct, you'll never get a word in. So what is it, Mr. Shaw?"

"Did you get my letter?"

"Yes."

"Did you read it?" Max controlled his speech before his tone raised.

"Yes. It was beautiful. Thank you."

Max seemed extremely unsure of himself. *Poop Head* had chinks in his armor.

He sighed. "I've been an idiot."

I snickered. "Yes, you have, for many years. Actually, you've been that way since the first day you entered our house."

"There you go again. I'm not that boy. You should know that by now. If I'm an idiot, then you're judgemental." Max stopped talking as though he was reading my face. I began to contest his contention that I acted like a judge, but I shut my mouth quickly. He was right. He turned and placed his left arm over the back of the bench slightly touching my back. "In fact, this is all new to me. I want a fresh start all the way around. So here it goes."

I wondered what he was doing. He removed his right hand from his pocket and extended it for a handshake. "Hi. I'm Max Shaw. And you are?"

What the heck was he doing? Fine. I'd play along.

I gave him my hand. "I'm Charlotte O'Donohue."

"It seems like everyone I run into is an O'Donohue."

I smiled. "It does seem like that some days."

Max remained quiet. I searched his face, but as usual I couldn't read him. I had to say something.

"Surely you're more articulate with a jury than this, right? I mean, you're supposed to be this great prosecutor, at least that's what my dad says."

"Your dad thinks I'm great?" His hopeful expression made me laugh.

"Don't let it go to your head. He thinks the dog is great. He thinks the mailman is great when he doesn't bring him a bill in the mail."

Max's hand went up to stop me. "I get it. Thanks for continuing to humanize me at any chance you get."

"You're welcome. Is this how you speak to a jury?"

"No, because I'm not trying to ask them out to dinner."

I blinked in shock. Why was I surprised that he wanted to go out with me? This is what I wanted, didn't I? He was opening himself up right here and now, and it was all too serious.

"You know, you can just show up for family dinner even if whatever this is doesn't work."

"I know. The old man already said that." His dark eyes began to crack any resistance I had. "I won't ever call you Charlie O again. We are beginning this the right way because this is important."

"Okay, I'm not sure what you really are saying, but I can guarantee I won't call you *Poop Head* again either." I began to laugh as I shook my head. "I'm sorry. I can't promise that. You've been my tormentor since childhood. Lately, you've been like the devil to me on my dark days of uncertainty."

Max reached over and took my hand in his again. Neither one of us had gloves on and our hands were cold to the touch. I stopped talking. Heck, I stopped breathing. I needed to be very careful.

"Max, I think you're asking me out, and I'm not sure why we have to be so serious about this. Just look at you. You're a mess. You shouldn't be stressed. Let's just have a good time. That way, if it doesn't work out, you can still show up for dinner. It's not like we're making a lifetime commitment."

Max's thumb stroked my hand. I watched the movement as it moved up and down. I could imagine his hand rubbing my back then moving its way to my neck, finally touching my hair as he slowly moved to kiss me. My imagination was getting the best of me. I looked up into his eyes. He was contemplative, and he seemed very upset. He tracked me down to tell me something.

"Max, I'll go out with you. Heck, every woman in this city would date you. But I'm not sure we're ever going to be more than Charlie O and *Poop Head* and that's okay." Just listen to me being the adult in this whatever relationship.

Briefly, he did nothing. Not one muscle moved. He moved a little closer to me, possibly for warmth or his weak attempt at any sort of intimidation.

His mouth moved near my ear. His breath was warm when he whispered.

"Remember, I don't usually doubt any of my decisions, but this is different. The odds are too high for this to fail. Listen carefully. I think I'm yours, Charlotte, but right now I need a friend."

Yours what? I paid no attention to his lament about friendship. We were friends, very good ones. I was shivering, and it wasn't from the temperature but from the timbre in his voice. I remembered Rose's words and suddenly understood. Perhaps this would work out, and maybe it wouldn't. It was all up to just the two of us. But at this moment, Rose was right about her grandson. *Family, Max, Charlotte. Yours. Charlotte.*

Chapter Twenty-Nine

Taylor Mansion

"How was the date of the century?" Gio Campano handed the cup of coffee to Max as he entered what would be the kitchen of the old Taylor Club. Now that all the signs had been removed, and the structure was to be a home, it was not a club. It would be a home; it would be a restored mansion.

Max looked up and smiled slightly. With the coffee in his hands, Max took a quick drink. "Is that what the city is calling it?" He looked at the bag in his grandfather's hand. "Are those cannolis?"

"They are, and you can have a couple of these if you tell me about your evening out with Charlotte." He held the bag up as a prize, but Max quickly grabbed it.

"Let's go to the other room. I set up a table there where we can sit. By the way, when are you moving in with me?"

Gio lowered his body on the folding chair. His knees were hurting more than usual, but he wouldn't tell Max. "I'm paid up through the end of the year."

Max dug into his midmorning treat. "You can't be paid up. Rent is monthly."

Gio laughed. "Not when you're my age. I have a nice little place, and I get a discount for paying for the year. If I die, they keep the money. All of my utilities are included. Do you even have central air ready for the house? Summer will be here before you know it."

Max wiped off the powdered sugar from his chin. "Did you get these from Constanza's?"

"No, I went to the bakery off the Plaza. I like the kids there. Now, what about the night out with Charlotte?"

Max put his pastry down. "Fine. It went fine."

Gio hit his forehead with his hand. "Boy! Fine? That's all?"

Max stood up and took his coffee with him to face the windows. The date would've gone better if he hadn't decided to delay any interaction with Charlotte O'Donohue. It was a difficult task as he thought about her smile. Even her slightest touch drew his eyes to fall on those lips, especially when she bit them. He wondered what her kiss would feel like in a more heated, private moment. Even when she hit his arm playfully with her fist, he became strangely aroused, wanting more of her touch in a much different way. No, he needed to keep Charlotte as Charlie until he received an answer. "Gio, was Judge O friends with my mom?"

"Of course, ask your father. Edward and the judge were best friends before your dad took the FBI job."

Max focused on the large untrimmed tree blocking the view of the Plaza. Landscaping was way down on his list, but he felt like cutting on something, or hitting anything. "Could my mother and Judge O'Donohue have been closer?"

Gio slammed his fist on the small card table. Max turned at the noise. "Max, what are you getting at?"

"Could he be my biological father?"

Gio hadn't felt this nervous in over thirty years. In those days, his age was showing and any young pup felt the need to show him up. He studied Max. The younger man's eyes were dark, his jaw was clenched. He was a man intent on discovering the truth. "Edward is your father."

"Not my biological father," Max answered plainly. "I had a physical exam before I left Atlanta. Imagine my surprise when my bloodwork showed that my father couldn't be my father."

"Edward will always be your father. That blood test must be wrong. Shame on you for even saying that."

Max returned to the table. His sigh resonated in the empty room. "Of course he'll always be my father, but the test wasn't wrong. Who made me? It wasn't Edward Shaw."

"And you think it's Judge O? Why on earth would you think that?"

"The blood results piqued my interest so I sent off my DNA, and I received the results the day of the date of the century. I'm half Irish. Edward Shaw doesn't have a bit of Irish in him, in fact that side of the family would consider it an insult to their English and Scottish ancestors. You know my mother isn't."

"But you're a little Sicilian and Italian," Gio added. His wide smile lightened Max's eyes.

"Yes, I know that now. I just figured there must be a reason why the judge seems to like me so much."

Gio shook his head slowly. "Max, he just likes you.

You can be charming. You got that from me. And you and he share a love for the law, right?"

"Yes, but he has a family for that."

"Not like you. Charlotte is the only attorney, and she sells real estate. It's just not the same. He and I talk about the old days, and we discuss various crimes and criminals, but you are special to him."

Max nodded. "Exactly. I think he might be my real father."

"Ask your mother," Gio suggested quickly. "She should know."

Max thought for a minute. "No. She can't know I'm looking into this. So, in the meantime, Charlotte O'Donohue is off limits."

"What are you going to tell her?"

Max's thin smile revealed his plan. "I'll be very busy until I get to the truth."

Gio shook his head. "Why now? Why care?"

Max sighed. How did this mobster weasel his way into his life so quickly? And why did he care for him so much? "I have my reasons."

Gio grabbed the bag of cannolis. "You're not getting any more of these until you tell me at least one reason."

The old man's voice changed. It was demanding and threatening. "Now, spill, kid."

"Someone is threatening my family." Max's hand flew out and grabbed the bag. "The cannolis are mine now."

Gio shook his head in disbelief. "What's the matter with you? Your father always has threats against his life. He's the head of the damn FBI. In your position, someone has to be mad at you or you aren't doing a good job. Why are you upset about this?"

Max withdrew one more pastry and shut his eyes. Should he tell Gio that he'd decided to live in his family home so he could be a target, so whoever was after him could find him easily? "My sister was almost kidnapped. She's been threatened. Yes, I've been threatened, but this time is different. It feels very personal, and I'm afraid–"

"That they'll go after Charlotte?" Gio saw the palpable fear etched on Max's face.

"Yes, that too. I can take care of myself, but I don't want people I love hurt."

Gio clapped. "You do love her. We all knew it."

Max shook his finger at the old mobster. "You all don't know anything. I love her like the sister she could be. I'm scared someone will be hurt."

Gio shook his head in disappointment.

"What? Now, what?"

Gio looked directly at the man across from him. "Max, you think you're a man, but you're a scared little boy who has been running all of your life. You've been running away from your mother and the duties she drops on you. You don't want to be in her society world, but that's how you can advance your career. You run toward charity work because you are a very generous soul, and you don't mind working hard to take care of others."

"Are you done?" Max crossed his arms in front of him and stared into Gio's eyes.

"No, not yet. Just sit there and listen. I've been watching you. You run toward a family, but you don't want one yourself. You take every burden onto your back and think you can do it all yourself. I thought that once." Gio looked away briefly. He learned so many things from Rose, but the greatest lesson had been to fall in her arms and to allow her into his heart. "Max, maybe it's time for you to reach out to someone who could take care of you properly, who could soothe that scared little boy's soul?"

"And who do you suggest to take on this huge job?"

Gio smiled. "In your heart, you know who. You're just scared of feeling, of having those feelings for her. She's the only woman I know for the job. God help her."

"If you're talking about Charlotte, then think again. She calls me the devil, and after the other night I'm sure she's plotting my demise. Do you want to throw me into the arms of someone like that?"

Gio cocked his head as he thought about it. "She's also said you're a vampire. I consider lawyers bloodsuckers so the girl is onto something. As for the devil, your attributes do remind me–"

Max's hands flew up. "Enough. Charlotte may be my sister. Until I have definite proof that she isn't, I'm not falling into her arms."

Gio nodded knowingly. The boy had already fallen. Max just didn't realize he needed a parachute before he crashed.

Max grabbed another cannoli and bit off a huge part of the pastry, the powdered sugar landing on his chin. With his mouth still full, he fired off one final salvo. "Charlotte means nothing to me. That is final."

Gio nodded, but one of his brows raised. "Keep telling yourself that, Max. You'll just fall faster and harder."

"Will not." As the two words came out of his mouth, Max sounded like the little boy Gio had accused him of being. Whose little boy he was was another question, and when he learned that answer his life wouldn't be the same. One way or another the future remained uncertain with a father out there somewhere, and a threat that seemed to grow every day. "And I'm not scared."

"Max, just ask yourself one thing," Gio said as he patted his new grandson's arm. "Why on earth would Judge O even allow you out on a date with his daughter if he was your father? Why jump to the conclusion that it's the judge?"

"Maybe he doesn't know. Maybe my mother didn't tell him. I just have this feeling deep inside that he's my father. We have this connection."

Gio shook his head. "Or you just want him to be the one so you can stop searching for God knows what. Max, he's not your father."

"I can't take any chances." Max left to retrieve another cup of coffee. Gio was right. Was he just wishing that the judge was his biological father? The judge did seem to be cheering him on, steering him into a relationship with Charlotte. No, he knew that the judge was the one. Any feelings he thought he was developing for Charlotte needed to be pushed aside. When he returned to sit across from Gio, the old man shook his head.

"You're being foolish, but I won't stop you from making your own mistakes. God knows I made my share," the elderly mobster murmured. He stared into Max's eyes. "I promise to keep quiet on all of this, but I believe that United States Attorney, The Honorable Maxwell Edward Shaw has invented the absurd idea that Judge O is his biological father because he so badly wants to avoid committing to the judge's daughter. How's my summation, counselor?"

He had his answer in Max's glare.

Gio felt the cool breeze flow through the room. He almost saw the outline of his love's body near one of the undamaged builtin cabinets on the far side of the room. Max was discussing the bump out he was planning for the north side of the kitchen. The room would be a large living area complete with an updated fireplace and mantle. Max was just keeping himself busy with projects.

"Danger is coming, my love. Protect our boy."

Gio blinked his eyes in understanding as Rose vanished before him. He would do his best to protect his family, all of his family.

A Sneak Peek Of What's Next For Charlotte...

My father sighed. "Charlotte, you don't have to answer, but I just have to ask. Your mother would ask. What the heck happened on that date?"

"Nothing. It was fine."

"Fine doesn't usually mean good."

"No, it doesn't, does it? He was a perfect gentleman. We laughed a little and ate a wonderful dinner, and then he took me home and gave me this weak peck on my forehead like he was the big brother taking out his forlorn little sister. It was like something happened somewhere along the way, but I don't know what it was."

My father was examining my face, but I remained stoic. I wasn't about to share my devastation. I had been examining what had happened for days. I thought...I didn't know what I thought now. "Saturday night at the charity auction, he was with that lovely girl. She works for one of the news stations."

"I saw, and you were with me."

I rolled my eyes. "Yes, you and I went together. Max kissed her. Her hands were all over him."

Dad's smile was infuriating. His happiness taunted me. "I saw the performance. He made sure you saw him, and what I saw was a man desperate to make you jealous."

I continued to chew the popcorn in my mouth. "I saw someone moving on and very quickly. He had no intention of a serious relationship with me. Max kissed her ferociously like he was devouring her." I shielded my face with my hand. Just the thought of Max kissing me in that way made me warm. I would only have my dreams of what that would feel like, how my body would feel when his hands roamed over my lower back…

"Charlotte, look at me."

I had been caught. I was flushed not out of anger but from lust. Why did Max Shaw make me feel? Couldn't another man do the job? I just needed a good…cold shower.

C.L. BAUER

"I always wanted to write romances. I read them, and our mom loved her soap operas. But at night, our family watched mystery and detective television shows. I was influenced to go in a different direction when I began my adventure in writing. I love a who done it that adds in a little humor, romance, and keeps you guessing."

C.L. Bauer's first cozy mysteries, A Lily List Mystery Series, debuted with The Poppy Drop featuring Kansas City florist Lily Schmidt. A spin off, A Lily List Mystery Exclusive introduced readers to the popular character, Gretchen Malloy. The premier event planner never met a pair of stilettos she didn't love!

Kansas City, Missouri native C.L. Bauer comes from a background in journalism and has received numerous awards as the owner of her family's wedding and event flower business, Clara's Flowers. (Many stories in A Lily List Mystery Series are based on true events.)

With Charlotte's Voices Of Mystery Series, C.L. Bauer has incorporated her love of mystery and romance with a bit of the paranormal. It's a little naughtier than your usual cozy, and with the introduction of the spirit world you'll never know what or who is just around the corner.

To contact the author or schedule special events/book club appearances, email clbauerkc@gmail.com. Visit her website at www.clbauer.com to join the newsletter for news about publications, contests, and upcoming events.

Other Books by C.L. Bauer

The Lily List Mystery Series
The Poppy Drop
The Hibiscus Heist
The Tulip Terror
The Sweet Pea Secret
The Magnolia Dilemma

A Lily List Mystery Exclusive
Stilettos Can Be Murder
Stilettos On The Run

CPSIA information can be obtained
at www.ICGtesting.com
Printed in the USA
BVHW081635130323
660320BV00014B/450